MURDER—
ON A WORLD
WITHOUT CRIME!

"My son should have been here by now," said Sarek. "Perhaps our guests overslept—"

The communications console buzzed loudly. Sarek flicked the switch, and Spock's face appeared on the communicator screen. "Father, there has been another power failure. Captain Kirk, Dr. McCoy, and I are with Storn—"

"I'm on my way!" Sarek cut him off, clamping control over the panic in his veins. It had happened twice now—and if it happened a third time, the victim would be Amanda!

Look for *Star Trek* fiction from Pocket Books

THE VULCAN ACADEMY MURDERS

JEAN LORRAH

A STAR TREK® NOVEL

PUBLISHED BY POCKET BOOKS NEW YORK

Another *Original* publication of POCKET BOOKS

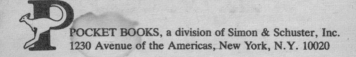

POCKET BOOKS, a division of Simon & Schuster, Inc.
1230 Avenue of the Americas, New York, N.Y. 10020

This book is Published by Pocket Books, a Division of Simon &
Schuster, Inc. Under Exclusive License from Paramount Pic-
tures Corporation, The Trademark Owner.

ISBN: 0-671-50054-6

First Pocket Books Science Fiction printing November, 1984

10 9 8 7 6 5 4 3 2 1

FOREWORD

I would like to thank Gene Roddenberry, the creator of *Star Trek,* which has been an important influence in my life,

D. C. Fontana and Theodore Sturgeon, who wrote the episodes which most inspired this book,

William Shatner, Leonard Nimoy, DeForest Kelley, Mark Lenard (Sarek), Jane Wyatt (Amanda), and all the other actors who brought life to *Star Trek* characters,

Star Trek fandom, which over the years has provided a forum for the stories I—and so many other fans—needed to tell,

Gordon Carleton, who has given me permission to use "T'Kuht," the name he invented and fandom adopted for Vulcan's sister planet, the "moon" of moonless Vulcan seen in Vulcan's sky in "Yesteryear" and *Star Trek: The Motion Picture,*

Jacqueline Lichtenberg, who read this manuscript in progress and provided exactly the right suggestion at exactly the right moment,

and the *Star Trek Welcommittee,* who for many years have served to bring fans who love *Star Trek* to know and share their interests with one another.

I have been a *Star Trek* fan since 1966, when the original live episodes first appeared on NBC. I learned to write fiction through fanzine writing, and made many wonderful friends through Trekfandom.

Trekfandom is not a "club" one "joins." It is friends and letters and crafts and fanzines and trivia and costumes and artwork and filksongs and posters and buttons and film clips and conventions—something for everybody who has in common the inspiration of a television show which grew far beyond its TV and film incarnations to become a living part of world culture.

In both Trekwriting and my other professional science fiction, I have a strong belief in the interaction between authors and fans. If you would like to comment on this or any other of my books, you may reach me in care of my publishers, or at P.O. Box 625, Murray, KY 42071. If your letter requires an answer, please enclose a stamped, self-addressed envelope.

But if you are interested in reaching fandom, the way is not through me, or any other author of *Star Trek* novels. You want that wonderful organization, the *Star Trek Welcommittee*. Be *sure* to enclose a stamped, self-addressed envelope, as this is a purely volunteer, non-profit organization of people who love *Star Trek* and are willing to answer your questions and put you in touch with other fans. The current address is:

Star Trek Welcommittee
P.O. Drawer 12
Saranac, MI 48881.

Keep on Trekkin'!

Jean Lorrah
Murray, Kentucky

THE VULCAN ACADEMY MURDERS

CHAPTER 1

"Fire photon torpedoes!"

Captain James T. Kirk leaned forward in the command chair, as if forcing the weapons of the USS *Enterprise* to fire by his very strength of will.

Nothing happened.

The Klingon warship on the viewscreen drew bead on the Federation starship and fired again. The *Enterprise* shook, but the screens held.

"Mr. Sulu, I want torpedoes!" The Captain's voice was firm but determined.

"No response, sir!" the helmsman replied, still struggling with the controls.

Kirk punched a button on the arm of his chair. "Auxiliary Control! Mr. Chekov, fire photon torpedoes!"

"Firing, Captain!" And the screen showed the torpedoes away at last.

The voice from Auxiliary Control, however, was not Pavel Chekov's. Ensign Carl Remington, fresh out of Star Fleet Academy, had replied. Kirk heard the fear in the boy's voice, and wondered if he would break under fire.

"Number One Phasers—fire!"

The Klingons were moving in for the kill—the short-range weapons caught them full blast, but their screens also held.

"Number Two Phasers—now!" Kirk pressed his advantage.

The Klingon vessel's port screens went down in a satisfying display of fireworks. "All weapons—fire!"

Remington responded at once. Torpedoes and phasers blasted the enemy ship; the *Enterprise* was peppered with return fire, her own screens shorting out for a long moment. Then the rest of the Klingon screens fizzled out, and the long-necked ship blazed in death glory.

"Cease firing!" Kirk commanded—and realized that the firing had stopped before his order. "Auxiliary Control!"

No answer.

"Chekov! Remington! Respond!"

There was a long pause. Then Chekov's voice, weak and choking. "Keptin. Medical aid—" A cough, then silence.

"Sickbay!" Kirk exclaimed, punching another button. "Bones, get someone to Auxiliary Control, on the double!" Then the general intercom, "Anyone in vicinity, take over Auxiliary Control!"

"Grogan here, Captain!" came a female voice as the AC button lit reassuringly. "Mr. Chekov's unconscious, and Mr. Remington . . . I think he's dead!"

"Grogan, man the console—power is out on the bridge!"

"Aye, Captain."

But the battle was over. The Klingon ship lay dead in space—scans showed all power out, life support systems nonfunctional. The gasps of the aliens, choking on fumes from the fires consuming the last of their air, rang in the ears of the *Enterprise* crew.

"*Enterprise* to Klingon vessel—crew prepare to be beamed aboard our ship! Scotty—"

The engineer's voice responded, "Aye, Captain, we'll try—but we scan only a dozen or so left alive, and they're dyin' even as we try to fix on 'em."

Kirk sat frozen now, listening to the reports coming in. The *Enterprise* had sustained major damage—they would have to put in at the nearest starbase for repairs. The computer monitored the ship; those damage reports were swift. But people had to care for people; the reports of deaths and injuries followed at a more leisurely, and trying, rate.

"We got three of the devils aboard alive," Scotty reported as he entered the bridge from the turbolift, "all sick as dogs from breathin' smoke, and well deservin' of it!" The Scotsman headed immediately for the sputtering helm console.

"Where are they?" Kirk asked.

"Sickbay. I suppose Dr. McCoy will patch 'em up well enough for interrogation."

Kirk stared at the viewscreen, which still displayed the Klingon vessel, now a tomb for all but three of its crew. "Why did they do it?" he wondered aloud. "I know they dispute our right to this quadrant, but to attack? All we did was warn them that they were in Federation space."

"They're Klingons," Scotty responded. "What do you expect?"

"But why risk their lives? One on one they knew they had a less than even chance against a starship. Why bother to fight over a hundred cubic light-years of vacuum?"

Mr. Spock, who had been silently manning his post throughout the battle, suddenly spoke up. "'We go to gain a little patch of ground/ That hath in it no profit but the name.'"

"Hmm?" asked Kirk.

"*Hamlet*," the Vulcan supplied. "Shakespeare understood the warrior mentality. 'Witness this army, of such mass and charge,/ Exposing what is mortal and unsure/ To all that fortune, death, and danger dare,/ Even for an eggshell.'" He paused, then added, "Or as a Klingon poet might put it, Captain, any excuse for a fight."

"Cynicism, Spock?"

"Observation, Captain. I have seen how the Klingons act, only too often. They are not logical . . . but they are predictable."

"Are you suggesting that I might have avoided this battle?" Kirk asked.

"No, Captain, quite the opposite. I am suggesting that given contact with the Klingons in a disputed quadrant, battle was inevitable."

But Kirk felt no better because his First Officer agreed he had had no way out. There *had* to be a better way than blasting away at one another. They were like children playing pirates—but with genuine loss of life and limb!

Finally McCoy reported from Sickbay. "Four dead, Captain. Rosen, Livinger, M'Gura, Jakorski. Ninety-three injuries, but only eleven serious enough to confine them to Sickbay. One of those, however—Jim, when you can, will you please come down here?"

"Remington?" Kirk asked, recalling that Grogan had thought the boy dead.

"Yes. I'd like to talk with you privately."

Scotty had the bridge console operating again; all final reports were in. "Mr. Spock, take command," Kirk instructed, and took the turbolift to Sickbay.

Those of his crew who were conscious managed to smile at the Captain, and he turned on his charm in return, assuring them they had all done a fine job, and would certainly soon be back on their feet with McCoy's help. But his enforced cheer dropped away like a mask when he followed the doctor into the intensive care unit, and saw Carl Remington lying pale and unmoving. He certainly looked dead. Only the life sign indicators on the board over his head showed life in the still form. "How bad?"

"It's hopeless," McCoy replied. "Dammit, Jim, the worst of it is, it'll take him days to die. He's totally paralyzed. His voluntary nervous system is burnt out—must have taken a freak burst of energy in those last blasts from the Klingon ship. His involuntary system is working—I took him off life support, and . . . he's alive, for the moment. But he can't do anything—and I do mean anything. He can't even blink his eyes. But if he stabilizes instead of dying in the next few days, he could go on like that for years."

"Dear God," Kirk whispered. "Does he know? I mean, can he hear us? Is he—aware in there?"

"I don't know. He hasn't responded—there's no increase in heartbeat or respiration to indicate emotional response—but maybe he can't even do that. Should I ask Spock to—?"

"No!" But after a moment Kirk sighed. "Yes. We have to know."

Mr. Spock, although always reluctant to use the mind

meld, agreed. "Yes—I understand that you must know whether Mr. Remington is aware before you can decide on treatment for him. I will meld with him, Doctor, if you will grant me privacy."

Kirk and McCoy retreated to the doctor's office to wait for Spock's report. Kirk slumped into a chair, for the first time that day allowing his state of mind to show in his posture.

"Maybe he's technically dead," McCoy offered. "I found no brain wave activity—"

"And maybe his body will just turn off, too, and save you the trouble—" Kirk cut off his angry retort, and rested his elbows on his knees, rubbing the palms of his hands over his eyes. "I'm sorry, Bones. You did everything you could."

"And so did you," the doctor said. "Here—my prescription." He held out a brandy. Kirk took it gratefully, without protest. After a moment McCoy sat down in his desk chair and said, "Jim, Remington's one of those kids you identify with, isn't he?"

"Bones, I—"

"I know—you care about your whole crew equally. But I also know that whenever you see one of these up-and-comers right out of the Academy and ready to take on the galaxy, you remember a certain James T. Kirk setting out to become the youngest Captain in Star Fleet—and doing it."

"That was a long time ago, Bones."

"And at times like these you wonder what it's all for. Why set yourself up for a day like today? They come only too often, don't they?"

Kirk nodded. "But somebody has to do it. Maybe we're protecting vacuum here—but if we let the Klingons have this particular piece of vacuum, they'd build a starbase that much closer to populated Federation territory. But dammit, that doesn't make it any easier to have people die, or be crippled for life."

He sat staring into his drink, and McCoy didn't prod him further, knowing the Captain would probably have another drink or two, sleep from exhaustion, and be up early for a workout in the gym before facing the funeral ceremony.

It was nearly half an hour before Spock emerged from the intensive care unit, pale and grim. "Mr. Remington is . . . there, Doctor. He cannot respond, but his mind is alert, trapped deep within himself."

"Oh, God," McCoy said softly, tears welling in his blue eyes. He didn't let them fall, but they roughened his voice as he said, "This is when I wonder why I'm a doctor—if I hadn't done anything for that boy today, perhaps he'd just have died. Instead, he is condemned to living death." He poured himself a brandy this time, hesitated, then poured one for Spock. "Don't argue— just drink it."

"I am not arguing, Doctor," said Spock, downing the drink in one swallow. Then he sat down in the last chair in the small office, and said, "Doctor McCoy, Captain. . . there may be a chance for Mr. Remington to recover."

"Spock," said McCoy, "there is no way to repair that kind of nerve damage. Nerves don't regenerate. If anyone was even working on a technique for nerve regeneration, I'd have heard of it."

"Not if it was happening at the Vulcan Academy of Sciences," Spock replied, "and was still in the experimental stage."

"Was?" asked McCoy, realizing that Spock's ever-perfect grammar would call for the subjunctive if he were speaking hypothetically. "You mean there *is* such a technique?"

"Yes, Doctor, there is."

"But—how can you know that when I don't? I read the Journal of the Vulcan Academy, too."

"They have not completed their research, and so cannot yet release the results," Spock explained. "However, I have a . . . personal reason for knowing about the experiments."

Kirk sat up, immediately alert with concern for his friend. "Personal, Spock? Is something wrong?"

"Not with me," the Vulcan replied in the flat tone that masked his feelings. Both human men recognized that it meant he was controlling carefully. "It is . . . my mother."

"Amanda?" McCoy asked, recalling the lovely lady whom he had gotten to know on the voyage to Babel. "Is she ill? Is there anything I can do, Spock?"

"She has degenerative xenosis."

McCoy held his tongue, knowing that expressions of sympathy would not be welcomed by his Vulcan friend. The disease was one of the products of star travel—it seemed to be a kind of allergic reaction to living for long periods on alien worlds. Once it had started, there was no cure; the nervous fibers dissolved away until the person simply died because the body could no longer operate. "How long?" he finally asked gently.

"We hope—my father Sarek and I—that she will not die, Doctor. She would have had only a few more months, but the regeneration techniques developed by the healer Sorel and his associate, Dr. Daniel Corrigan, were tested successfully on Dr. Corrigan."

"Sounds like a man after your own heart, Bones," Kirk commented, "trying his experiments on himself."

"Although he is only a few years older than my mother," Spock explained, "Dr. Corrigan began a few years ago to age very rapidly—physically. Fortunately, his mind remained untouched, and he and Sorel were able to develop their methodology. Sarek tells me that Dr. Corrigan recovered completely—including nerve regeneration. At this point they are trying the technique only on people who cannot be cured by any other means. My mother is in the stasis now; in a few days she will be released. The latest communication from my father says that the monitors show almost total regeneration. She will be well, and will have many more years with my father."

"Spock," said Kirk, "I'm very happy to hear that. But why didn't you tell us before?"

"I intended to—but the communication came just before the battle. I was going to ask for leave on Vulcan, and request that you come with me, Dr. McCoy. I have complete faith in Dr. Corrigan, who has been my mother's physician for many years. However—"

"Thank you, Spock." McCoy felt warmth at Spock's trust in him. "I would be honored. Do you think they'll accept Remington? Jim—the *Enterprise* will have to be drydocked for repairs anyway—"

"Take Remington to Vulcan, Bones. That's an order. And of course your leave is granted, Spock. For once you'll get shore leave at home—we're not even that far from Vulcan!"

"Since you will also have leave time, Captain," Spock said formally, "may I invite you to my home? I am certain my father will be honored to have both of you as guests—and when my mother is released from stasis, she will surely be pleased to see you again."

So it was settled, with relief all around. Now the only problem was McCoy's: keeping Remington alive until they reached Vulcan.

CHAPTER 2

Sarek of Vulcan stepped out of the sonic shower and pulled on the light clothing suitable to Vulcan's summer. The day was already giving promise of being torrid enough to make even native Vulcans uncomfortable. His students would surely be restless; how had he ever allowed himself to be coerced into teaching the entrance-level computer course always three-quarters filled with offworlders?

The house was empty, but he had become used to that this past month. If Amanda had to be in stasis, it was fortunate that she was missing the hottest part of the summer. Despite all her years on Vulcan, she still minded this kind of heat.

Remembering that he would have human guests arriving this evening, Sarek set the cooling unit several degrees below the temperature necessary for his own comfort. Even Spock would undoubtedly require a few days to reaccustom himself to the fierceness of Vulcan's summer. It was nearly two years since Spock had last set foot on Vulcan, under such regrettable circumstances—

No, Sarek refused to let himself dwell on the past. Amanda had been right. He had been wrong to disown his son. He deeply regretted not standing with Spock for what should have been his marriage, but what was done was done. And on the journey to Babel father and son had found one another again—yes, he could look forward with equanimity to seeing Spock once more.

Nonetheless, he did not miss the sardonic quality in Spock's coming home to face his father flanked by the same two men he had taken to his Koon-ut Kali-fi. Having gotten to know the crusty doctor and the brave, if impetuous, captain on that same trip to a most disputative excuse for a peace conference, Sarek highly approved of his son's choice of friends. He hoped, however, that soon Spock would not feel a need to bring protectors into his family home.

Sarek walked from his home on the outskirts of ShiKahr to the Vulcan Academy, where he taught and did research when he was not off-planet on diplomatic missions. Sorel insisted that he take at least that much exercise daily, to be certain that his heart maintained full function after the emergency surgery performed by Dr. McCoy. Sarek had not felt so well in years as he did now that he had recovered. The walk was pleasant, not a chore—although he would wait until the cool of the evening to walk back.

Amanda's illness had come as a shock—Sarek had faced his own mortality on board the *Enterprise*, but despite the probability that he would outlive his human wife, he had never before truly faced Amanda's. His relief at the reports Sorel and Corrigan had given him

11

the past few days was un-Vulcan, he knew, but he did not care. Amanda was going to be well again!

In Sarek's office, his teaching assistant, Eleyna Miller, was going through the programs designed by the class he was about to teach. "Good morning, Sarek," she said formally. "I think you'll want to go over Mr. Watson's attempt at a starship navigation program. At least, I deduce that that is what it is supposed to be."

Sarek leaned over her shoulder to study the screen. The columns of numbers should have been totally familiar to him; after all, he had taught this same course and assigned these same problems for years. Mr. Watson's answers, however, were always unique. "Using this program, plot a course at Warp 4 from Vulcan to Earth," he instructed the computer.

"Not possible," the computer replied nasally.

"You can't get there from here," Sarek told Eleyna, deadpan, and was rewarded with one of her disapproving looks.

Although as human as Amanda, Eleyna did not share Sarek's wife's sense of humor—on the other hand, even after more than a year of working closely with Sarek, perhaps she did not believe a Vulcan could possibly be joking with her. On the third hand, it could be part of that "I am more Vulcan than Vulcans" attitude that some humans put on when they studied here. Every so often Sarek wanted to tell Eleyna to be herself—but then, he could never be sure that the strictly formal façade she wore was *not* herself, and so he curbed the remark.

He sorted through Watson's program, highlighting the errors, and added marginal notes to explain where his student had gone wrong. By the time he had finished, it was time for class. The temperature was already rising. The classrooms were several degrees cooler than the outside air, but that was not enough for many offworlders' comfort. Sarek looked out across a sea of perspiring, squirming humans, punctuated with an occasional Andorian, Hemanite, or Lemnorian. The handful of Vulcans sat properly, paying strict attention, taking notes, and still—after a month of the class— looking faintly disapproving when the rest of the class laughed at Sarek's occasional jokes.

The two Tellarites, Sarek noted, were absent— undoubtedly holed up in their quarters with the air-conditioning on full.

Sarek finished his demonstration of the new assignment, and asked for questions. As usual, Mr. Watson's immediate response showed that he had missed the point. Patiently, Sarek explained again, wondering once more how Watson had passed the Academy entrance examinations. T'Sia, a Vulcan girl from one of the colonies, then asked an insightful question, and the class came to life with interest—the discussion continued until time was up.

Two humans, Mr. Zarn and Mr. Stevens, left with T'Sia, still debating. Sarek wondered if the young woman had the slightest notion of her appeal to the human males. Although she appeared to be full-grown, T'Sia would not reach sexual maturity for at least twenty more years. The young humans, finding total lack of response or even comprehension, would soon lose interest. He had seen new students go through this same process time and again.

Human women were more subtle—and far more likely to know or surmise the facts of Vulcan biology. They didn't waste time on Vulcan students; those few looking for a real challenge focused their interest on their male professors. But because male Vulcans who had attained sexual maturity were either bonded or married, no such attempt had ever succeeded, to Sarek's knowledge.

Returning to his office, he found Eleyna working at the computer. For the first time, he wondered what she did in her time off. Did she ever take time off? It was a rare occurrence for Sarek not to find her in his office. Her dissertation was proceeding admirably—he could not fault her for her work or for her assistance. Yet . . . he could not seem to get to know her. Many of his human students, both male and female, had become friends, but Eleyna was an enigma.

Thinking of his human students playing their mating games, Sarek considered whether at Eleyna's age she should not have a male consort. Matchmaking was routine in Vulcan society. Only last year, Sarek and Amanda had helped find a suitable bondmate for his cousin's daughter. But humans did not operate that way.

Ah, but Eleyna seemed to be trying to act Vulcan. Sarek wondered if she would appreciate introductions to some of his human male graduate students. Perhaps it would be better, though, to wait and ask Amanda's advice.

"Eleyna, I am going over to the hospital," he told her.

She looked up, startled—she had been so engrossed that she hadn't heard him enter. Her composure slipped for once, and she blushed, catching her lower lip between her teeth. Then her façade was back. She cleared her screen, and put her hand over the cartridge in the slot. "Your students' programs are graded, Sarek. I can work on my own console in my room if you—"

"No, Eleyna—go ahead with what you were doing. I will be back in approximately one-point-three hours," he replied, for he had seen that she was working with a green cartridge that accessed the main Academy computer. At Eleyna's level of work she often needed programs from the main system that were unavailable to student consoles, but easily keyed up on those in faculty offices. Pleased to allow his student the time she needed for her own work, he set off across the campus toward the medical buildings.

Sarek wended his way into the cool depths of the hospital complex, to a door marked STERILE FIELD ONLY. He entered the airlock, removed his clothes, waited for the rays to bathe his body, and put on the disposable sterile gown that slid out of the slot. Barefoot, he went to the inner door, and spoke into the lock that he had insisted be keyed to his voice as well as the physicians'. "Sarek to see Amanda."

The door slid open, and he stepped into the sterile chamber. Lights came on over the bank of gauges on the left-hand wall, but Sarek was interested only in the dim light they threw into the mass of fluid in the center of the room. The bluish mist was in a colloidal liquid-gaseous state. Within it, Amanda drifted, suspended by antigrav units. Nothing touched the mist but her body. There were no walls enclosing the liquid; a force field held it in a roughly rectangular box-shape.

In six more days Amanda would be removed from the fluid and brought back to consciousness. By the end of the month, Sorel had promised yesterday, she would be released from the hospital, completely cured.

As her body drifted slowly within the mist, her long silver hair forming its own aimless patterns, Amanda seemed a mythic creature from the oceans of her mysterious home planet. Sarek could not see her clearly enough to note any changes; although the treatment was specifically to stop and reverse the nerve degeneration that had begun crippling her, it would also have the effect of reversing aging, as it had done for Dr. Corrigan.

Amanda had laughed when Corrigan told her that. "Why, you'll make it look as if Sarek's robbed the cradle!"

"No—but when it's all over, you'll probably look much the way you did in your mid-thirties," the doctor had reassured her. Sarek had been pleased to hear that. Although Amanda had been in her early twenties when he met and married her, he felt that she had improved with age; he preferred the grace and wisdom of maturity.

The door behind him swooshed open, and someone else padded on bare feet to the wall of gauges. Sarek remained where he was. He knew better than to ask about the readings; delaying one of Sorel's technicians might give the healer an excuse to rescind the visitation privilege he found so illogical.

But the intruder did not leave after studying the dials; instead he came to Sarek's side—and Sarek discovered that it was Sorel himself!

Although they were about the same age, Sorel always seemed much older to Sarek. Healers were the most formal and controlled of all Vulcans; they had to be, as they had the strongest ESP, and had to deal with sick minds as well as sick bodies.

Sorel was as tall as Sarek, but much thinner. His straight black hair showed only the first traces of gray, while Sarek's had been silver for years. But it was Sorel's eyes that made him inscrutable. The irises were so black that they became indistinguishable from the pupils, making it impossible to read them. Since he did not allow his face to reveal his feelings either, it sometimes felt to Sarek as if he were being treated by a computer . . . and a disapproving one at that.

He waited for the healer to open the conversation. If there were any change in Amanda's condition, Sorel would tell him; if not, there was no point in asking.

After a few moments, Sorel said abruptly, "Sarek, I must apologize."

Startled, Sarek waited until he could speak impassively. "You have given no offense, Sorel."

"I made no effort to understand your request for visitation privileges, merely because it was illogical. Now . . . *my* wife is in stasis."

"T'Zan? I did not know she was ill."

"An accident, last night. She was repairing a neural stimulator; it short-circuited, and she sustained extensive nerve damage. We fear . . . even the stasis chamber may not assure total regeneration."

"Who is her physician?"

"Corrigan."

Of course. Sorel's partner, the human doctor who had come to Vulcan with the first human scientists invited to the Academy . . . and who had found a home here, as a few rare humans did. Sorel and Corrigan had first teamed to bring Spock to term alive, and the partnership had flourished over many years. They were generally regarded as the best medical team on Vulcan.

Sorel continued, "Daniel did not ask me—he simply keyed the door of T'Zan's stasis chamber to my voice. I did not think I would do anything so illogical . . . and I have been there already this morning."

Thinking the healer might be embarrassed at admitting an emotional act, Sarek suggested, "Naturally, you wished to inspect Dr. Corrigan's work."

A faint smile—the first Sarek had ever seen on the healer's face—tugged wryly at Sorel's mouth. "No, Sarek. I looked at the dials, but I do not know what they said. I went to do what you do: to be with her, to look at her. I envy you the knowledge that when your wife is released from stasis she will be well."

"If T'Zan is not well when she is released, Corrigan will find a way to make her well. Humans are like that. When they have exhausted all logical approaches, they apply illogical ones until they succeed."

Sorel frowned, and looked into the stasis tank, then back at Sarek. "I sometimes wonder if your bonding with a human has not changed you. Yet—I have never known Amanda to act illogically, while you—"

Sarek expected to be reminded once again of how stupid—although no Vulcan would use such a harsh term—he had been to take on the Babel assignment when he had had two heart attacks. Instead, Sorel said, "I hear that your students think you something of a . . . comedian." He had to use the English word; Vulcan had no such term.

"Offworld students respond to different techniques from those most successful with Vulcans," said Sarek.

"And yet Amanda is very successful at teaching Vulcans."

"Indeed. However, you do know one illogical act on Amanda's part."

"Indeed? Enlighten me."

"She married me," Sarek explained.

"Ah. Indeed." Sorel stared into the blue mist again. "You deliberately provoke the universal Vulcan failing of curiosity, Sarek. How did you come to marry her? Forgive me. I do not expect you to answer."

The awkward moment was broken when the door swooshed open a third time, to admit Dr. Daniel Corrigan. The human physician was short and stocky, genial and gregarious. He had never tried to adopt Vulcan ways, and yet somehow he had managed to keep up his association with Sorel, the most formal of

Vulcans. "I might have known you'd be making rounds as usual, Sorel," he greeted his partner. "Good morning, Sarek."

"Good morning, Dr. Corrigan. If you wish to consult with Sorel—"

"No, there's nothing to consult about—but good news, Sorel. T'Zan is responding much better than we could have predicted. Prognosis is now complete recovery. But I suppose you checked that out for yourself."

"No, Daniel. I read the dials, but I was unable to interpret the data."

Sarek was surprised to hear the Vulcan healer admit to emotion before a human. Then he realized that the surprising thing was that in all the years he had seen them working together professionally, he had never known that they had a personal friendship as well.

"Thank you, Daniel," Sorel was saying. "Can you estimate how long T'Zan must stay in stasis?"

"Twenty to twenty-five days. We'll keep her carefully monitored—but it's only a matter of time now."

"I am pleased to hear that T'Zan will be well," said Sarek. "Does her absence leave you alone in your home, Sorel?"

"Yes," replied the healer. "My children have all left home, although Soton has rooms here at the Academy. My daughter T'Mir will be coming home tonight, however."

"And my son," said Sarek. "Two of his friends will be with him, and I plan to take all of them to Angelo's for dinner. Would you and your daughter care to join us, Sorel? And you, too, Dr. Corrigan?"

"We have a new patient coming in to be set up in stasis," said Corrigan. "A starship crewman with severe nerve damage. Our technique may be able to help him."

"Yes," said Sarek, "I know—that is why Spock and

his friends are coming here. Once you have the unfortunate young man installed in the stasis chamber, perhaps we can all have dinner together."

"T'Mir will arrive too late to join us," said Sorel, "but I would be honored, Sarek."

"Dr. Corrigan?"

"I'd be pleased to join you. And call me Daniel— only my human patients call me Dr. Corrigan."

Returning to his office, Sarek found that Eleyna had left. He was late—she had undoubtedly left ten minutes ago, when his one-point-three hours were up. More Vulcan than Vulcans indeed!

Settling down to his own work, he said, "Computer."

"Working. Do you wish to continue with the program in progress?" The screen displayed a code which Sarek recognized as the Academy medical programming. "If so, insert cartridge A slash S."

Sarek had no such cartridge; it must be one of Eleyna's. But her work had nothing to do with medicine—Then he realized, as he read the code on the screen, that she had been studying the new stasis techniques. Checking on Amanda's progress, no doubt. So she wasn't as cold as she tried to appear.

In his privacy, he allowed himself to smile at the girl's refusal to show that she cared by asking him. He could not tell her that his discovery made him feel a certain paternal warmth toward her. There was one thing he could do, though. Come to think of it, Dr. Corrigan was unmarried. Now that the man was back in perfect health. . . .

CHAPTER 3

*L*eonard McCoy had been on Vulcan only once before in his life, and he would have preferred to forget that occasion. However, he did not think he had forgotten the gravity or the heat until the transporter sparkles dissolved into the Academy Hospital Central Transporter Terminal, and waves of hot air caused sweat to pop through his skin as if he were being cooked.

Beside him, Captain Kirk echoed his thought, "I don't remember it as being *this* hot!"

"It is midsummer," Spock said calmly, and stepped down from the platform to greet his father.

Spock might appear totally emotionless to anyone else, but McCoy saw him swallow hard as he lifted his hand in the Vulcan salute. "Peace and long life, Sarek."

But Sarek no longer accepted the formality of

strangers from his son. He crossed his hands at the wrist, palms out toward Spock, as McCoy had seen Amanda do on the *Enterprise*. "Welcome home, my son."

Spock did not hesitate to touch hands with his father. "I am pleased to be here. Mother?"

"She will be well soon." Sarek turned to the others, now offering the Vulcan salute. "Captain Kirk, Dr. McCoy, may you live long and prosper."

"Thank you, and the same to you, Mr. Ambassador," said Kirk, managing to force his hand into the proper position.

McCoy didn't even try. "We appreciate your hospitality, sir, but I've got a patient—"

"Of course. Please have him beamed down at once. All is in readiness."

There were orderlies waiting with an antigrav gurney to take Carl Remington from the beamdown point into the central hospital complex. There McCoy met for the first time the famous medical team of Sorel and Corrigan—a mismatch if he had ever seen one, yet their amazing contributions to medical science had filled Federation medical journals for decades.

Corrigan was as jolly as McCoy was misanthropic, a short, balding Irishman with laughing blue eyes and a stocky build—yet he seemed hardly old enough to have worked with Sorel all these years. "Let me see," he said when McCoy asked his age. "I forget to think in standard years, I've lived on Vulcan so long. I'm seventy- . . ." he trailed off, calculating.

"Seventy-three-point-six-one years, precisely," supplied Sorel. The healer seemed more of a walking computer than Spock at his worst.

"Then the fact that you appear to be in your thirties is the effect of the stasis treatment?" McCoy asked Corrigan.

"That's right. Cosmetic effects were not the intention. I was dying, Doctor. However, the fact that I *feel* thirty-five again is indeed a blessing."

"Do you think your stasis field will become a standard geriatric treatment?"

"It is far too dangerous," Sorel answered. "Interruption of stasis for even a millisecond causes the field to collapse—and causes the occupant, whose entire life support depends on that field, to die."

"But surely you have a backup system?" McCoy asked.

"Indeed," replied the healer. "There are two power sources operating simultaneously, for even the few seconds it would take for a secondary source to cut in would be too long—once the field collapses, it takes approximately twenty-seven-point-nine minutes to reform after power is restored. In that time, the patient would be dead."

McCoy was watching the blue mist slowly taking form around the body of Carl Remington, already suspended by antigrav units in the middle of the small room. "But Mr. Remington was alive without life support before we put him in there."

"The stasis field is still forming—he is still surviving on his own," Sorel replied. "Only after the field is complete will it substitute for his own involuntary nervous system."

"But there's nothing wrong with his *involuntary* system," McCoy protested.

"It would interfere with the healing process," Corrigan explained, "preventing regeneration of the damaged nerves of his voluntary system. The field shuts off the body's nervous defenses just as certain drugs shut off the chemical immune system when a transplant is done. Just as that technique leaves the patient vulnerable to every kind of infection until his immune system is restored, the stasis field leaves the patient vulnerable to having his whole body shut off, until his own nervous system is restored to function."

"You understand, Dr. McCoy," said Sorel, "that we are taking into this program right now only those patients who would otherwise die in a very short time—or who, like Mr. Remington, are not alive in any sense of the word except bodily function. It is not available to people who simply want to reverse the aging process, and probably never will be."

"Why not? You haven't lost any patients yet, have you?"

"I'm the only one who has been through the entire process," Corrigan replied. "The other three patients have not yet undergone the most dangerous part of the procedure, which can be done only by a Vulcan healer."

"Or by a similarly-trained telepath," Sorel amended. "To release the patient from stasis, a healer must meld with him and bring his mind back into contact with his body. It is a most delicate procedure, Doctor, extremely difficult and even painful. Daniel trusts me completely, and yet I had great difficulty establishing that meld with him."

"He means I put him through hell," Corrigan interpreted.

Sorel continued calmly, "When it is time to bring Amanda out of stasis, Sarek will enter the meld with me, as they are bonded. We assume that that will make it easier, but as we have no such experience yet, we are merely hypothesizing. T'Par will be primary healer to bring my wife out of stasis, but I will also enter the meld, for the same reason."

"The bush Sorel is beating around," Corrigan interrupted, "is this: we are almost certain that we can regenerate Carl Remington's voluntary nervous system. What we cannot guarantee is to rejoin his mind and his body afterward. You've seen the results of sensory-deprivation experiments, Doctor?"

McCoy shuddered. "Yes. Paranoia, hallucinations, delusions—"

"Precisely. I am not exaggerating when I say I put Sorel through hell getting me back. To me, he seemed the devil himself—and he is my closest friend. If I can't trust Sorel, then I can't trust anyone in the universe. So . . . how do we get Remington to trust Sorel or T'Par or any other healer trying to bring him back to his body? He doesn't know any of them. He may retreat into permanent catatonia. We just don't know yet."

McCoy looked from Corrigan to Sorel, unable to read anything in the unfathomable black eyes. But then the healer said, "We must try. We are all healers, and it is our duty to save lives. We have warned you of the potential danger, Dr. McCoy—but Vulcans and humans have one philosophy very much in common. Where there is life, there is hope."

CHAPTER **4**

James T. Kirk could no longer count the number of planets he had visited in his lifetime of careening about the galaxy, but he knew of very few with any size of human population that did not have an Italian restaurant. The one on Vulcan was, naturally, situated near the campus of the famed Vulcan Academy of Sciences. It was called Angelo's, and was run by a human couple who had immigrated from the Deneb system. Perhaps it would have been taken for granted by a less-traveled patron that an Italian restaurant would be run by humans, but Kirk had learned to check out such things after experiences with Andorian pizza and Tellarite linguini.

Of course, since Sarek had chosen the restaurant, Kirk knew the food would be safe for human consumption; however, knowing Spock's tastes, he wondered whether it would be palatable. The moment the party of six walked in the door, though, the humans knew they were in the right place. The air was filled with delicious aromas, and Angelo himself, a swarthy human with an infectious laugh and an Italian accent as thick as Chekov's Russian or Scotty's highland brogue, came bustling to seat the Ambassador's party.

Although most of the customers were human students, Kirk spotted several Vulcans as they were led through various rooms. It was one of those marvelous family jumbles, clearly expanded over the years as business had grown. A back room was set up for them, with linens, china, and crystal imported from Earth— and the temperature set considerably lower than any Kirk had yet encountered today. With a sigh of relief, he settled into a chair and decided maybe he could eat after all, now that he wasn't using all his energy for sweating.

McCoy and Spock were fairly quiet, but Sarek was more outgoing than Kirk had ever seen him. Sorel, the Vulcan healer, was even more intimidating than Sarek, but the little human doctor, Corrigan, was a pleasant surprise. How could such a man live out his life in a place like Vulcan?

But as he watched them interact, Kirk realized how: Corrigan simply remained himself. There was a Vulcan saying, "I rejoice in our differences." Kirk realized that he was seeing it in action.

Although meatless, the food was excellent. Kirk sat back and enjoyed the company—particularly watching Spock watch his father.

"One problem with being a doctor," said Daniel Corrigan as he helped himself to another slice of bread, "is that I don't have time to cook. You know, Sarek, I will be glad to have Amanda out of stasis just so I can taste some of her bread again."

"Sam's bakery has a wide variety of breads," said Sarek, "far superior to computerized goods."

Kirk wondered if "Sam" was a Vulcan or a human name.

"Their kreyla is very good," agreed Corrigan, "but they don't do justice to Earth-style breads."

"This discussion is most illogical," Sorel objected. "Nutrition is nutrition. A perfectly balanced diet can be provided by any kitchen computer."

"That from the man who has just eaten eggplant parmigiana *and* two helpings of spaghetti," observed Corrigan. "Don't tell me you taste no difference between real food and computerized nutrition."

"If he doesn't, *I* do," McCoy interjected. "I haven't had such a good meal since my last leave on Wrigley's. Thank you, Mr. Ambassador."

"Sarek," Spock's father corrected. "I am not on a diplomatic mission now."

Corrigan, however, was not giving up on his Vulcan associate. "Are you going to tell me you would have eaten that much if you had dialed up something from the computer?"

"I had not eaten since yesterday morning," the healer replied with unruffled dignity.

"I never have been able to get you to eat lunch," said Corrigan.

"Vulcans don't eat lunch," chorused Sarek, Spock, and Sorel, and the three humans all laughed.

"What you need, Daniel," said Sorel, "is to marry a woman who is a good cook."

"All right, all right—I'll stop trying to get you to eat properly if you'll stop trying to marry me off!"

Kirk recalled that all male Vulcans were married— had to be—and glanced at Spock. His First Officer, however, was very busy inspecting the almost untouched wine in his glass. Lest Sarek take up the subject of his unbonded son, Kirk decided to turn the discussion back to food. "This was the best meal I've had in a long time, too, Sarek. In fact, it almost tops a little place on Rigel Four—"

They lingered over the last of the wine, enjoying the company and conversation as Kirk had never thought possible in such a mixed party of humans and Vulcans. It looked as if it was going to be a pleasant shore leave after all—if he could just manage to stay out of the heat!

Suddenly Sorel stiffened. His face went pale and he clutched at his chest.

Corrigan was immediately on his feet, medical scanner in hand. "What is it?" he asked.

Sorel gasped once, and then gained a shuddering control. "T'Zan."

"Sorel, she's in stasis," said Corrigan. "She can't feel anything."

"She is dying," the healer said, his eyes focused on something not in the room with them.

"No!" exclaimed Corrigan. "Oh, God, no—it can't be! But come on—let's get back to the hospital."

Kirk and Spock went ahead, clearing a path for the healer, who stumbled, leaning heavily on the small human doctor. Sarek stepped to Sorel's other side to help support him.

They had come in two ground cars, Kirk, Spock, and McCoy with Sarek, and Corrigan and Sorel together. Now, as Sorel was close to passing out, Sarek shoved them both into the back seat of the car they had come in, saying, "Take care of him, Daniel. I'll drive. Spock —you take my car."

"Come on, Spock!" said McCoy, hurrying toward Sarek's car. "If something has gone wrong with one of the patients in stasis, it could happen to all three!"

CHAPTER 5

The monitors!" Daniel Corrigan said from the back seat. "There can't be anything wrong, or by now the hospital would be paging both of us!"

"Trust a bonding over monitors," Sarek said grimly, swinging into the wrong lane to pass two slower vehicles. Fortunately, the oncoming car was driven by another Vulcan, who avoided them easily. If only they encountered no offworlders!

Sarek felt nothing, but forced down fear for Amanda with a Vulcan meditation formula. How could something go wrong in only one stasis chamber? How could he have allowed his wife to undergo the treatment when they knew so little about it?

She would have been dead in only a short time without it, he reminded himself. *Perhaps by now.*

As they careened around a corner two blocks from the hospital, Daniel's communicator began to beep, and within seconds Sorel's was also signaling.

"Corrigan here. What's going on?"

"Power failure to Lady T'Zan's stasis chamber. Please come, Doctor!"

"I'm on my way. Sorel is with me."

At that moment Sorel gave a strangled gasp, the most horrifying sound Sarek had ever heard. He came to a screeching halt before the emergency entrance, and turned to find Daniel supporting Sorel, who had buried his face in his hands. "We're here," Daniel told him. "Come on—we've got to help her!"

When Sorel lifted his head, Sarek did not have to be told. The healer's face was frozen, immobile, expressionless. "We are too late. She is dead."

"Then we'll resuscitate her!" Daniel insisted. "Sarek —please take care of Sorel." And the human doctor left the car and ran into the building.

Sarek had lived with a human long enough to know that no logic would stop Daniel's efforts to save T'Zan. He also knew that his efforts would prove futile; the system had been carefully explained to him before Amanda entered stasis. With her nervous system blocked from functioning, T'Zan could not be revived by even the most advanced life support.

The life that now must be supported was Sorel's. The unexpected severing of his marriage bond could destroy his mind. Death of the body might follow more slowly, but it would be inevitable if he did not get the healing meld he needed now.

When Sarek said, "Sorel, you must come into the hospital," the healer followed him without protest, an automaton. The unreadable eyes were no longer inscrutable—just blank.

The healer T'Par was already coming toward them as

Sarek guided Sorel through the entrance. She touched Sorel's face lightly, then said, "We must have one of his family."

"I'll call his son," said Sarek, and went to the communications console at the desk. The nurse provided Soton's code for him. A young man with features similar to Sorel's appeared on the screen.

"This is a recording," he said. "My sister T'Mir is returning from off-planet today. I will meet her at the spaceport, and take her to the home of my father, Sorel. I can be reached there." The image gave Sorel's code—but all Sarek got at that number was an image of Sorel saying he was off duty, and that the hospital would page him in case of emergency.

Frustrated, Sarek said unnecessarily, "They have not yet returned from the spaceport." Then he realized that James Kirk was standing at his shoulder, watching his efforts.

"May I?" the human asked, and punched in a new code. "Vulcan Space Central, this is Captain James T. Kirk of Star Fleet. Emergency Code 3B. I must find a passenger just arrived on Vulcan." He turned to Sarek. "Do you know what ship she came in on?"

"No."

"Well, her name, then."

"T'Mir. Her brother Soton is meeting her."

"Code 3B," Kirk repeated. "I must locate incoming passenger T'Mir, a young Vulcan woman, or her brother Soton, who is in the spaceport to meet her. They are needed at the Vulcan Academy Hospital, family emergency. We will hold this channel open."

"Vulcan Space Central extends all courtesy to Captain Kirk of Star Fleet," a voice answered. "We are paging T'Mir and Soton on all channels."

"Thank you, Captain," said Sarek. He could have achieved the same goal—but not without precious time lost going through intermediaries. "I hope Soton and T'Mir are not in transit."

"Car?" Kirk asked.

"I do not know. They may be aboard public transit."

"Damn!" said Kirk. "Why didn't the girl beam directly home?"

"T'Mir has no military or emergency priority. She must go through immigration, so she could not beam directly to ShiKahr."

"Well, she's got emergency priority now, if we can reach her. Come on," he said illogically to the blank screen, "answer that page, kids. Your father needs you."

If the situation were not so grave, Sarek would have been amused at the human's illogical behavior, so much like Amanda's. Kirk was a starship captain, Amanda a noted scholar. They were successful, efficient . . . and totally human.

As if in response to Kirk's demand, two young Vulcan faces filled the screen, one Soton, the other a woman, clearly his sister. Their composure was admirable, but Sarek could see the strain in their eyes. Their family bond was obviously strong, the news he gave them of their mother's death only a confirmation of what they had sensed.

"You must come to the Academy Hospital at once," Sarek said. "Your father—"

"We understand," said Soton, looking at his sister, then back to Sarek. "I have Father's ground car. It will take three hours—"

"Too long!" said Sarek.

"I'll arrange to have you beamed here," said Kirk. "Where are you?"

The scene on the screen expanded to show a Vulcan woman in Star Fleet uniform. "We called them to Space Central, Captain."

"Excellent. Patch me through to whichever orbiting station is in position to pick up those kids and send them here. Stay on the channel, Lieutenant—you have all the coordinates at your end."

"Yes, sir," the Vulcan woman replied.

Her picture faded, and was replaced by the face of a male Vulcan in a plain beige tunic with a red badge. A scientist. There were few military personnel on Vulcan's space stations, and those few not in command. Sarek stood ready to back Kirk if necessary.

But the human's attitude changed at once from command to diplomacy. "Orbit Station Two, Star Fleet requests emergency assistance in aid of Vulcan civilians."

"How may I be of assistance, Captain?"

"Soton and T'Mir are at Vulcan Space Central. Their mother has just died. Their father is at the Science Academy Hospital—"

"I understand, Captain. We will beam them aboard Orbit Station Two, and from here directly to the Academy Hospital Central Transporter Terminal."

The scientist and the Star Fleet Lieutenant began giving coordinates to one another. Finally the Lieutenant returned her attention to Kirk. "Soton and T'Mir are being escorted to the transporter."

"Very efficient, Lieutenant . . . ?"

"T'Vel, sir."

"I will see that there is a notation in your record. And from me, personally—thank you."

"You're welcome," she replied at once, as Sarek would have done—using the courtesies of human culture when dealing with a human, just as Kirk had slipped without effort from command stance to the deference required when requesting assistance of a civilian scientist.

Sarek was aware of Spock standing behind Kirk, and

hoped he had noticed the flexibility of the Vulcan woman as well as the human Captain.

Both Kirk and T'Vel were reaching to cut off transmission. Sarek asked hastily, "How long, Lieutenant, until Soton and T'Mir will arrive?"

"It takes approximately five-point-eight minutes to walk from here to the transporter," she said, supplying the only piece of data she had.

It could still be too long. Transporting, changing coordinates, transporting again—then the long walk from the Academy transporter. . . .

"Thank you, Captain Kirk," Sarek said. "I could not have arranged their transportation as quickly as you did . . . and at this moment Sorel's life must be counted in minutes."

As they turned from the desk, Corrigan and McCoy came down the corridor. "It was a failure to one unit only," McCoy announced. "Both Amanda's and Remington's are working fine. Engineers are swarming all over the place trying to trace the failure."

"But T'Zan is dead," Corrigan added. "Where's Sorel? His children—"

"They're on the way," Kirk supplied.

"Thank God!" said the doctor.

Just then a young Vulcan man wearing a laboratory coat came in from another hallway and went to the reception desk. "I heard. . . . that the Lady T'Zan. . . ."

"She is dead," the nurse told him.

"What happened?" the man asked, his voice tense, although otherwise he maintained decorum.

Sarek recognized him as Sendet, a student who had done excellent work in his advanced computer class a few years ago. Now Sendet wore a green badge with a red slash across it, indicating that he was part of the hospital's medical technology staff.

"Until the Lady T'Zan's family releases the information," the nurse was telling Sendet, "I cannot tell you any more."

"We worked together in the neurophysics laboratory," Sendet told him. "I was with her last night, when she was injured. I was told that with the new stasis equipment, there was no danger to her life."

"Sendet." Daniel Corrigan looked up at the tall young Vulcan. "There was a power failure in the stasis unit. That is all anyone knows right now. Please—go and tell T'Zan's colleagues what has happened."

Sendet studied the human doctor for a moment, then said stiffly, "Yes, Daniel. And T'Zan's family—?"

"T'Par is with Sorel, and his children are on the way. There is nothing you can do here."

"No . . ." Sendet said softly, "I am not a member of Sorel's family."

Sarek could not identify the odd tone with which the young man spoke. But Sendet turned and left them.

Daniel started toward the suite of offices he and Sorel shared, just as the healer T'Par emerged.

"Daniel," she said, "Sorel is dying and resists my meld. His children—"

"They will be here in approximately twenty-two minutes," Sarek estimated as he joined the doctor and the healer.

"Too long," said T'Par. "Sorel is retreating from life."

"No!" gasped Daniel. "He can't! I won't let Sorel die, too!" He started toward the office.

T'Par's soft voice stopped him. "He cannot see or hear you, Daniel. There is only one way you can help him: meld with him."

Sarek saw the doctor's face pale—saw T'Par back off a step as her healer's ESP picked up his primal fear. She regained control instantly, and continued as if she had not noticed Daniel's reaction. "You are as close to him as a brother, and you have melded before. You must try, Daniel—if you can keep his mind from retreating only for a few minutes, until his children arrive, you will save his life."

There was stark fear in the human doctor's blue eyes. "I can't do it. I'll—I'll drive him away, T'Par, with the pain and fear I feel at the very idea of melding again. I'm *not* Vulcan!"

"Nor is Sorel human," said the healer, "but he melded with you to bring you out of stasis—suffered your pain and fear that you might live. Do you not owe Sorel something, Daniel?"

The doctor squared his shoulders. "I owe him my life," he said, "many times over. Very well, T'Par . . . I will try. Whatever it takes, I'll hold him here for his family."

CHAPTER 6

*D*aniel Corrigan entered Sorel's office quietly —although there was no reason to tiptoe. The end of the world would not disturb the healer now.

On the lounge used for mind melds, Sorel lay, body limp, eyes open but unfocused. He looked dead. Automatically, Corrigan used his medscanner. Sorel was alive . . . barely. His vital signs were fading even as Corrigan read the scanner.

T'Par had said all he need do was touch his friend's face, and the meld would form if Sorel accepted him as family. If he did not. . . .

Deliberately, Corrigan thrust the negative thought from his mind. He had learned some Vulcan techniques in his years here, and took a moment to compose himself as he sat in the healer's seat. Then he focused on positive memories: Sorel and T'Zan accepting him as a friend all those years ago; the rapport he and Sorel had found in uniting their medical skills; the many times Sorel had been there for him in his times of trouble, accepting his human differences without the judgment of so many other Vulcans.

I rejoice in our differences, Corrigan repeated as he braced himself to accept the one difference that unnerved him: the mind meld. He was not alone; few humans could endure that invasion of self without fear—yet he must not let his fear drive Sorel deeper into himself, further from life.

Delving into his memory, Corrigan called to mind the first time he had been invited to Sorel's home—a scene in the garden, Soton a child playing with his baby sister T'Mir, both guarded by the family sehlat, a great fanged bearlike creature the Vulcans had bred to be as loyal and gentle as a dog.

Corrigan could hear the bells on the toy the children played with, feel the soft evening breeze, smell the blossoms in the garden. . . .

He touched Sorel's face.

Despair!

Emptiness!

Death!

Fighting the instinct to pull away, Corrigan insistently filled the vacuum with the pleasant family scene.

Sorel's powerfully trained mind grasped control—Corrigan fought down terror, then found that Sorel had no interest in invading his mind now. Instead Sorel was yearning toward someone else with memories of T'Zan, wanting only to see her again, touch her again. . . .

As if Corrigan's memory were the catalyst to release a flood of healing memories, the pain and despair faded. The point of view on the remembered scene shifted from the children playing under the watchful eye of the gentle beast to their mother, watching them with the pleasure every Vulcan knew in the presence of children.

Corrigan had always recognized that T'Zan was beautiful, the warmth in her soft brown eyes making it seem, in those days, as if she accepted him more than her husband did.

But through Sorel's eyes Corrigan saw a different T'Zan, just as warm, but far more beautiful. He felt the support of their marriage bond, something he had never understood but merely accepted as a Vulcan fact of life.

Nothing he had ever experienced in a mind meld was like this. Instead of intrusion, embarrassment, invasion of privacy, it was completion, acceptance, homecoming.

Sorel's memories took over. The bonding of Sorel and T'Zan. As if it were his own memory, Corrigan knew that Sorel had been bonded in childhood, but that the girl had died only two years later of a rare fever. They had hardly known one another; the severing of the childhood bond had been painful, but nothing compared to the ending of the full marriage bond of adults.

Sorel's lack of a bondmate had been an advantage during his training as a healer. No one else's feelings intruded on his, nor did the painful mental experiences he had to learn to accept, block, or alleviate, cross over a bond to torment another person before he learned a healer's full control. But his dedication had been cold, ambitious, determined. He was living without something vital to the Vulcan makeup . . . but he did not feel the lack until he met T'Zan.

She was also in training at the Academy, studying neurophysics, the relationship between the chemical and physical elements of the nervous system and sensory and emotional perceptions. She gave a demonstration lecture to Sorel's class of healers-in-training one day, and for the first time in all his years at the Academy, Sorel was unable to keep his mind on the lesson.

Afterward, he followed her into the research area of the hospital. She turned at the door without entering the laboratory, her warm brown eyes studying him, a question in their depths although her face remained otherwise controlled.

"You are not bonded," were the first words he spoke to her.

"Nor are you," she replied, watching him warily.

"Your lecture—" he fumbled.

"You did not hear it," she responded.

"I— Yes, that is correct. May I—borrow your notes to study? Forgive me—" He felt like an utter fool. He had no idea what to say to her, and yet he did not want to leave her presence.

The attraction was not sexual—could not be, as both of them were physiologically immature. They were mentally attuned. Unbonded, they were drawn inevitably to one another despite their differences.

"There is a concert tomorrow evening," T'Zan said. "Will you attend it with me?"

He had never been to an Academy concert, knew nothing of music except what was routinely taught to children, but he said yes eagerly, and left with the printout of her lecture notes clutched tightly in his hands. Only when he got back to his room and spread the notes out on the desk, unable to see anything but her name at the top of the first sheet, did he remember that he had not told her his.

But he looked up the time and place of the concert, and T'Zan's rooms at the Academy, and the next evening knocked at her door to find her waiting. She had done some research herself, for she knew his name already, and also, "You are of the same family as the poet Soran. Did you know him well?"

Soran was a distant relative whose works through most of his life had been considered too far from tradition. A few years ago, just when he had begun to achieve acceptance and recognition, he had died. Being somewhat cynical about the arts, Sorel suspected that the adulation Soran's work had received since his death was *due* to his death—but he did not say so to T'Zan. In a short time he was glad he had said nothing, for she knew and understood Soran's poetry, and had the gift of making it comprehensible to others. He came to appreciate the sensitivity of the man, and now regretted having missed the opportunity of discussion with him at the rare family gatherings.

Sorel's relationship with T'Zan was built upon paradoxes. T'Zan, who had an outgoing warmth uncommon among Vulcans, was working in the sterile, clinical field of neurophysics, which attempted to define feelings in terms of chemical or physical reactions. Sorel had the very strong ESP required of a healer, but lacked the empathy to work well with the patients who most needed his help—until he met T'Zan. Although he barely passed his exam on neurophysics, his teachers noted a steady improvement in his sensitivity to mental and emotional problems as their relationship advanced.

While T'Zan's family might not have the long and heroic history of Sorel's, which could be traced all the way back to the small community of philosophical rebels founded by Surak, it was a respectable line—and Sorel's parents were relieved not to have to search for a suitable bondmate for their son.

So Sorel and T'Zan were bonded, moving easily from

the closeness they had known for months into the unity they had had to deliberately resist until the ceremony which made it proper and accepted.

They were adults, not children, under Vulcan law; their bonding constituted a marriage, and they set up a household together, even though sexual maturity—and children—would come years later. They finished their training, began their careers, and lived in harmony.

Sorel's memories shifted, carrying the human along on the power of his mind to the terror of madness in first pon farr, the sweet assurance of T'Zan's steady sanity. There was no question of a challenge as they endured the ritual of fire and bells. At last they had proved the unity in the eyes of the world that they had known privately since their bonding. Sorel caught T'Zan in his arms, quenching his flame in her welcoming coolness.

T'Zan bore him a son, Soton, and later a daughter, T'Mir. Corrigan appeared in Sorel's memories—alien but respected, then friend, then brother. They first united their medical skills to bring to term the first Vulcan/human hybrid, Sarek and Amanda's son Spock.

But when that infant, a child of such impossibly different heritage, was thriving . . . Sorel's third child, a girl, was born premature and sickly. Despite their combined skills, she died only hours after birth.

By that time Corrigan understood the value of children to Vulcans—each one a precious link with the future. Child abuse or neglect was unheard of here; every child was wanted, and if Vulcans claimed not to know the meaning of the *word* love, they certainly demonstrated that they knew the *feeling* in their care for their children.

So when he spoke the formal words, "I grieve with thee," to Sorel and T'Zan, he meant them with all his heart. Now, reliving the memories from Sorel's point of view, he found that the healer had truly felt his sympathy. He also found that that was when Sorel began wondering why he did not marry.

Sorel's Vulcan curiosity focused on his memories of Corrigan . . . how strange to see himself through alien eyes!

At first Sorel dismissed Daniel's single state because of his youth. Humans did not bond, so his colleague would have to find a wife as he had. There were not many choices; few human women came to Vulcan, except as students at the Academy.

There had been a visiting professor, Theresa Albarini, with whom Daniel had spent a great deal of time. But she did not want to stay on Vulcan, and Daniel was already established here. Sorel had sensed the sorrow in his friend at their parting, but not known how to deal with the human's emotion.

Daniel had not shown serious interest in a woman again for many years, until he became involved in the case of Miranda Jones, a blind human telepath who had come to Vulcan for the training to control her ability.

Sorel knew Daniel was attracted to Miranda, and hoped that the young woman would understand how fine a man he was. He had somehow doubted that she could, yet mistrusted his assessment of a human woman on such a matter. When he spoke of it to T'Zan, who had worked closely with Miranda in designing the sensor web which allowed her to "see," she had said, "Do not encourage Daniel, my husband. I do not think Miranda is capable of appreciating him."

And some days later, Sorel had found Daniel sitting dejectedly in his office, his face in his hands. "Are you ill, Daniel?" he asked.

His friend looked up, and attempted a smile that did

not succeed. "No, I'm not ill, just stupid. *You* knew better—Miranda Jones must be the first human woman in years that you and T'Zan haven't thrown at me. I'm just a foolish old man, Sorel, to think that a sweet young girl like Miranda could have any interest in me."

And that was the first time Sorel realized that his friend was growing old. Their relative stages of life had changed drastically; when Daniel had first come to Vulcan, he had been younger than Sorel, not just in literal years of life, but in the stage of his life. Now Sorel was entering his middle years—and Daniel had passed through his and was on the brink of old age!

In the next few years, the rapid encroachment of age on his friend—far more rapid than was normal for humans—drove Sorel to work even harder on the stasis technique they had begun experimenting with years before. At one time they had hoped to try to regenerate the nerves whose atrophy caused Miranda Jones's blindness, but she had left Vulcan long before their technique reached even the stage at which it might be used as a last resort for a terminal patient.

It had saved Daniel . . . but T'Zan!

T'Zan!

The overwhelming grief surfaced again, Corrigan unable to do more than add his own personal sorrow at the loss of a beloved friend to Sorel's soaring despair.

It was not our technique, he tried to tell Sorel. *It was a power failure.* But his own uncertainty about the cause interfered with his reassurance of his friend.

There was no guilt in the healer's sorrow, however, and no blame to Corrigan, either. There was nothing but bleak emptiness where T'Zan had been—an emptiness that could be only partly filled with memory. For memory inevitably came around to the fact that she was gone. Dead. Beyond reach. . . .

Father.

Another presence entered the meld, gently joining in the sorrow—and then a second, less certain, no less grieving. Soton, with the sure mental touch that would make him as fine a healer as his father one day, and T'Mir, coming home after years off-planet to such a terrible welcome.

I grieve with thee. The response was so natural Corrigan hardly had to think it—and both young people touched his mind with gratitude and shared sorrow.

Sorel accepted the meld with his children. Corrigan felt the natural bonds of family reaching out to him, too. How strange in the midst of such grief to know joy in their acceptance!

Then the contact lessened, and he became aware of the physical world again. T'Par had lifted his hand from Sorel's face. Soton and T'Mir each held one of their father's hands, and each touched Corrigan while T'Par disentangled him from the meld.

"They will care for him now," T'Par said softly. "Come, Daniel—you must rest. You have done well. Sorel will live."

Reluctantly, he let go—and staggered against T'Par when he tried to stand. He realized that his face was wet with tears, but the healer merely wiped it with a soft cloth, and guided him to his own office. He was too exhausted to try to go home. He lay down on his own couch.

T'Par pulled his shoes off and put a blanket over him, then touched his forehead. "Shall I—?"

"I'll sleep," he said, now wanting only for her to go away so he could give in to the wracking sobs that were the human way of cleansing grief. T'Par nodded, and left.

Alone, Daniel Corrigan wept for the loss of a dear

friend, and for the loss of something he had never known before this night: the family he had had for a few moments in a depth of love and joy such as few could ever have experienced before. The family which now shut him out of their shared sorrow.

After a time, alone, he slept.

CHAPTER 7

Sarek woke at his usual hour, but after being up late last night in the heat and gravity, in air thinner than they were accustomed to, his human guests showed no sign of stirring. Even Spock was still sleeping soundly.

So Sarek went into the home office he and Amanda shared, and called his office at the Academy. As he expected, Eleyna was already there. When he came on-screen, she started. "Sarek!"

"Please take my morning class, Eleyna."

"Of course," she replied. "But Sarek, are you all right? You are not ill?"

"No, I am not ill. However, there was an emergency last night which kept my guests up late."

"An emergency?"

"One of the stasis chambers malfunctioned and the patient died."

"Not . . . your wife?" The young woman's voice carefully hid her emotions.

"No. T'Zan, wife of the healer Sorel."

Eleyna looked away from the screen for a moment, then back. "I did not know anyone else was in stasis. I am . . . pleased that Amanda is safe." There was a slight tremor in her voice.

"She is safe. But my guests will want to go to the hospital this morning, and I wish to check the data myself. Take my class, Eleyna—you can teach it as well as I can." He suddenly realized that Eleyna could give him a way out, at least until she completed her degree and left Vulcan. "In fact," he told her, "I shall recommend to Senek that you teach the course next term. You are fully qualified, and teaching experience will be a useful addition to your credentials."

"I am honored by your confidence in me, Sarek," she said neutrally, and he wondered if she realized he had found a logical way to foist a thankless task off on her.

Sarek went to the kitchen—Amanda's kitchen, smelling of the spices and herbs she kept in loose-lidded containers. His wife was an excellent cook; Sarek found it easy to eat two meals each day when Amanda prepared them. On his own, he was likely to have nothing but a piece of fruit for breakfast, and there were days when he entirely forgot about an evening meal.

But with guests in the house he dialed up the list of meals Amanda had prepared and frozen before entering stasis, selected a savory vegetable stew which would keep, even if they were late getting home, and programmed the kitchen computer to thaw and heat it for that evening. Then he set out kasa juice, and put on coffee to brew.

Surprisingly, Spock was still not up. He expected the

humans to be late risers, but his son usually awakened early, and Sarek was hoping to have some private time with him this shore leave, Spock's first since father and son had "mended their fences," as Amanda put it, on the journey to Babel.

Sarek had heard the human expression before, knew what it meant, but when it was applied to the situation between his son and himself he had pondered the literal meaning. "My wife," he had asked, "why is placing a fence between two people a symbol for improving relations between them?"

They had been aboard the *Enterprise*, after Sarek was released from Sickbay. In a few hours they would reach Babel, where Federation history would be made.

"Are you not about to make peace by placing a fence around Coridan?" Amanda asked.

"Please elucidate."

"On Earth, if one farmer was raising corn and another cattle, if the fence between their lands was broken the cattle would eat and trample the corn. The farmers might have many arguments about it—but if together they mended the fence, both the incidents and the arguments ceased."

"So," said Sarek, "if we put the 'fence' of Federation membership around Coridan, we keep the Orions out of the dilithium—"

"Like cows out of the corn," Amanda replied, her blue eyes twinkling. Then she sobered. "When people have irreconcilably different philosophies, such as the Federation's belief in freedom and the Orions' belief in slavery, there is nothing to do but place a 'fence' that both sides will respect between them. It also works between individuals."

She had called up for him from the ship's library a twentieth century poem, "Mending Wall," by Robert Frost. Sarek had read it carefully, and thought he understood the concept, "Good fences make good neighbors."

Now, though, it was the first line of the poem that repeated in his mind: "Something there is that does not love a wall." He did not want a wall between himself and his son. Surely their differences were not irreconcilable. Now that Sarek had accepted Spock's choice of Star Fleet as a career, he was not at all certain that they *had* any differences.

Yet the rest of the journey to Babel, and one other time Sarek had traveled aboard the *Enterprise*, Spock had buried himself in his work and avoided seeing his father except in public gatherings.

Two moments stood out in Sarek's memory, moments when he had hoped the restraint was dissolving. The first was in Sickbay, after his surgery, when father and son had spontaneously closed ranks to tease Amanda. The other was at a poker game—a simple human card game based on mathematical probability. Several of Spock's colleagues had invited the two Vulcans to join in. Sarek recalled Spock's astonishment—indicated, of course, by no more than one raised eyebrow—when his father agreed.

Ship's rules prohibited gambling for money, so the stakes had been mostly consumable items. Between them, Spock and Sarek had accumulated a considerable horde—including several bottles of very old Scotch.

But the moments of camaraderie had been fleeting— as if each time Spock regretted letting his guard down, and reasserted his formality . . . perhaps fearing he had offended his father.

We must not go on this way, Sarek thought. *Spock is my son. Why can we not also be friends?*

CHAPTER *8*

*D*aniel Corrigan woke with a start—his physician's reflexes brought memory instantly clear, and he looked at his chronometer with a rush of guilt. Mid-morning. He had missed three appointments already! And he had to cover for Sorel. . . .

No patients waited in the outer office, but T'Sel, who arranged schedules for both Sorel and Corrigan, was at her desk. She looked up as he entered, and reported, "Sorel is recovering in healing trance. The two occupied stasis chambers are functioning normally. T'Par and M'Benga are taking your patients today. T'Par instructed me to give you theris tea and call her when you woke."

Corrigan knew better than to argue. By the time he had drunk his tea, T'Par arrived. She took him into his office, and touched his face—the cold, impersonal mind touch he had always known until last night. He struggled not to flinch.

"You seem to be unharmed, Daniel. I do not want you to work today, though. Sleep again if you can—and take comfort in the knowledge that however painful that meld might have been for you, you saved Sorel's life."

"It was not painful," Corrigan replied. "I've never known anything like it before."

"Sorel accepted you as family—I hoped he would. But I did not know you would perceive a difference in the meld. When I entered, it seemed you were experiencing the same discomfort. . . ." She trailed off as she realized, "That was a response to my intrusion, then. Forgive me, Daniel. I should not have drawn you out of the meld so abruptly."

"I'm all right. The kids—uh, Sorel's children?"

"They have purged their grief with their father, and are resting. As you should rest."

"I'm slept out for the moment," he told her. "What I need is a shower and some coffee. Then I want to see the engineering reports on what happened in the stasis chamber."

"Daniel—" she began reprovingly.

"I won't see patients today—it is possible that my judgment could be off. But I must satisfy my curiosity about what went wrong last night."

Curiosity was one emotion Vulcans admitted, and even approved. "I understand," said T'Par. "Do not overtire yourself, Daniel."

He showered and shaved. The sonics quickly cleaned his clothes, and he put them back on, feeling much more like himself. He had his own coffee brewer in his office, and soon sat sipping the fragrant beverage while he studied the reports on his computer screen. They told him nothing. He frowned, punched buttons, frowned again. There was no evidence of malfunction . . . yet a woman had died.

The more he concentrated on the figures on the screen, the less they told him. Quelling annoyance, he called the hospital engineering section. Storn, chief of engineering services, came on-screen immediately.

"I have been expecting your call, Daniel. My people have spent the night trying to trace the malfunction, and they are still working. Thus far we have been unable to trace the source of the power failure."

The Vulcan spoke calmly, but Corrigan saw the traces of frustration in the olive smudges under his eyes, the deepened frown lines. Concentration was an art Vulcans learned early, but concentration without results took its toll on any sapient being.

"Please keep working on it," Corrigan told him, "and call me when you find out what happened. Meanwhile, the other two stasis chambers—"

"Are being monitored visually as well as by computer," Storn assured him. "We will continue to do so until we have found and corrected the malfunction."

"Thank you," Corrigan said grimly, and cut off. Damn Vulcan efficiency anyway! He would have welcomed an excuse to shout at someone.

Instead, he went through the private door joining his office to Sorel's, to look at his partner lying in trance. The healer's face was pale and blank, but that was normal for the trance, as were the life signs on the monitors, which showed heartbeat and respiration far below normal. There was nothing he could do for Sorel now. He felt cut adrift, wanting to take action, frustrated every way he turned.

As he reentered his own office, T'Sel came through the outer door. "Soton and T'Mir would like to speak with you, if—"

"Send them in, T'Sel."

But as Sorel's son and daughter seated themselves on the other side of his desk, all Corrigan could tell them was, "I have no answers for you. So far no one has been able to trace the source of the power failure to your mother's stasis chamber."

"We did not come to question you, Daniel," said Soton. Sorel's son was a younger version of his father, except that he had his mother's warm, expressive eyes.

"Daniel, we came to thank you," said T'Mir, and the new maturity in her voice made Corrigan look at her closely for the first time. To all outward appearances, she was the same young woman who had left Vulcan seven years before, to serve an apprenticeship in xenobiology. But exposure to other cultures had given her a certain . . . sophistication. No—that was not the right word. . . .

He dismissed his search for a descriptive term and accepted the gratitude of the two young people he had watched grow up. Soton had been ten years old, T'Mir just a baby, when Corrigan had come to Vulcan. He was not stranger or alien to them—he would have known that from the acceptance he had felt in the meld if he had not already known it for many years.

"You saved our father's life," said Soton. "Daniel, you have acted as Father's brother to us many times before, but never as you did last night. T'Par should not have pulled you out of the meld as she did."

"No!" agreed T'Mir. "We could not stop her, as Father needed our attention—but we felt your pain of separation, Daniel. Just because Father accepted you and not T'Par—"

"No, T'Mir," Corrigan corrected, "T'Par wished only to free me from what she assumed was a painful experience. It was she who insisted that I try the meld when Sorel rejected her. You must not accuse her of negative emotions when she acted in every way as a healer, for the benefit of her patient."

"Forgive me, Daniel," said T'Mir, lowering her eyes and accepting his admonition as she would have her father's. Then she looked up and added, "My concern is for you."

Her brother's eyebrows rose, but he said only, "As is mine. Now that Father is recovering, I suppose T'Par has already—"

"Yes, she examined me as soon as I woke, but you may check for yourself that I have no ill effects, Soton."

Sorel's son was completing his residency as a healer. In less than a year, he would join his bondmate on the other side of the planet, where he planned a private practice in a small community, quite unlike the research post his father held here at the Academy.

"One . . . does not have many opportunities to examine humans," he said—which was true enough. Humans in ShiKahr came to Corrigan or one of the other human doctors. But he knew perfectly well that Soton wanted to confirm his condition for himself, exactly as Corrigan had had to examine Sorel this morning.

He steeled himself for another impersonal mind touch—but what he felt as Soton's hand was positioned on his face was the gentle familial warmth he had known last night . . . a healing touch, soothing away the abrupt break and suppressed sorrow. "Thank you," he murmured as Soton withdrew as gently as he had made contact.

T'Mir looked curiously at her brother. "Perhaps I should have become a healer, too."

Corrigan did not know what to make of that remark. All the reports of T'Mir's progress during her apprenticeship had been laudatory, and her letters home enthusiastic.

Soton gave T'Mir a look Corrigan could not interpret, then said, "Mother's memorial will take place tomorrow. Daniel, will you stand as Father's brother?"

"I shall be honored. But you must instruct me as to what I will have to do."

"I will instruct you," said T'Mir. "Tomorrow, before the memorial."

When the two young people left, Corrigan went back to his study of the engineering reports. Somewhere in those figures there had to be an answer to how two power systems to a single chamber could fail without warning. But what was it?

CHAPTER 9

The chiming of a grandfather clock penetrated into James T. Kirk's dream. He was visiting his grandmother's farm. It was July, and the heat was oppressive, but he and his brother Sam would be off to the fishing hole. . . .

As he opened his eyes, the dream vanished. No dappled shade filtered through the branches of an apple tree into *this* bedroom. Harsh desert sunlight glinted off the light walls, making him squint for a moment.

Kirk had been given Spock's room and McCoy the guest room in Sarek's house—a house far from anything Kirk would ever have imagined as the home Spock had grown up in. He had envisioned either a sterile, unadorned "environment," or a castlelike ancestral residence. Instead, the house on the outskirts of ShiKahr was a simple single-family dwelling. The architecture was ubiquitous throughout the galaxy; only the occasional curve where a human might have put an angle—or vice versa—marked it as Vulcan.

The furnishings, though, made it both unique and homelike, a comfortable mixture of Vulcan pieces and Amanda's family heirlooms. The clock was one—made of dark rubbed walnut, it stood in the hallway, its pendulum swinging majestically, neither the time its hands told nor the phases of the moon shown at the bottom of the dial having anything to do with time on moonless Vulcan—or so Kirk had thought.

"I hope the chimes will not disturb you," Sarek had said as he showed Kirk and McCoy to their rooms last night, "but Amanda would not forgive me if I allowed her clock to stop."

"How would she know?" McCoy asked. "It can't tell Vulcan time."

"Ah, but it does," Sarek said. "When my wife first came to Vulcan she adjusted the clock until midnight and noon corresponded to Vulcan midnight and midday. The other times are meaningless."

"Not to Mother," Spock put in. "Nor to me as a child. Do you remember, Father, how you stopped the clock when I relied on its chimes, not developing my time sense?"

Kirk had seen a look of shared memory pass between father and son, and then Sarek had said, "I need not have been concerned. However, at the time I feared you would inherit no Vulcan abilities."

Spock had not answered, and Kirk guessed that he feared to say the wrong thing. Sarek was completely hospitable and congenial, showing nothing of his famed temper. But Kirk had seen that temper released once— and once was enough, when Sarek had casually thrown the persistent Tellarite ambassador against the wall in the *Enterprise* reception room.

This morning Kirk moved quietly through the house. McCoy's door was still closed. The smell of coffee drifted from the kitchen, but when he found his way to it the room was empty.

Freshly-brewed coffee steamed on the counter beside a pitcher of blue-green juice. Knowing neither Sarek nor Spock would put out anything harmful to humans, Kirk tasted a small glass of juice. The flavor was tangy—somewhere between pineapple and cranberry. He drank it down, then poured himself a cup of coffee and walked to the window to look out at the garden.

In the heat, the plants were withered and dry. Kirk guessed that they could come quickly to life with a little water, like desert plants the galaxy over. He savored the coffee, but was about to turn away from the dull outdoor scene when a movement caught his eye. At the back of the garden was a greenhouse—and someone was moving about inside.

When Kirk opened the back door, the morning heat flared over him like the blast from an oven. He almost retreated, but curiosity got the best of him, and he made his way down the path to the greenhouse.

It was deliciously cool inside. "Good morning, Captain Kirk," said Sarek.

"Call me Jim," he replied. "I'm off-duty, too. This is quite a setup."

The cool, dim interior focused as his eyes adjusted after the bright sunlight. At the far end of the glass enclosure were miniature fruit trees, citrus, apple, peach. Then there were a few tomato plants, peppers, onions, beans—not many of each, but a wide variety. A tub held a strawberry vine, twining all over itself in a display of blossoms and fruit.

"A little piece of Earth," said Kirk, breathing in the moist, oxygen-rich air.

"Literally," Sarek replied. "We brought the soil,

seeds, and slips from Earth many years ago. The intention was to make certain that Amanda, and the few other humans in ShiKahr at that time, had foods with the trace elements required to maintain health. There are so many humans here now that there is a commercial establishment growing Terran foods—but my wife likes being able to pick what she needs from her own garden."

And you enjoy puttering with something like this just as much as your son does, Kirk thought as he watched Sarek tying up tomato vines with practiced skill. "Where do you get enough water at this time of year?"

"ShiKahr is built over artesian wells," Sarek explained. "With solar power, water is easily pumped to all parts of the city. We do not irrigate the outdoor gardens while the water table is low—but there is adequate water for this small greenhouse. It is all recycled, of course, as is the water from the shower, which is cleansed and filtered and added to the system here."

"Shower?" Kirk asked, trying not to pounce. Water showers were a shore leave luxury he had not expected to find on Vulcan. The bathroom between his room and McCoy's was equipped with sonics, like the ones aboard ship.

"Many humans prefer water to sonics," Sarek observed. "When the plumbing for the greenhouse was installed, I had water run into the master bathroom for Amanda. If you or Dr. McCoy would care to use it—"

"I'm sure you know humans well enough to be sure we'll take you up on that offer," said Kirk. "On board ship, water showers are by prescription only!" He wandered along, examining the green plants. "Everything is so alive in here, compared to outside."

"On Vulcan, it is in the heat of summer that the vegetation dies. Before you leave, the rains should come—and you will see the garden come to life. Just now, though, only the carnivorous plants out in the desert are at their best; in the season of drought they catch many animals weakened with thirst."

Unlike the hydroponic gardens on the *Enterprise,* Sarek's greenhouse contained no purely ornamental plants. "No room for roses," Kirk observed.

"Some are grown in the commercial greenhouses. Amanda was pleased when she could have some again. . . but once they are cut, they die quickly here. So she does not buy them."

"Vulcan respect for life," Kirk suggested.

"And human," Sarek replied. "My wife does not reject her heritage. You did not have time to become well acquainted with her before. I know she will be pleased to find you and Dr. McCoy here, off-duty. She will expect Spock, of course."

"Just in case," Kirk commented. "I know, Vulcans consider worry an inefficient use of energy—"

"Did my son tell you that?"

"He once suggested that one of our young officers have his adrenal gland removed," Kirk recalled.

Sarek's eyebrows rose, and Kirk stifled a smile at the expression so much like Spock's. Then, "Worry is unprofitable. Concern, however, can prepare one for emergencies, expected or unexpected. Spock is here now out of concern for his mother and for me. We have ended our differences, Jim."

"I know. I'm glad."

"Will you wish to join us today in inspecting the engineering report on last night's power failure?"

"Yes—I'd like to see that report. I wish Scotty were here. Not that I don't trust your engineers— it's just that I don't know them the way I do Mr. Scott."

"And our engineers are Vulcan," Sarek added. "They will study all the logical sources of the malfunction, but they will not . . . play hunches."

At the Academy, Kirk felt odd man out. McCoy wanted to study the medical potential of the stasis procedure, Spock and Sarek set to work at Sarek's computer terminal, and Kirk had nothing to do but watch, although he itched for action.

Daniel Corrigan, looking slightly pale and puffy-eyed, but otherwise none the worse for whatever he had gone through last night, was eager to show McCoy around. "T'Par won't let me work today—but that leaves me free to show you our facilities."

"I'd like to look in on Remington first," said McCoy, "and Amanda, too, if you don't mind. She's not my patient, but she is a friend . . . and the mother of a closer friend—"

"No apologies necessary, Leonard," said Corrigan, falling into the Vulcan first-name habit. Before the two doctors left, though, he turned to the Vulcans. "Sorel will remain in seclusion until the memorial for T'Zan tomorrow—it is set for midday. You are family, Sarek—"

"We shall be there," Sarek replied, "to honor the memory of the Lady T'Zan."

When Corrigan and McCoy had gone, Kirk watched Spock and Sarek playing the computer console in total rapport, frowning in unison as each new display appeared—apparently without the information they were seeking. Within half an hour they had gone beyond the universal computer symbols and were calling up diagrams with notations that were Greek to Kirk . . . except that he understood the standard

Greek symbols, and so concluded that these were Vulcan.

He was considering taking a walk—but dreading the blistering heat—when a woman entered Sarek's office. She was exquisite—exactly the physical type that made Kirk's blood pound in his arteries. Human, blond, petite, with a soft, innocent face and huge blue eyes. Her lightweight summer garment, although it covered her from throat to ankles, did not hide the contours of a perfect figure.

She moved confidently, obviously belonging here, and set a pile of cassettes on the work table. Glancing at the two Vulcans so engrossed in their work that they did not notice her entrance, she favored Kirk with a smile. "Like father, like son, it appears. That is Sarek's son, is it not?"

"Yes—and I'm James T. Kirk."

"Captain of the *Enterprise*. I'm pleased to meet you. I am Sarek's assistant, Eleyna Miller."

Sarek's assistant—that meant a fine brain to go with the lovely exterior, and Kirk's heart beat even faster. He found most compelling the kind of highly-intelligent woman who looked as if she could get anything she wanted just by batting her big blue eyes. Come to think of it, that certainly wouldn't work at the Vulcan Academy of Sciences!

Nor did Eleyna bat her eyes at Kirk. After the single smile, she donned an air of Vulcan composure and approached the computer terminal. "Excuse me, Sarek —may I interrupt for a moment?"

"Of course," Spock's father replied, and proceeded to introduce his son to his assistant.

Giving Spock only the barest acknowledgment, Eleyna asked, "Shall I take your students' assignments to correct on the terminal in my room, Sarek?"

"No, you may have this one. We have not found the information we need at this terminal, and are moving closer to the source."

Spock said, "Jim, we are going to examine the monitors at the stasis chambers. The engineering section has been unable to find the source of the malfunction, but—"

"But you may see something they didn't. Go ahead, Spock. I'll join you later."

But when they had gone, Eleyna sat down before the computer terminal and began programming in the revision mode. Kirk asked, "How about some lunch before you go to work on those?"

She looked up at him and flashed the smile again. "I wish I could, Captain, but teaching Sarek's class has put me behind in my own work. I would enjoy hearing about your adventures in Star Fleet. Perhaps we can find a time before you leave Vulcan."

But she did not suggest a time, and Kirk recognized a polite brush-off when he heard one. He received them seldom enough not to let it be a blow to his ego . . . so he left Sarek's office with just a small regret. Eleyna Miller was the most attractive thing he had yet seen on Vulcan.

The Academy complex was huge, but directions were well marked in several languages. Kirk found his way to the hospital easily enough, and soon located Spock and Sarek with another Vulcan named Storn, studying the guts of a wall-sized computer whose panels they had removed.

"These monitors recorded no fluctuation in power," Storn was saying, "and yet the power failed completely. That is not possible. There are far too many safeguards."

"So I see," Spock noted.

"Until we find the source of the power failure, though," Sarek observed, "we cannot guarantee that it will not happen again."

And your wife will be in danger, and my crewman, thought Kirk. *Damn, but I wish Scotty were here!*

CHAPTER **10**

Leonard McCoy was beginning to dislike his second visit to Vulcan almost as much as his first. What the devil was he doing at the funeral of a Vulcan lady he'd never even met?

As many of the members of the family as could get there were supposed to attend, Spock had explained, and would have gone into a detailed genealogy to show how his family and Sorel's were distantly related had not McCoy stopped him by growling, "Well, *I'm* not related to 'em!"

"You and Captain Kirk are guests in our home, Doctor," Spock had explained patiently. "Guests are traditionally treated as family. Please understand that none of us will be expected to participate in the ceremony. That is the duty of the immediate family, while we are very distant relatives. However, the larger the number of friends and relatives in attendance, the greater the honor shown the deceased."

That lady sure has plenty of honor, McCoy thought as he looked around the auditorium where the memorial was held. It was packed. He and Jim were high up on one side. A few rows away he saw another human, Dr. M'Benga, whom he had met briefly yesterday. Like McCoy, he was a Star Fleet physician, but he had spent the last three years here at the Vulcan Academy, learning to treat Vulcans. Quite a number of them were now in Star Fleet, but it was almost impossible to get Vulcan healers to enlist. Hence the training program for human doctors.

Could I ever have used someone with that training when I had to operate on Spock's father! McCoy thought. But he had managed, he reminded himself with deserved pride. Sarek was obviously in robust health these days.

The crowd was quiet already, but fell completely silent as Sorel and his family appeared on the platform below. His immediate family was small: Sorel, his son, his daughter, and—McCoy was surprised to see—Dr. Daniel Corrigan.

Through another entrance on the opposite side came a small but imposing figure: T'Pau. Leaning on her cane, the aged Vulcan matriarch approached the family and spoke in the ancient ritual dialect which McCoy's translator interpreted as a rather arcane form of English.

"Thee claims this outworlder as kin, Sorel?" Her voice dripped scorn.

Unemotional Vulcans, indeed! McCoy thought, remembering how this woman's prejudice had almost cost James Kirk his life.

Before Sorel could answer, Corrigan spoke up for himself. "I am no outworlder, T'Pau. I am Vulcan."

He forced her to answer, and thus acknowledge him. "You have Vulcan citizenship. A piece of parchment does not change your blood."

Sorel's daughter took a step forward, but her brother on one side and her father on the other pulled her back. *That's right,* thought McCoy, *let him show up the old battle-ax by himself!*

"Blood is blood," the human replied. "Mine sustains life as does yours. Human and Vulcan alike honor life. Today I have come to honor the life of a dear friend, now gone from us. Why have you come here, T'Pau?"

She stared at him haughtily for a long moment. Then her whole demeanor changed. "Thee speaks wisely, Daniel Corrigan. We are here to honor the memory of T'Zan. Sorel, hast thou been comforted by thy brother and thy children?"

Well I'll be damned! thought McCoy. Come to think of it, when he had pushed her she had let him give Jim that shot he had claimed was tri-ox. *You've just got to prove you're not afraid of her,* he surmised, and settled back to watch the ritual below.

The memorial service was simple and restrained, as he supposed a Vulcan funeral ought to be. Spock had explained that Sorel and his family were feeling neither the sharpness of fresh grief nor the false numbness that humans often knew before a loss was accepted. Supposedly they had done their grieving already, joined together in a mind meld. After this memorial they would return to their duties, their grief worked through and their loss accepted as if it had happened years ago.

McCoy hoped it was true. He didn't like the lack of answers he had gotten so far on the stasis chamber failure. It made him nervous to have two patients life-dependent on machinery that could fail again.

Just four more days, and Amanda would be released. That was some relief—he liked Spock's mother very much, and had seen enough of her interaction with Sarek to know that their unlikely marriage had a solid foundation. God forbid some mechanical malfunction should end that relationship just in the promise of a new beginning!

When the memorial ended, people began filing quietly out of the auditorium. As Sarek, Spock, and McCoy moved toward an exit, though, Jim Kirk turned in the opposite direction, toward the family group on the central platform. Sarek noticed, and changed course, saying, "It is appropriate to pay respects to the family."

As they worked their way down to the platform, a young Vulcan man approached Sorel's family. "My respects, Sorel. I grieve with thee."

"Sendet," Sorel acknowledged, and McCoy remembered where he had seen the man before—inquiring about T'Zan at the hospital. "Your presence honors us."

"Indeed?" the young man asked, his finely-chiseled features narrowly avoiding a sneer. "I would have been honored to stand with your family, Sorel."

McCoy caught the young man's look toward T'Mir, and saw her lower her eyes. So. A suitor.

They would certainly make a *beautiful* couple, he thought. Sorel's daughter was slender and delicate, and moved with a dancer's grace. Although she maintained Vulcan dignity in her bereavement, McCoy could not help noticing her beautiful, expressive eyes. No wonder she veiled them now, lest they reveal something inappropriate to the occasion.

Sendet was tall and well-built, with dark brown hair and large eyes fringed with thick black lashes. He had the kind of handsomeness McCoy had envied as a callow youth—the kind that had only to exist to attract every girl in sight. Aristocratic features, his mama would have called them.

But McCoy had long since outgrown that kind of envy . . . so what was it he didn't like about this young man he didn't even know? The pride, the air of being better than those around him?

Sorel was saying, "If your place is among us at some future time, you will be welcome, Sendet. For today, we appreciate your attendance as T'Zan's colleague and friend."

As Sendet moved to one side, staring at T'Mir—who still refused to meet his eyes—McCoy decided what it was he didn't like: Sendet's mind was obviously on his own concerns instead of on the poor dead lady and the needs of her family. He had seen people like that at funerals back home in Georgia, much more concerned with being granted their proper "place" than with consoling the grieving family.

With Sendet out of the way, McCoy worried that Kirk might create further disruption of the peace the ceremony had brought. Of course it was possible Kirk intended only to pay his respects as representative of Star Fleet . . . but McCoy suspected the Captain had something else in mind.

Sure enough, although he spoke formal phrases to Sorel and his family straight out of the Star Fleet manual, it was the wizened T'Pau who was Kirk's true target. She stood to one side, as if dissociating herself from the family contaminated by a human in its midst. McCoy saw disapproval on her face as Dr. M'Benga stopped to express his sympathy.

What ever happened to IDIC? McCoy wondered as he felt T'Pau's eyes rake over him, then glance elsewhere as if he did not exist. M'Benga left without approaching T'Pau, and McCoy had no desire to try to talk to her. But James T. Kirk went from his formal remarks to T'Zan's family straight across the platform to the Vulcan matriarch.

"T'Pau. We meet again."

Only when he spoke did she deign to look at him—and for a moment McCoy thought she would refuse to recognize him. Finally she said, as if she were accusing him of a crime, "You live, James Kirk."

"No thanks to you," Kirk replied with enforced calm.

As if she had not heard, T'Pau looked beyond Kirk to Spock and McCoy. "You live, and Spock lives." McCoy felt her eyes pierce him like a phaser beam. "Humans mock our traditions." And she turned and walked away.

Her slow pace could not take her far before Kirk recovered from the snub—but he took only one step after her before McCoy caught his arm. "Jim—let it be!"

"Dammit, Bones, I was giving her a chance to apologize! What happened to Vulcan respect for life?"

"We don't understand all their traditions. Obviously they hold some things higher than life. So do you—so don't quibble just because what T'Pau holds sacred isn't the same thing you do."

Kirk's anger abated, but he said, "I thought logic was supposed to do away with prejudice."

"T'Pau's the older generation," McCoy observed. "Look around you—we're accepted by everybody else. Your actions will reflect on all the humans who live here, long after we've gone back to the *Enterprise*."

"You're right, Bones," said Kirk. "Still . . . I'd like to teach that woman a lesson someday!"

CHAPTER **11**

After the memorial, most of the audience scattered to their work. Soton's bondmate T'Pree had been seated in the front row, along with cousins, aunts, uncles, Sorel's grandfather, and T'Zan's parents. This extended family, T'Mir had explained to Corrigan, would now go with the principals for a traditional meal.

Corrigan knew all of these people, although some of them only from the memorial for Sorel's parents some fifteen years ago, when he had sat in the ranks of friends and not participated in the banquet. For the first time, he wondered if they thought one of Sorel's male relatives should have enacted the role of brother. No doubt had crossed his mind when he stood up to T'Pau: if Sorel wanted him, he was there for his friend. But family disapproval might fall on Sorel. . . .

He could feel the steely disapproval of Sendet, but

dismissed it, as he was not a family member. The young man finally turned his icy stare away from Corrigan and said to T'Mir, "We must speak together soon, now that you have returned to Vulcan."

"We have nothing to discuss, Sendet," she replied, her voice as gentle as if she spoke to a child she did not wish to hurt, yet had to discourage.

"It has been seven years, T'Mir. We have both matured. Your father—"

"Sendet, this is neither the time nor the place," Sorel interrupted him. "The family must leave."

Sendet's eyes fell on Corrigan once more. "You claim this outworlder as family, and insult a member of one of Vulcan's most noble clans?"

Soton on one side and T'Mir on the other moved in to flank Corrigan. Soton said, "There is no offense where none is taken."

T'Mir added, "Nobility lies in action, not in name."

Both were quoting Surak. Sendet could not answer without denying Vulcan tradition. It was obvious Sorel was not going to invite him to the traditional meal . . . and the clan was gathering to back the small family group.

Spelak, Sorel's grandfather, approached. He was as old as T'Pau, and as imposing, with Sorel's inscrutable black eyes still clear and alert in a face that had otherwise turned to parchment with age.

"Sendet," he said regally, "you came to do honor to your colleague. Do not remain to dishonor yourself. What happens now is within the family."

Sendet could not defy that imperious command. Without another word, he turned and walked away.

Spelak turned to Corrigan, who steeled himself to face a similar dismissal. He determined not to disgrace Sorel's choice with a display of emotion, no matter what the old man said.

"Daniel, you have brought honor to our family today. T'Pau tested you, and you withstood the test."

Corrigan forced down astonishment, and did not allow the human "Thank you" to pass his lips. Instead, he replied formally, "I am the one honored, Spelak."

The old man's mouth twitched, almost smiling. "You are as welcome as anyone of our blood. I would gladly claim thee kin."

He regally handed Corrigan over to T'Mir, and went on to talk to Sorel. T'Mir leaned close and murmured, "Now no one can object—no matter what you do."

Corrigan had no intention of doing anything to offend, however. He had lived on Vulcan more than half his life, spoke the language with all its nuances— although he would never lose his accent—and knew what foods at the banquet he could eat, and how to handle them.

Conversation flowed pleasantly, and he forgot about trying to maintain formality as he and Sorel were asked about their work. It was clear that Sorel's relatives were as ready as his immediate family to accept Corrigan and rejoice in their differences. T'Pau, fortunately, was not there.

As they left the banquet, though, Sorel's aunt T'Peyra stopped to have a word with Corrigan. "How is it that you remain unmarried, Daniel? You may not have a Vulcan's need of a bondmate, but surely you would benefit from the companionship of a wife. And children—"

"My work is fulfilling," he replied, "and occupies most of my time. I have no objections to marriage, T'Peyra, but you must understand that my choices are severely limited—"

"Not at all," she insisted. "You are esteemed in your profession, you are of good health and character—any eligible woman would surely be honored to have you as husband. Do not be concerned; the family will find someone suitable."

"Oh, no!" Corrigan said to T'Mir as T'Peyra left them. "It's bad enough with your father trying to marry me off. What do I do if your whole family gets into the act?"

T'Mir gazed into his eyes—on a level, as they were about the same height. "I believe I can save you from being auctioned off on the marriage mart, Daniel. Let me talk with my father about it—for I think I know an acceptable solution."

Corrigan and Sorel spent the rest of the day caring for patients, together and separately. Amanda and Remington were still being monitored visually, as the source of the malfunction had not been located. Everything was normal in the stasis chambers, as well as among all their other patients. After their final rounds, both physicians found themselves free to go home.

T'Mir was with her father in his office when Corrigan stopped to say good night. "I will walk home with you, Daniel," she said, "and tell you my solution to your problem."

"Problem?"

"Aunt T'Peyra."

"Oh—I had forgotten about that. By all means— come along and tell me your plan."

But as they walked through the twilight, T'Mir's talk was of other things—her apprenticeship, her experiences on other worlds, the friendships she had formed with other apprentices of diverse races, with whom she had spent the past seven years.

Corrigan lived in the complex of apartments available to faculty and staff at the Academy—had, in fact, lived in the same small apartment all his years on Vulcan because he had never needed anything more elaborate. He had brought few mementos with him from Earth all those years ago, not having the diplomatic allowance that had permitted Sarek and Amanda to transport heavy pieces of furniture across the galaxy.

The largest item Corrigan had brought from Earth was a painting, a tall ship on the ocean, sails billowing in the wind. Vulcan had no oceans. He recalled how fascinated T'Mir had been with that painting as a child, demanding endless stories about his ancestor who had been a sailor. How disappointed she had been to learn that Corrigan had never sailed on such a ship himself!

When they entered his apartment, T'Mir went immediately to look at the painting, just as she had always done. Corrigan went into the small kitchen unit, saying, "We certainly don't need a meal after that banquet today, but I have some of those biscuits you like, and I'll make some tea."

"I would prefer brandy, Daniel."

Surprised, Corrigan got out the glasses and poured drinks for both of them. T'Mir still stood before the painting. "I traveled on a sailing ship," she said.

"What?"

"On Earth. Two years ago—we had a month's leave there. The other students suspected I had gone mad—a Vulcan wanting to sail on the ocean? But I found that there are still ships sailing, mostly for tourists and vacationers, but a few cargo vessels. I think . . . perhaps the vessel I sailed on might have been smuggling something that couldn't go through the transporters."

"T'Mir!"

"I wanted to sail as a crew member," she explained, "and that was the only ship where I wasn't laughed at. They didn't question my credentials—and I sailed from Italy to Ireland just the way your ancestor did."

"And how did you like it?" Corrigan asked.

"I spent most of the journey soaking wet. It was impossible to keep warm. My hands blistered from hauling ropes. And . . . I would not trade the experience for ten comfortable voyages on a starship."

They were standing side by side before the painting. Now T'Mir turned to Corrigan . . . and he was suddenly very much aware of her warm presence invading his private space. He blushed—for no good reason except that he realized he had made a serious error. No longer could he casually play uncle to his best friend's unbonded daughter. Although T'Mir looked to all outward appearances as she had when she left Vulcan seven years ago, during that period nature had breathed life into the sculptured perfection of her beauty. She had reached her sexual maturity.

No longer could Corrigan think of T'Mir as a child; he was only too aware that she was a woman, a most desirable woman. . . .

He stepped away from her, but she followed, remaining as if within his aura. Of course she could have no idea what she was doing to him. . . .

"T'Mir, I have just remembered some work I have neglected these past two days—"

"It will wait until tomorrow," she replied. "Tonight I shall give you the answer to your problem."

"Oh, yes," he said with a forced laugh, turning from her to sit at the end of the couch. "Tell me how to keep T'Peyra off my back."

He expected T'Mir to take the chair opposite, leaving the small chest which served as a table between them. Instead, she sat down beside him on the couch. Could she possibly know her effect on him? He felt like squirming, dared not lest she realize he was reacting to her as a woman, destroying their friendship forever.

Nervously, he began to talk. "If you don't come up

with a solution, every human woman who comes to Vulcan will find herself being thrown at me."

"Why do you think only of human women, Daniel? Today even T'Pau admitted that you are Vulcan."

"No Vulcan woman would—" What was he saying? He had never allowed himself to think of a Vulcan woman . . . before.

T'Mir's soft eyes studied him over the rim of her brandy glass. "I may not have inherited a healer's ESP, but I have enough, Daniel—enough to know that you desire me but are afraid to speak. I was also afraid— afraid that you would *not* desire me, that you could see me as nothing but the daughter of your friend."

"You *are* the daughter of my friend," he told her. "If your father knew—"

"Father said you might be difficult to persuade."

"Sorel *knows!?*" He almost spilled his brandy, and set it carefully down on the chest, trying to control the shaking of his hands.

"Daniel, our family keeps tradition. I sought my father's permission today. He was most pleased. If you agree, he will offer me to you as bondmate and wife."

"Sorel was . . . pleased?" One shock on top of another.

"Indeed. Daniel, you are the only man I have ever wanted to marry. When you were . . . aging so rapidly, why do you think I left Vulcan? I knew that my maturity would come soon—and I did not want to be pressured into marriage with another while you lived. Had you and Father not found a cure, I would not have returned to Vulcan . . . until you were dead."

"T'Mir! These are a child's fancies."

"No," she said firmly. "Father did not bond Soton or me as children, because his free choice of our mother was so felicitous. Soton easily found someone whose mind is compatible with his . . . as did I. I have known since childhood why you turned down every opportunity for marriage: you were waiting for me to grow up. Now . . . it is time, Daniel."

"I cannot believe this," Corrigan murmured, although his experience of the meeting of Sorel and T'Zan through the healing meld told him it was indeed possible . . . but between Vulcan and human?

"Surely you felt it," T'Mir whispered, "when our minds touched even briefly in the meld with Father? It confirmed what I have known ever since I was old enough to understand it."

"But what about Sendet?" he asked, suddenly realizing the source of the young man's resentment.

"Sendet? He has nothing to do with us."

"Obviously he thinks he has. With you, anyway."

"Sendet does not want *me,* Daniel; he wants to join his family with ours. His parents tried to persuade Father and Mother to bond me to him when we were seven years old. But my parents were determined that my brother and I be free to choose. Before I left Vulcan, Sendet tried again to persuade me to bond with him. I had hoped," she added softly, "that by the time I returned he would have found another. He is correct in claiming that his is an old and honorable family. There are many Vulcans to whom that is of utmost importance; Sendet could easily make a good marriage."

"Yet your parents did not encourage you to choose him?"

"They would never try to persuade me against my wishes. Furthermore, they recognized that Sendet's adherence to tradition is to forms and names, not to actions and beliefs. Daniel, I do not want Sendet, and I do not want to spend my time with you talking about him. Let us plan *our* future together."

"T'Mir, I am old enough to be your father."

THE VULCAN ACADEMY MURDERS

"Not anymore. You will live for many years, strong and healthy. It is illogical to state objections you do not mean, Daniel. This is not a hypothetical exercise. I would bond with thee, never and always touching and touched."

He could feel his own emptiness yearning to be filled with the sweet presence of T'Mir. He didn't *want* to argue—she was right that he raised objections only out of form, wanting to be talked out of them. That *was* illogical. "I . . . would be bondmate and husband to thee, never and always touching and touched."

Although her lips did not, T'Mir's eyes smiled. "Tomorrow," she said. "We shall bond tomorrow, before my brother's bondmate leaves. Father and Soton and T'Pree will witness. Father will help us bond if necessary—but I do not think any help will be required."

Corrigan looked into T'Mir's eyes, and saw the promise of a future such as he had never dared dream of. The emptiness he had recognized in himself since T'Par tore him out of the family meld would be filled. Only now could he admit how much he wanted it.

"I love you," he said, resorting to English for the term.

"I cherish thee," T'Mir replied, using a Vulcan word with levels of meaning Corrigan was only beginning to comprehend. "Until tomorrow, Daniel."

"Tomorrow," he replied . . . and kissed her.

She accepted the gesture, and responded by putting her arms about him—exactly as she must have seen human women do in life or in drama. But it was mere acceptance now, and it was not the time to teach her what kissing meant to humans.

He released her, and smiled into her questioning eyes. "It gets much better than that."

The smile found her lips this time. "I know

. . . although I have never experienced this touching before. After tomorrow you will teach me, Daniel—and I will show you Vulcan ways. But I should go home now."

He nodded. "I must perform surgery in the morning, and I have a full day's schedule. So has Sorel. But in the evening—"

"Yes, Daniel. Until tomorrow evening, my husband-to-be!"

She left him. He resisted the urge to prolong contact by walking her home. It was not a Vulcan custom, as since the days of the Reforms there was no crime of any sort on Vulcan. Inside the city, a woman or a child was safe alone, any time of the night or day.

There was no lock on Corrigan's door, or on any other door to a home, for no Vulcan would invade another's privacy uninvited. Only such areas as the stasis chambers, where an inadvertent intrusion might cause damage or death, were locked.

When T'Mir had gone, Corrigan prepared for bed, knowing it would take every meditation technique he had ever learned to calm his overflowing heart. The face that looked back at him from the bathroom mirror was as unprepossessing as ever. He was the same short, stocky, balding human male he had been an hour ago . . . but T'Mir wanted him.

Happiness lurked in the blue eyes twinkling from the mirror. Corrigan looked back at the image and laughed aloud with sheer joy.

CHAPTER **12**

The next morning, James T. Kirk was the last to shower before going back to the Academy. Spock was ready, and McCoy was dressing when Kirk padded through the master bedroom, a serene haven of blues and greens in pleasant contrast to the beiges and whites of the rest of the house. Amanda's touch was strongly evident here. A holograph of young Amanda holding an elfin baby Spock smiled from the dresser. On the wall over the bed was fastened a brass head-board—another antique, judging by the dents in the rungs.

Sarek had already left to teach his morning class, so there was no hurry. Spock would drive Kirk and McCoy, for although they were beginning to adjust to the air and gravity, the humans were not yet up to a long walk under Vulcan's merciless sun.

Kirk felt good this morning—better than he would

have hoped for, actually, for if there were not that unexplained power failure hanging over their heads, he and McCoy would have spent last night sampling ShiKahr's nightlife. He was certain there would be some interesting establishments around the Academy, with its mixture of students, faculty, and staff from a hundred different worlds.

Instead, they had spent an unexpectedly pleasant evening with Spock and Sarek. After Sarek's evening class they had come home to a good meal, then sat around the main room of the house, talking. McCoy, Kirk noticed, restricted himself to a single glass of wine—the doctor, too, shared the sense of being "on call."

But no calls came, and Kirk and McCoy related those tales that were unclassified about the missions of the *Enterprise,* especially adventures in which Spock had played a heroic role. "It's too bad," Kirk observed, "that we can't tell you some of the best stories."

"I understand," said Sarek. "Because the details are classified, I cannot tell you about the time Amanda almost traded me away for a handful of dilithium crystals. However," he continued serenely as the two humans choked back astonishment, "I *can* tell you of the time we were sent to trade with a Dorkasi warlord for latium."

"What's latium?" asked Kirk.

"It's a plant," McCoy responded, "that for over a century was the only source of immune system support serum. The chemical was finally synthesized about twenty-five years ago, but until then the rare natural sources were the best hope for victims of immune system failure."

"Yes," said Sarek. "Our mission took place when latium was the only known source. Spock had just begun school, so we left him in my mother's care. The

Federation had decided to send a delegation from Vulcan because the Dorkasi had scorned the first delegates as weak and puny. Their idea of congenial entertainment is hand-to-hand combat; they stand well over two meters tall and have the strength to match their size.

"The Federation also wanted the head of the delegation to take his wife on the mission, as there had been some difficulties on the unsuccessful first mission when the ambassador insulted Malko, the warlord, by refusing the Dorkasi woman offered to him as a gift."

Kirk chuckled. "Customs and mores. I've had my share of such problems."

"Problems?" asked McCoy. "Seems to me you'd just take the lady in question and run, Jim."

"There are *other* local custom problems, Bones. Seems to *me* I recall your hiding behind desks and chairs and potted plants when we had to beam down to Solaris Three. The whole planet is a nudist colony," Kirk added for Sarek's benefit. "No clothing allowed— they have a belief that it's sacrilegious to cover nature's handiwork."

"As I recall, it was *you* who insisted on carrying the tricorder," McCoy growled, "and holding it in a most unusual position. Why don't you let the ambassador get on with his story?"

Unperturbed, Sarek continued, "We assumed that since I already had a wife, the Dorkasi would consider it redundant to offer me another. As for physical combat . . . while we hoped to escape it, a party of Vulcans would have the physical strength to avoid the ignominious defeats suffered by humans. We *thought* we had anticipated all possible problems, and would be able to negotiate a trade agreement."

"What happened?" asked Spock. "You never did tell me about that mission, Father. I was very young

. . . but I recall that you returned home with vestiges of a . . . black eye."

"True, but I also returned home with your mother."

"Oh, no," Kirk chuckled, "I think I know what's coming. The warlord thought you had brought Amanda . . . as a gift for him?"

"You should consider a career in the diplomatic service, Jim," said Sarek. "That is precisely what he thought—and no one had anticipated it. Malko arranged an evening's . . . entertainment . . . for the diplomatic party. Since that is a universal custom, and we had no way of knowing that the socio-ethnic structure of the native community called for public indulgence in what are in our culture considered private activities—"

"It turned into an orgy," McCoy interpreted.

"I believe I said that," Sarek responded. "When the diplomatic party showed reluctance to participate, and when Malko was not presented with the gift he believed should have been forthcoming, he took matters—and Amanda—into his own hands. In that society, there was only one response I could make."

"You . . . had to fight for Mother?" Spock asked, his voice giving away his astonished disbelief.

"Would you have had me allow Malko to take her, Spock?"

Spock swallowed hard. "Surely there were logical alternatives—"

"Malko was inebriated. He was determined to have what he wanted, then and there. He had no desire to negotiate . . . and your mother had no desire to become one of the terms of the trade agreement. Tell me, Spock—what would you have done?"

"Your mission—"

"You would have traded your mother for the latium?"

"No, of course not. But attacking your host—!"

"Created a diversion. In the midst of the ensuing battle, one of my aides called the starship that had brought us, and had us all beamed out of the hall. Not before Malko and I had inflicted considerable damage on one another, though . . . and Amanda had impressed upon Malko that she was not the pliant concubine he sought. In fact, he concluded that such a spirited woman had to be a witch!"

"So your mission failed," said Spock. Kirk wanted to throttle him for obstinately missing the point of his father's story, but Sarek remained unperturbed.

"Not at all," he said. "Malko decided that any man with the temerity to take on your mother as a lifemate —'tame her' was the term he used—was a hero in his eyes. My actions had gained his respect, and the treaty was concluded to the satisfaction of all parties."

"That was one of your earlier missions," observed Kirk. "Those of us who contact new peoples run into surprises constantly at first, until we get some experience. Then the surprises may come further apart, but they don't stop."

"They never stop," Sarek agreed. "In that sense, your job, and mine when I am acting as ambassador, are very much alike."

Kirk looked over at Spock, wondering if his Vulcan friend actually heard what his father was saying—for of course Spock's job aboard the *Enterprise* was very similar to Kirk's. But Spock sat impassively now, listening politely without comment.

"Carl Remington, the young man we've put in stasis," Kirk continued, "faced one of those surprises on his first landing party. I took him along to see how he would handle himself. There should not have been any serious danger, as we had Spock with us, and three security people."

"The planet was uncharted, mineral-rich, but with a variety of large life forms, although sensors showed no signs of civilization," Spock explained. "We were to survey several different areas to determine whether the planet could be opened to mining and colonization, or whether it was already populated with intelligent beings, however primitive."

"Our data was ambiguous," said Kirk. "There was a sort of big catlike creature that lived in groups, but didn't build shelters. The translator interpreted their sounds as possibly being language, and the computer asked for more samples. So that's what the various landing parties were trying to do—get close to the creatures with tricorders and record enough of their sounds for the computer and the translator to interpret. If it were language, the *Enterprise* would put a warning buoy in orbit, and the planet would be left to develop on its own.

"It was a nice place—mild climate, warm sunshine, soft breezes. We knew the cat-creatures preyed on some of the other animals, but they hunted in pairs, bringing their prey back for the group to enjoy. There had been no other large predators observed, and . . . I guess I got careless," Kirk admitted. "Our landing party circled a group that was busy eating. That should have meant they'd finish their meal, make a lot of the sounds we wanted to record for a while afterward, and then all go to sleep."

"That was their observed behavior," Spock explained. "In this particular group, however, one member was not eating. It kept lifting its head and sniffing the air. Then it would call out, pace back and forth, and call out again."

"It was doing this close to where I was," Kirk continued. "I saw a chance to record some new sounds the translator hadn't had to work on before, so I crawled up as close as I could. Remington was off to my right, the only other member of the landing party I could see. We didn't dare use our communicators, because the cat-creatures might hear us. We were all bathed in anti-scent spray, of course, so as long as the creatures didn't see or hear us, we were perfectly safe.

"I waved to Remington, signaling him to move forward and record from his angle. He shook his head—and gestured to me to move back! That annoyed me—this wet-behind-the-ears kid not only disobeying the captain's order, but trying to give his own orders to the captain!"

"You should've listened," put in McCoy.

"Yeah, well—never too old to learn. I should have realized that with his splendid record at the Academy, Remington was the last person ever to be insubordinate. But I didn't know what the cat-creature's actions meant, so I motioned Remington forward again. He shook his head again, and started crawling toward me.

"Now I was getting angry. This was the kid's first landing party, and he was acting as if he was the one running things. I tried to wave him back, getting up on my knees—and when I did, there came this awful squealing from behind me.

"I turned—and there was a cub! A little cat-creature, maybe a quarter the size of the others, looking at me with big, terrified eyes and screaming for mama—and mama, of course, was the one that wasn't eating! She came charging over the knoll to see what was attacking sonny—and there I was, an alien monster to her, between her and her baby!

"We had phasers, of course, set on stun. I grabbed mine, aimed—and she hit me like a photon torpedo before I could fire. My phaser went spinning off God knows where, and I rolled over, pain splintering through me from broken ribs before it started to burn where she had ripped the skin off my chest. I was in no shape to fight—I could hardly move.

"Remington kept his nerve—I heard his phaser hum, but the cat-creature just shook its head and yowled. Different nervous system; phaser stun didn't put it out!

"Meanwhile, the baby is screaming and the mama cat is ready to pounce on me—and I know what Remington's going through. He has orders not to kill anything on this planet. And if he doesn't stop that cat-creature, it's going to kill his captain! The other members of the landing party are on the way—but so are the other cat-creatures! There's no time to waste, and I can't help him. . . .

"And then I see him start to run. I try to shout—but I can't get a deep breath with broken ribs stabbing me. He runs for the cub, yelling like a banshee!

"The mother turns from me to defend her baby. Remington picks it up—getting his arms clawed up in the process—and throws the cub at the mother. She just has to take the time to examine her baby—and by that time our security team is on the scene. They've seen that phaser stun won't work—but they've got a harpoon net and know how to use it. The three security guards zap that net out in front of the oncoming cat-creatures while Spock calls the *Enterprise*—and we're all beamed out of there before the cats can untangle themselves from the net!"

"If you had only recalled that Mr. Remington comes from a planet which is a wildlife preserve—" Spock began.

"Yes, I know," Kirk replied. "I should've remembered that he knows lots more about wild animals than I do. But he saved the day and his captain, and got a commendation on his first landing party—and it turned out that the cat-creatures do have a primitive form of language. So we didn't kill any intelligent creatures, and the planet is quarantined so they can develop naturally. And except for Bones swearing at me for getting myself almost killed again, it all ended happily."

"It sounds to me," said Sarek, "as if your Mr. Remington is a most valuable addition to your crew."

Kirk had agreed. This morning, as he showered, he hoped again that nothing would go wrong with the boy's treatments. Even if the stasis regenerated his nerves, there was still the danger that the healers wouldn't be able to reach his mind and pull him back. No—too early to worry about that problem. The stasis system seemed to be working fine again after the power loss—

"Jim! Jim, can you hear me? *Jim!*"

A pounding on the bathroom door, and McCoy's voice.

Kirk turned off the water. "Yeah, Bones—what is it?"

"The Academy just called. There's been another power failure! Get dressed and come on!"

Kirk hurriedly toweled off, and stuffed his still-damp limbs into his clothes. Who was it this time? Amanda? Remington? Or . . . both?

CHAPTER **13**

Sarek finished teaching his morning class, and returned to his office. Eleyna was waiting for the assignments he had just collected.

The computer console was on, but the screen was blank. There was no cassette in the slot.

"Have you finished your work, Eleyna?" Sarek asked. "Please feel free to use my console; while I have guests, I will not be working on my own projects."

"Thank you, Sarek," she replied. "I will grade these assignments first, and then go on with my project."

"My son should have been here by now," said Sarek. "Perhaps our guests overslept. They have been kept very busy with the events of the past few days, while trying to adjust to Vulcan's summer."

Eleyna, he noticed, appeared as adjusted as any Vulcan. Her blond hair was fastened up off her neck, her dress was loose and of light material, and she did not even seem to perspire as most humans did. She had never expressed a preference as to where she would go to use the expertise in computer science that she had learned on Vulcan, saying only, "I must choose from the positions available when I complete my studies."

But a degree from the Vulcan Academy of Sciences, along with recommendations from Sarek and her other teachers, would take her anywhere she wanted to go.

Perhaps . . . she didn't want to go. She had studiously adopted Vulcan ways—and with expanding enrollment, the Academy could use more teachers. He would speak to Senek, he decided. And he would definitely talk with Amanda about—

The communications console buzzed loudly. Eleyna started—she must have been concentrating deeply on the student assignment on her screen.

Sarek flicked the switch, and Spock's face appeared on the communicator screen. "Father, there has been another power failure. Mr. Remington is dead. Captain Kirk, Dr. McCoy, and I are with Storn—"

"I'm on my way!" Sarek cut him off, clamping control over the panic in his veins. It had happened twice now—and if it happened a third time, the victim would be Amanda!

Eleyna was watching him. Sarek steepled his hands at his waist, took a careful calming breath, and forced his voice into normal tones. "You heard. If the failures were in the monitoring systems, my son and I may be able to trace them before another failure occurs."

"Is there anything I can do?" she asked.

"We would welcome your assistance."

"Of course, Sarek. You go on ahead. I will shut down the systems here and follow you."

So she had seen his impatience—or assumed it from

what she would have known in his situation. A repeating malfunction meant only a matter of time before it struck Amanda, unless they could find it or repair it first—or get her out of stasis.

When he arrived at the hospital, Sarek first sought Sorel and Corrigan, finding them together in the empty stasis chamber recently occupied by Carl Remington.

Without preamble, Sarek told the physicians, "I want Amanda out of stasis at once."

"I started the procedures immediately after we abandoned attempts to resuscitate Carl Remington," Sorel replied. "However, the difference is only a few hours, Sarek. Preliminaries for Amanda's release from stasis were already scheduled for late this afternoon."

Corrigan's face was pale and grim. "The process cannot be hurried. It takes two days to reach the point at which her body can function independently of the field. If we removed her from stasis prematurely, she would die."

"And if the power were to fail during these preliminaries?" Sarek asked.

"The risk diminishes with each passing hour," Sorel replied. "However, until the process is complete, the risk of death will remain. Even an hour before the process is terminated, there will be a 22.83 percent chance that the patient would die were the stasis field to collapse."

"And the risk now?" Sarek asked, taking refuge in cold figures.

"99.21 percent."

Again he controlled his breathing before he spoke. "Have you located the malfunction this time?"

"No," Corrigan replied. "A technician was here in the chamber, monitoring the dials. They did not fluctuate. She *heard* Remington's body fall to the floor, turned, *saw* that the field had collapsed—and *then* the heart monitor alarm sounded. Look at these connections," he said, gesturing toward the circuit board he and Sorel had exposed. "Every one is in perfect working order. What happened *couldn't have!*"

"But it has," Sorel said flatly. "Twice."

Corrigan turned away from the two Vulcans. "It's my fault," he said. "Using untried techniques on my patients—"

"Daniel!" Sorel reproved, "it is my technique as much as yours, and it was *not* the stasis field that malfunctioned. It was the incoming power."

"Show me," Corrigan replied. "How can it be the incoming power when there is no evidence of a drop, let alone an outage? We *assumed* that a power failure caused the field to collapse. If there was no power failure, the field collapsed for some other reason—something we didn't test thoroughly before we began to use it."

"Nothing but a power failure could make the field collapse," insisted Sorel.

"Nothing *that we know of,*" Corrigan replied flatly. "Oh, God." He sat down heavily on the cabinet that housed the stasis equipment, for there were no seats in the chamber. "I was lucky," he said, "just plain dumb lucky to survive my own ineptitude." He rubbed his face with his hands. "T'Zan. I know why you can't believe it's the technique gone wrong, Sorel—but I know it. I killed her as surely as if I'd performed surgery and left her bleeding!"

Sarek didn't know what to say. Sorel was likely to see the situation more logically than Corrigan—but would he be willing to consider the possibility that the failure of his technique was responsible for his own wife's death? Corrigan might take the emotional human attitude, but his idea that when one avenue of research produced no results they must explore other possibilities was certainly sound.

Finally Sarek suggested, "If you have thoroughly examined both the stasis machinery and the power source, and not found a malfunction in either, then should you not try yet another possibility?"

"What possibility?" asked Corrigan.

"You said that the collapse of the field—no matter what the cause of that collapse—did not appear on the monitors. It was only when the patient's heartbeat faltered that the alarm sounded. You have already checked the connections between the stasis unit and the monitors and found them all in order. Thus one malfunction must lie in the monitor system. Perhaps finding that will lead you to the cause of the primary malfunction."

Sorel and Corrigan looked at one another. The human doctor nodded. "Thank you, Sarek," he said. "Sorel?"

"Let us call Storn in here. His engineers built the monitor board."

Spock was with Storn, Leonard McCoy, and Jim Kirk, testing power input to the stasis chamber. "We have determined that there was a malfunction in the monitor board—apparently in both chambers," said Sorel. "In both instances, no alarm sounded when the field collapsed. I . . . knew when my wife's life began to ebb, several minutes before anyone here at the hospital knew. The monitor failure cannot be the source of the field collapse—but as Sarek suggests, finding one malfunction may lead us to the other."

"Good idea," said Kirk, "if we're really dealing with malfunctions."

"Please explain, Jim," said Spock, and Sarek received the distinct impression that his son was relieved to have the human point out something he was reluctant to say himself.

"You're talking about four separate malfunctions—two which caused stasis fields to collapse, and two which caused that collapse not to appear on the monitors. And now you can't find any trace of short circuits, broken connections, blown-out breakers—anything? That's too much for the long arm of coincidence. Somebody *planned* those malfunctions, and carefully removed the evidence."

Everybody stared at him. To Vulcans without experience of other worlds, or even to the few carefully-screened offworlders who chose to live here, such a conclusion, however logical, did not come easily. Sarek realized that he himself, for all his experience of violence in other worlds, other races, had never let the possibility cross his mind here, in the safety of home. *And that is . . . illogical.*

It was Corrigan who finally asked, "But . . . *why?*"

"If we knew why, we'd know who," Kirk replied. "You go ahead and look for mechanical malfunctions—and for God's sake *fix* any you find! I don't want Amanda to die, any more than the rest of you! But I want to find out why one of my crew members died—did someone try to get him first, and accidentally kill that poor Vulcan lady? Or was Lady T'Zan the intended victim, and Remington's death meant to make it appear that the stasis units are at fault?"

"Jim," said Spock, "you are speaking of homicide. There is no such crime on Vulcan. The last murder on this planet occurred over three thousand years ago."

"Well, the last *attempted* murder wasn't so very long ago," Kirk replied, and Sarek barely controlled his anger at the man's bringing up his son's—

And then he recalled that James T. Kirk, who still remained Spock's faithful friend, had very nearly been the victim of the ritual homicide which tradition allowed, although modern custom had not permitted for many generations. And it was T'Pring who should know the blame and the shame of it, not Spock nor Kirk.

Kirk did not make any further reference to the incident as they returned to their investigation.

Sorel's son Soton joined them, accompanied by his sister T'Mir. "Spet told me of the latest malfunction, Father. I will take your patients if you wish to remain here."

"Yes, Soton, I do want to test the equipment further. Daniel, please go with Soton—"

"No!" the human doctor said emphatically. "This is not the time for me to get my mind off the problem."

Sorel said gently, "Daniel, I did not mean that. It would be better for our patients if at least one of us were there for them, and your engineering skills—"

"Are just as good as yours!" Corrigan countered. "Look—Storn is the expert, but he worked from *our* design. You *or I* may spot something an engineer wouldn't see."

"Very well. Soton, please see if one of the human doctors is available to help you," said Sorel.

"I'll go," said McCoy. "I feel like a fifth wheel here with all this electrical stuff. I'm a doctor, not an engineer."

McCoy and Soton left, but T'Mir stayed. Sarek wondered what help she could be. She was a xenobiologist, he recalled. Then he forgot her as Storn suggested, "Sorel, watch the monitors inside the stasis chamber. Sarek, take the stasis box—see if the power indicators fluctuate. Spock, I have studied the circuits inside that panel"—he gestured toward the circuitry revealed behind the wall—"None of my tests show anything. Perhaps you will see something I do not."

For the next several minutes, Storn ran varying levels of power through the circuitry panel and into the empty stasis chamber. As it was supposed to, the equipment leveled the power supply before it entered the chamber. Sarek tried cutting one, then the other power source off at the stasis cabinet; each time the alternate source remained steady, while an alarm rang on Sorel's panel to indicate the failure.

The third time everything worked perfectly, Daniel Corrigan came in, saying, "Let me see that!" He lay down, his head inside the open cabinet, and shouted, "Run a surge through here again, Storn—make it a strong one. I want to see if the circuit-breakers move."

Storn looked around the door, saw Corrigan's position, and said, "Not with anyone in there! I'll get the meters—"

As he left the narrow opening to look for his equipment, T'Mir entered the chamber. "Daniel, you mustn't endanger yourself!"

"The power's off," he replied, stubbornly poking at the circuits as if he expected to find a loose connection in solid-state machinery.

Storn was coming through the outer chamber with a set of voltage meters. Sorel was saying, "Sarek, do you know how to read these—"

The air buzzed, sparked, and spat.

Daniel Corrigan screamed. The panel of gauges before Sorel and Sarek exploded with a flash, showering them with sparks. The stench of overheated insulation filled the small room.

Sarek caught Sorel, who had thrown his hands over his eyes. Both men ducked their heads and shielded their faces as shards of plastic battered them. Coughing, Sarek opened his eyes cautiously, and pulled Sorel's hands from his face. "Are you hurt?"

Although his face was blackened and his eyes were

watering, Sorel replied, "I am unharmed," and looked past Sarek to his partner. "T'Mir—no!" he gasped, and thrust Sarek aside.

T'Mir was kneeling beside the unconscious Corrigan, her hands positioned against his face for a meld. "Daniel," she murmured, concentrating. . . .

Corrigan's eyes opened, widened as he saw T'Mir. Sarek saw guilt and horror cloud the human's face as Sorel reached to break his daughter's concentration—too late.

T'Mir started back, pulled her hands away as if they were contaminated—and just as Kirk, Spock, and several technicians came pounding through the doorway into the smoke-filled chamber, she gasped. "No! Oh, no! Daniel—you killed my mother!"

CHAPTER **14**

James T. Kirk studied the tableau in the tiny stasis chamber. Everyone who had been inside when the power surge blew out the stasis machinery was covered with grime. The place stank of burning plastic, and the ventilators had stopped. Only dim emergency lighting was on.

Sorel moved first, lifting his daughter away from the human doctor and bending over him to feel for the pulse at his throat. Corrigan began to cough, and Sorel said, "You'll be all right, Daniel."

"But, Father," T'Mir protested, "he—"

"He is human!" Sorel silenced her as he picked up his partner. "You do not understand! Let us through," he said to the others. "Let us into the clean air."

Kirk followed. He had heard T'Mir's accusation, and wondered what she could have seen in Corrigan's mind.

Why would he sabotage his own equipment? It didn't make sense.

In the hallway, Sorel laid Corrigan down on a bench, and pulled out his medscanner. Kirk saw him recalibrate—then the instrument hummed, and Sorel said, "No serious damage. But you must rest, Daniel."

Corrigan was looking past Sorel to T'Mir. She would not meet his eyes, saying, "Father, how can you treat him as your friend when he—"

"Silence, Daughter. You do not understand—and if you know so little of humans, how could you presume to think of marrying one? Do you not know that your accusation harms him more than anyone else's possibly could? If you cannot be logical, be silent."

The young woman subsided, but not before Kirk put two and two together and got five. T'Mir had wanted to marry Corrigan? Her father certainly didn't sound keen on the idea—what if her mother had refused permission? If Corrigan wanted the girl—and why wouldn't he, a lovely thing, as beautiful as T'Pring but without her coldness—could he have taken the opportunity to rid himself of an obstacle when T'Zan was placed in his care? As Kirk recalled, T'Zan had been placed in stasis after an accident. Could Corrigan have engineered the accident?

He kept silent, having no evidence for his theory—but he remembered from studying psychology back at the Academy that most murders were committed by members of the victim's family or close friends. Apparently Corrigan qualified as both.

What about the rest of the family? T'Mir had been in transit from off-planet when her mother died. She could not have had anything to do with it.

But her brother—could he disapprove so strongly of his sister's marriage plans that he would do anything to discredit Corrigan? Including murdering his own mother?

No—no, that made no sense at all. What about Sorel himself? Among humans, the husband would be the first suspect. Since it would put his own life at risk, a Vulcan was unlikely to murder his wife . . . although from what Kirk knew, that might be his only way of ridding himself of her. Once in seven years the wife had the option to challenge—but he had never heard of a way for a Vulcan husband to divorce his wife.

Then there was T'Zan's co-worker—what was his name? Sendet, he remembered. He had showed up at the hospital, and later made some kind of fuss at T'Zan's funeral. Something about being part of the family? And the way he had looked at T'Mir. . . .

Had T'Zan been blocking his hopes to have her daughter? Now *there* was someone who could have arranged the original accident, and when that didn't kill her he could have tried the power failure. . . .

Yes, he must question Sendet.

Kirk realized that his thoughts were straying because he did not believe Corrigan capable of murder, despite T'Mir's accusation. The girl was not a trained healer like her father. She could very well have misinterpreted what she saw in Corrigan's mind.

Storn, the engineer, emerged from the stasis chamber. "That power surge came through circuits that were off. The malfunction had to occur in the incoming power source. Daniel, Sorel, it could not have been caused by your equipment."

"But now we have an even wider range of possibilities," Kirk observed. "Where does the power to this area originate?"

Stepping to his office on the other side of the hall from the stasis chambers, Storn called up diagrams of the hospital circuitry on a computer screen.

Everyone gathered to look, although Kirk suspected that to most of them, the flashes of patterns followed by rapidly changing columns of figures, meant as little as they did to him.

Sarek said something in Vulcan. The translator did not translate—and Kirk realized that it was a word which had no English equivalent. He wondered if it was an expletive, for Spock's father followed it by saying, "That power surge was not recorded! There is a computer malfunction."

"A most serious one," agreed Spock, "and occurring only in connection with the stasis chambers. Storn, have there been any other power surges or outages in the hospital complex?"

"No," replied the engineer. "They would have been reported to me."

"Is it possible . . . ?" Spock began.

". . . that someone has tampered with the programming?" his father finished the thought.

"No one has access to our terminals," said Sorel. "Everything is locked under my code or Daniel's, so even if someone entered our offices—"

"A computer expert could access from another terminal," said Sarek. "Spock learned very young how to break the simple codes protecting his fellow students' programs."

"Father—"

Kirk looked at his First Officer, and saw him concealing embarrassment. Sarek said, "I did not intend to remind you of childish pranks, Spock, but to indicate that your talent is such that with the experience you now have you could break the most complex codes available today. As could I," he added. "However, neither of us has any reason to do so." Kirk made a mental note to ask Spock at a more propitious moment about those childish pranks.

"This latest malfunction was not in the stasis programming," said Storn. "Possibly neither were the previous ones. But this one was definitely in the power circuitry programming, perhaps less complex than the stasis programming, but not selfcontained."

Kirk asked, "Why are not vital programs like that accessed only by retinal pattern ID? Or hand prints?"

"That is the very programming which appears to have been forestalled," Sarek told him. "A computer is a machine; when it is instructed to ignore its own safeguards by someone who knows its innermost language, it obeys."

Spock said, "I will examine the power circuitry programming records for the past three days for evidence of such tampering. Father, would you be willing to work with me?"

"Certainly."

"You work on the 'how,'" said Kirk, picking up a tablet and stylus, "and I'll work on the 'who.'"

Sorel and Corrigan left with T'Mir for their offices, Storn and his crew began putting the circuitry panels back together, and Spock and Sarek remained at the computer terminal. Their cryptic comments and the clicks and beeps of the machine were just enough to make Kirk lose his concentration. He left the office, looking for one of the private meditation niches scattered throughout the hospital.

Eleyna Miller was coming down the hallway. Wrinkling her nose at the acrid smoke coming from the stasis chamber, she asked, "What happened here?"

"Murder, I do believe," Kirk replied.

"What?!" Her exclamation was quick and sharp. Then, "There is no murder on Vulcan," she said more calmly. "Captain, this is the most peaceful planet in the Federation. Whom do you think has been murdered?"

"The Lady T'Zan, and Ensign Carl Remington."

Her smile had a hint of condescension. "A Vulcan scientist and a Star Fleet officer, neither of whom knew the other? Who would have reason to kill two such different people? Or are you suggesting two murderers?"

For a moment his theory seemed ridiculous. But then a new idea struck him. "T'Zan and Remington were the victims. I do not think either one was the target."

"I . . . beg your pardon?" Eleyna's coolness was gone. She was focusing on Kirk now with genuine interest—and although he appreciated it, he did not allow himself to be distracted from his purpose.

"I think Daniel Corrigan is the target," he explained. "Someone is trying to discredit his work, break up his partnership, and drive him off Vulcan."

"Fascinating," said Eleyna, but her tone was warm. "Tell me how you came to this conclusion."

They found one of the meditation areas further down the hall. It had a fire-pot like the one in Spock's cabin aboard the *Enterprise,* and a bench large enough to be comfortable for three or four people. As no one else was there, Kirk felt free to talk.

"What seems to have happened," said Kirk, "is that a party or parties unknown caused the power failures to the stasis chambers, killing T'Zan and Remington. There is only one connection between the victims: the treatment they were undergoing."

"Logical," said Eleyna. "But I thought they died as a result of malfunctions in the stasis machinery."

"Storn has pretty well ruled that out." Kirk turned on the electronic tablet—the on-off switch was obvious enough, but the other controls were marked with Vulcan symbols. "Damn," he muttered as nothing happened when he drew the stylus across the screen. It *looked* just like the tablets on which reports were tendered for his signature aboard the *Enterprise*. Why didn't it work the same way?

"Here," said Eleyna, "this yellow button activates the screen. What are you writing?"

"Actually, I'd prefer a tricorder," Kirk explained, "but this will do to make a list of suspects on. Then I'll borrow a tricorder and start interviewing."

"Just like a detective," Eleyna said with a smile.

"Well, why not? Oh—we should call in the police, shouldn't we?" He belatedly recalled that he was far out of his own jurisdiction here.

"Police?" Eleyna asked. "The closest thing to a policeman you will find on Vulcan is the old lady who fines students who park their vehicles in the wrong places or forget to return equipment borrowed from the supply center. She also runs the lost-and-found department, and has plenty of time left over to write some rather well-received poetry."

"All right," said Kirk, "I may see her to check out a tricorder, but not to investigate murder."

"I'm afraid you'll have to play Sherlock Holmes all by yourself," Eleyna agreed. She moved closer to him on the bench as he divided the small screen into three areas, labeling them "T'Zan," "Remington," and "Amanda." As he put down the last, Eleyna asked, "Amanda? But nothing has happened to her."

"And I hope nothing will," Kirk replied. "But if there is a pattern to the killings, she is the next potential victim. Now—who are the suspects for Remington? That's the easy one." He wrote "Kirk," "Spock," and "McCoy" under Remington's name.

"I don't understand," said Eleyna.

"I don't, either," said Kirk. "I know *I* didn't do it. Only Spock and McCoy and I even *knew* Remington, and none of us knew him well. Actually, I'm damn sure neither Spock nor McCoy had anything to do with his death, and since nobody else could possibly have both motive and opportunity, that leaves Remington as innocent victim in a pattern killing. If Sendet killed T'Zan because she stood in his way with T'Mir, for example, the second killing was to place the blame on the machinery. Or possibly the murderer is out to discredit Corrigan and/or Sorel, making both T'Zan and Remington innocent victims."

"Isn't murder a rather extreme way to discredit someone's work?" Eleyna asked.

"To a deranged mind, it could seem a completely logical thing to do. I'll investigate that theory—find out who else has it in for Sorel and Corrigan . . . besides T'Pau."

"T'Pau!" The young woman's blue eyes grew round with astonishment.

"Were you at T'Zan's funeral?"

"No. I did not know her. I have never officially met Sorel," she replied. "Dr. Corrigan is my physician, although I have been to him for treatment only once. Sarek recommended him—and he diagnosed a nutritional deficiency common among humans living for long periods on Vulcan. Now I take a dietary supplement, and have not been ill since."

As long-winded as Spock! Kirk thought, recalling his First Officer's habit of answering a simple question in full detail . . . yet Eleyna's answer was not Vulcan in character. She had turned the subject to herself.

"You think Corrigan's a good doctor?" Kirk asked.

"Oh, indeed!" Eleyna replied. "At least his reputation is undisputed. And surely Sorel would not have as a partner anyone whose abilities he doubted."

"Do you think Vulcan judgments infallible?"

"What a peculiar question!" Eleyna said with a smile that showed a dimple in her cheek. "Is it because you suspect T'Pau of being involved in this somehow? I know she disapproves of the large number of offworlders living on Vulcan. I would assume she disapproves of Dr. Corrigan's association with Sorel—and Sorel obviously approves. Now, Captain, how could Vulcan judgment be infallible when two Vulcans take opposing views on the same issue?"

"Touché," he said with a grin. "But there you are, giving me that point-by-point logical argument, just like a Vulcan. I thought maybe you were one of those people who admire Vulcans so much that you've practically tried to become one."

"Oh, no, Captain," she said warmly, "I am human. Quite human."

"And, like other humans, you take time off for . . . recreation?"

"Indeed."

"Amanda will be out of stasis in two days," said Kirk, "or we may solve the mystery of the malfunctions before then. I'll be on Vulcan for over a month yet. May I call you?"

She gave him her code number, and he settled back to the business at hand, listing suspects. Eleyna wasn't much help, as she knew few of the people at the center of the situation, and only Sarek well.

When Kirk listed Sarek's name under Amanda's, Eleyna gasped, "Oh, Jim—he couldn't!"

"That's what I think, too—but I've got to start with all possible suspects. It looks as if the murderer has to be a computer expert. That includes Sarek . . . and you, too."

". . . me? I have no motive," she said. "I did not know either of the victims."

"You could be after Sarek."

"What?!"

"If the pattern is meant to end with Amanda's death,

Sarek could die. How's your dissertation coming, Eleyna? Students have plotted against their professors before."

"Sarek will verify that my work is progressing satisfactorily," she said stiffly. "However, I did promise to help him with his part of the investigation." She stood.

"Hey," said Kirk, "I'm sorry! I told you I'm listing *all* possible suspects. Anyone else doing the investigating would keep *me* on the list, too."

Her stiffness eased. "Yes, of course. I understand. But I really must go."

"Well, before you do, tell me where to find the lady who dispenses tricorders—and show me how to store my notes in this gadget."

Kirk looked carefully at the Vulcan squiggles on the buttons she showed him, to be sure he remembered which was "erase" and which was "store." After Eleyna had gone, he made several pages of notes and stored them, then went to borrow the tricorder.

He discovered that T'Sey, the woman in charge of supplies, already had him on a list of guests to whom the Academy was to accord all courtesy, and did not have to check with Sarek as he had expected. She found him a tricorder of the same design as Star Fleet issue, and he was ready to start his investigation.

He decided to have lunch first, and in the cafeteria tried to transcribe the notes from the electronic tablet to the tricorder, so he could return the tablet to Storn's office.

The tablet was blank.

"Damn!" he said loudly, attracting the attention of three Andorians at a nearby table. One of them came over and offered to help. But he could not get anything to come up on the screen either.

"It happens to all of us," the student said in sibilant

Andorian tones. "You erased instead of storing. I hope it wasn't notes for an examination."

"No, not for an exam." said Kirk. "Thanks for trying to help."

And he left, feeling incredibly stupid at getting Eleyna's simple instructions backwards. *Some detective I am—can't even hold on to my notes on the case!*

However, he had a familiar tricorder now, and he remembered his list of suspects, so he set off for the hospital neurophysics laboratory for his first interview.

He found Sendet at a computer terminal, manipulating three-dimensional diagrams of humanoid nervous systems. The young man continued with his work long enough for Kirk to recognize a comparison between Vulcan and human systems on the screen.

Trying to figure out why that jolt this morning didn't kill Corrigan? he wondered.

Finally Sendet blanked the screen and turned to Kirk. He rose, imposingly taller than the human—but Kirk refused to be put at a psychological disadvantage by tall men.

"We have never met, Captain Kirk," Sendet said formally. "Why did you request to see me?"

"I am assisting in the investigation of two deaths of patients in the stasis chambers," Kirk replied.

"Two deaths?" Sendet raised one eyebrow. In Spock, that would have meant genuine surprise. How good an actor was Sendet?

"Carl Remington, a member of my starship crew, died this morning," Kirk replied.

"I see. Of course it is your responsibility to determine the cause of his death. However, I can be of little help to you. The Lady T'Zan worked with her husband on the neurophysical aspects of the stasis procedure. I was still an apprentice at the time the major work was done, several years ago. I can provide you with T'Zan's notes if they will be helpful."

My, he certainly is cooperative, Kirk thought, *as long as he is leading away from the real reason I'm here.*

"Thanks, but I believe Sorel and Corrigan already have all that information."

"Then . . . what do you seek from me?" Sendet seemed genuinely puzzled.

"I'm trying to find out *why* T'Zan and Remington died . . . that is, whether their deaths were accidental, or whether someone arranged them."

Sendet's face composed itself into purest Vulcan inscrutability. "I do not understand," he said in the flat tone Kirk knew meant that a Vulcan understood only too well.

"Let's take a hypothetical situation," said Kirk. "Suppose someone wanted something, and T'Zan and Corrigan stood in his way—T'Zan because she denied it to him and Corrigan because T'Zan and her family chose to give him what our hypothetical person wanted for himself."

Sendet's face became even more set in its expressionlessness. Kirk continued, "Now suppose further—still speaking hypothetically—that this person saw a way to get rid of T'Zan as an obstacle, and have Corrigan take the blame. An elegant solution. And fate played right into the hands of such a person, you see."

"No, I do not see," Sendet said obstinately.

"T'Zan's accident—you were there, you said. Perhaps her equipment was sabotaged. But it didn't kill her—maybe it was intended only to injure her severely enough to put her in stasis. It doesn't matter; she ended up there. Our hypothetical person now has the chance to kill T'Zan with Corrigan's equipment. Sorel, against whom he also has a grudge, will be discredited, too. It could break up their partnership. To make it seem even more convincing that the stasis procedure is at fault, he plans another failure, this one to the chamber of an insignificant offworlder—"

"Stop!"

Sendet glared at Kirk. His hands, gripping the edge of his desk, were white-knuckled with the intensity of his control. Remembering Vulcan strength, Kirk hoped he could maintain it.

Sendet took a deep breath, removed his hands from the desk, and folded them behind his back as Kirk had often seen Spock do. "You do not know what you are saying," the Vulcan told him stiffly. "You are suggesting the taking of other people's lives for personal gain. No Vulcan would ever contemplate such a thing."

"I told you it was hypothetical—"

"Do not mock me, Earther! I know very well that you are accusing me—but only the undisciplined mind of an outworlder could conceive such an obscene notion. I forgive you for not knowing who *I* am, but you cannot be forgiven for accusing *any* Vulcan of such an act. Leave me!"

"Sorry, Sendet, but you won't get rid of me by acting offended," said Kirk. "I don't care how many people I offend in search of the truth. If, in fact, you had nothing to do with T'Zan and Remington's deaths, *why* are you offended at my questions? Enlighten me."

"Then you do accuse me?"

"You are a prime suspect," Kirk affirmed, "and you will remain so until you give me some—logical—answers."

"And if I refuse? You have no authority here."

"Then I'll go ask Sarek the procedure for assembling an investigative tribunal and hauling you up in front of it. For the moment, I plan to keep my investigation private—but if you want it public, I can arrange that."

Sendet stared at him for a long moment, then asked, "What do you want to know?"

"How well can you handle that computer?"

"I can perform any function necessary to my research."

"No—I mean, can you go into its guts and change the programming on things not supposed to be accessed by you? For example, could you locate and change the stasis chamber programming?"

"I know the theory," Sendet replied. "I would not do such a thing."

"Did you?"

"I told you—no. In fact, I could not have done so."

"Why not?"

"If I understand your accusation, this programming you suggest would have been done after T'Zan was placed in stasis."

"Not if you arranged the accident that put her there," Kirk suggested.

"Captain, there was no stasis equipment set up until there was a patient to use it. Any of the hospital's isolation chambers may be adjusted for any of the medical techniques we have available. There are seven isolation chambers. *If* I had caused T'Zan's injury, and *if* I had known that her particular treatment would be with Sorel and Daniel's stasis equipment, there is no way I could have known beforehand which isolation chamber she would be placed in. Theoretically, I could have programmed in an order simply to disrupt the stasis field—but in that case the program would disrupt the first field it located. Depending on which chamber T'Zan was placed in, there is a 50 percent chance that the field disrupted would be that in the chamber occupied by the Lady Amanda."

Sendet cocked a supercilious eyebrow at Kirk, and

added, "I would have missed my target and killed an innocent person. Or do you assume that I regard any human life as valueless?"

I've met some Vulcans who seem to feel that way, Kirk thought, but what he said was, "I assume that anyone willing to take another person's life has little regard for *any* life form."

Sendet nodded. "You are right, of course. Anyone capable of conceiving of murder could not have the Vulcan respect for life. However, he would not want to risk missing his true victim, I would assume."

"So you waited until you knew which chamber T'Zan was in," suggested Kirk, "and then you programmed the computer to sabotage it."

"Such programming would have taken several hours of work," said Sendet. "With Lady T'Zan in stasis, the rest of the staff worked extra hours here in the laboratory yesterday. T'Ra and Skep were with me all day. They can tell you that I did not spend any time isolated with the computer."

"You realize that I plan to check that out?" Kirk asked.

"Certainly," Sendet replied. "You will quickly discover that I had no opportunity to do what you accuse me of."

"Sure you did. You had all night after T'Zan was put in stasis. And don't bother to say you weren't in the laboratory—there are terminals all over campus hooked into the main computer."

"I had no access to a computer terminal that night," Sendet said.

"Oh? None in your home?"

"I did not go home," the man replied stiffly.

Kirk pounced. "Where *did* you go? Were there witnesses?"

"I . . . do not know if anyone saw me or would remember," Sendet replied. "I went to meditate. At the . . . Shrine of T'Vet."

"Where is that?" asked Kirk. "Even if you were seen, can you prove you stayed there all night?"

"The Shrine of T'Vet is far across the desert, at the foot of the L-Langon Mountains. A tram makes the journey every evening, and returns at dawn. There are no computers at the shrine."

"But possibly no one noticed you," said Kirk. "All right—I have no more questions for now—but I will check your story. I assume you have no plans to leave town?"

"Why should I?" Sendet asked. "I have done nothing wrong. If you should discover that Lady T'Zan's death was not accidental, you will at the same time discover who is responsible. It is not I." ·

CHAPTER 15

Sorel instructed T'Sel to continue sending patients to T'Par and McCoy, and led his daughter and his partner into his office. Daniel Corrigan moved numbly, unable to think clearly. In fact, his head was spinning so it seemed he could not think at all.

He and Sorel washed the grime off their faces without a word. Then the healer made Corrigan sit beside T'Mir on the couch, and sat in his desk chair, studying them with his unreadable black eyes. Finally he said, "Daniel, have you thought through what happened?"

My whole world just fell apart, Corrigan wanted to answer, but he didn't. "T'Mir saw the guilt in my mind. It doesn't matter that logic will tell her I did not deliberately harm anyone—the strength of my emotion repels her."

T'Mir stiffened, and turned her head to look at

him. Although her face remained neutral under her father's scrutiny, her eyes were sad. "Daniel, I regret having caused you pain. It was foolish of me—you could not have melded with Father and saved his life if he had seen in your mind that my mother's death lay on your conscience. Nor could you have hidden such a thing from him in healing meld. I was indeed illogical to misinterpret your pain."

"You did not misinterpret it," Corrigan said flatly. "It was guilt."

"But . . . why?" T'Mir looked from Corrigan to her father, a host of unspoken questions between them.

Sorel went directly to the point. "Is Daniel correct that you are repelled by his emotions?"

"I . . . have lived for seven years among offworlders who give free vent to their feelings," T'Mir replied. "I thought I understood and accepted."

"And now?" her father prompted.

"I did not know . . . what it would mean to experience a human's feelings directly."

A *human's* feelings. Corrigan wished he could sink through the floor. How foolish he had been to let himself hope to end his loneliness. No Vulcan could live intimately with human illogic!

"Daniel," Sorel was saying, "I must consult with my daughter alone. You require rest. Shall I arrange a bed for you here and put you to sleep?"

Corrigan replied, "I'll go home, Sorel."

But in the outer office T'Sel was calling up the records of one of Corrigan's patients for Leonard McCoy, whose voice would not activate the program. The Star Fleet doctor frowned as he studied the computer screen. "Gout?" he asked in puzzlement.

"Gout in a thirty-two-year-old human male on a vegetarian diet?"

"Whose chart is that?" Corrigan asked, moving around the desk to see the screen. "I have no patients with gout."

The records on the screen were for David Fein, a geologist whom Corrigan was treating for a foot injury suffered on a recent expedition. "Dave's never h'ad gout!" he said as he stared at the misinformation on the screen. "He had surgery ten days ago for torn ligaments. This diagnosis is completely wrong! T'Sel—"

The woman was already calling other information onto the screen. "Medical history and surgical records appear to be correct, Daniel. The error occurred just now when I programmed in David's current symptoms."

"Never did trust machines!" grumbled McCoy. "It takes a doctor to diagnose a patient, not a computer."

"I agree, Leonard," said Corrigan. "However, it is standard procedure to run a patient's symptoms through the diagnostic program. Occasionally it provides suggestions I might not have considered—but I have never known it to be so outrageously far from the facts. T'Sel, pull that program and—"

"Wait!" said McCoy, a sudden gleam in his blue eyes. "It could be evidence. Is this computer tied in to the one that monitors the stasis chamber?"

"It is all one system," T'Sel replied.

"That's it! I've got to tell Spock! Leave that program just as it is until he looks at it. Daniel, can you take over here now?"

"Of course," Corrigan replied, his mind on his patient. "Leonard—you didn't mention gout to Dave Fein?"

"Hardly talked to him," McCoy replied over his shoulder. "He's waiting in your office. Is Spock still over at the stasis chamber?"

"In Storn's office, across the hall from the chambers."

McCoy grinned. "Good. I think I'm about to get the last word again!"

CHAPTER 16

Sarek watched his son trace the circuits from the stasis chambers to the main computer, calling up all commands the machine had been given. "Data lost," reported the computer when Spock requested this morning's log.

"Recover and enhance," Spock instructed, his long fingers playing nimbly over the keys. He was calm, his voice controlled, yet Sarek could sense tension in his son. There was a time, years ago, when he would have considered that tension a lapse from the Vulcan ideal. He had been so concerned that his son be a model Vulcan that he had driven him away, ultimately, into Star Fleet.

I was wrong. No Vulcan can live up to every ideal, or they would be customs, not goals. Surak himself said, "The cause is sufficient," when one of his followers exhibited emotion under stress. I placed Spock under stress from earliest childhood.

He remembered forcing Spock to control his emotions when he was five, and his schoolfellows taunted him for being "different." Under his father's tutelage, Spock had refused to cry when the others shut him out of their games, calling him "Earther" and "halfbreed." Amanda had hidden her tears from their son, and Sarek had hidden his anger.

Or had he?

Perhaps I directed it at my son instead, he realized. He had intended to prepare Spock for whatever lack of acceptance he would face in life. *And the message Spock received was that his own father did not accept him as he was, had to mold him into something he deemed acceptable.*

Just before the boy's Kahs-wan, his test of manhood, Sarek had been at his strictest—out of fear, he now knew, that his son would die in that desert endurance test. *The other children were tough and hard and full of fight. Did I realize then that I had disarmed my son by making him control too soon?*

But for all his quiet control, Spock had found the fortitude to endure. He had passed Kahs-wan with honor, and Sarek had said, "You have not disappointed your mother or me," driving down a secret desire to echo Amanda's, "Spock, we're so proud of you!" when the judges announced their decision.

Amanda had accused Sarek of pride in Spock aboard the *Enterprise* on the journey to Babel— "almost human pride," she had called it—and he had denied it. It was not human pride he felt; it was the universal satisfaction of a father who saw his son succeed.

Spock was succeeding now, his computer skills easily the equal of his father's—yet their combined skills had so far failed to find where the problem lay. Spock had on screen what could be recovered of the lost data—

hardly anything. That unexplained power surge had wiped the memory banks.

"There is no recognizable pattern," Sarek said. "However, if we look at the data for the period just before the failure to T'Zan's chamber—"

"—we should find a pattern to guide us in reconstructing today's data," Spock finished the thought.

But what came up on the screen showed no power failure.

"A computer cannot lie," said Spock. "Nevertheless, this one is giving false information."

"Why don't you try playing chess with it?" came a voice from the doorway. Sarek turned to find Leonard McCoy, bouncing on his toes and grinning.

"A valid suggestion, Doctor," Spock replied. "Unfortunately, if the programming has indeed been deliberately changed, it is difficult to predict what programs will show the effects."

"In an institution the size of the Academy," Sarek explained, "hundreds of programs could have been in use at the time this one was changed."

"All the more reason," Spock said thoughtfully, "that a person tampering with the records might inadvertently create errors in other programs without being aware of it. If we found such errors, we would know that someone had bypassed the security measures, opening any number of programs to change."

"But which other programs?" Sarek asked. "Is there a particular reason you suggest chess, Leonard? It is true that there are chess games in progress at any hour of the day."

"A crew member once changed the *Enterprise* computer record to falsify his death and blame Captain Kirk," McCoy explained. "I caught Spock playing chess while Jim faced court martial."

Sarek looked toward his son. "An error in the chess program?"

"That is correct," Spock replied. "Benjamin Finney's tampering with the bridge record had affected the chess program—the most recent permanent program entered into the system before the ion storm which he used to discredit Jim. If we can find out what programs have most recently been entered or changed in the Academy computer—"

"Since the computer itself is unreliable, we must ask all users to report their work," Sarek began.

"Thereby alerting the person who is doing the tampering," objected Spock.

"You are right," Sarek agreed. "How did you determine that the *Enterprise* chess program would hold the clue to the unlawful program change?"

"I . . . played a hunch," Spock admitted in a tone of quiet defiance.

Why did I try to stifle all the abilities he inherited from his mother? Sarek wondered. "And thereby, it appears, you discovered what had been done to the computer—"

"—and saved Jim's career," McCoy put in.

The doctor seemed ready to offer a suggestion, but Sarek quickly asked his son. "Have you any . . . hunches . . . now?"

"You won't need any," said McCoy. "I came to tell you what program's acting up."

Spock's eyebrows disappeared into his bangs. "Then why did you not *say* so, Doctor?"

"I just did. It's the hospital diagnostic program— specifically the one designed for human physiology. Diagnosed torn ligaments as gout!"

"Of course," said Sarek, "the original changes were made in the area of medical programming."

"And this is evidence that there actually *were*

changes made," Spock added. "We are not searching for something that does not exist."

"Well, I'm going to find Jim and tell him his theory's right," said McCoy.

When the doctor had gone, Spock had T'Sel transfer the faulty diagnostic program to their screen. While they waited for the safeguards to be cleared, he turned to his father. "When we had no hard evidence, why did you join me in what could have been a fruitless search?"

"You have not achieved command rank in Star Fleet through what your mother would call 'wild goose chasing.' Your ideas must, logically, be worth pursuing."

"It was actually Captain Kirk's idea," Spock pointed out.

"I respect your judgment of his opinions—and your judgment has just been validated. Where shall we begin to—"

The lights went out.

The computer screen blanked and the function lights flickered out. The hum of the ventilators died away, leaving the two men in total silence and utter blackness.

Sarek reached automatically for the communicator switch, and encountered his son's hand. "I have it, Father," Spock said, and the click of the key followed. However, no information came over the communicator, and no emergency lighting had yet come on.

"Amanda," Sarek murmured, and started toward the door.

Spock said, "Wait for the emergency system to come on. You cannot get through the airlock into her stasis chamber until it does. The secondary power source to her stasis field is independent of both primary and emergency power systems."

Logical, his son.

Also illogically comforting, reminding him of what he already knew.

And . . . he already knew Amanda was safe. He remembered Sorel, sensing his wife's death through their bonding. Sarek felt nothing—nothing but the silent presence of Amanda's unconscious mind.

"Your mother is unharmed," he assured Spock. "There is no need to go to her. It has already taken too long, however, for emergency power to come on."

"We are in the chief engineer's office," said Spock. "I saw a battery-powered lamp—"

Sure enough, after some shuffling noises a bright lamp illuminated the small room. By its light, Spock and Sarek found battery-powered torches and a communicator in one of the cabinets.

Storn's voice came over the communicator, "—keep this channel open. All engineering personnel locate battery-powered light sources and report to central power. All others in windowless areas remain where you are until emergency lighting is restored."

It was already becoming stuffy in the small office. Sarek said, "We have torches, and Storn can undoubtedly use our help."

"Indeed, Father," Spock replied. "We can do no more with the computer until power is restored."

As they walked toward central power by the light of their torches, though, Spock added a thought that Sarek had been suppressing. "Do you suppose this power failure . . . might somehow *not* be a coincidence?"

CHAPTER **17**

It is with deepest regret that I must inform you of the death of Ensign Carl Remington us the result of injuries sustained in battle with the Klingon Empire, in defense of our Federation. He wus a fine and courageous member of the crew of the USS Enterprise. *He will be sorely missed.*

Mr. Remington was unconscious from the time of his injury, and suffered no pain. . . .

James T. Kirk recited the words of the formula condolence message to Carl Remington's family—the most painful duty of a starship commander. It had not taken him long to recall that duty, and once recalled it had to be performed. Kirk was not a man to procrastinate.

He had gone back to the meditation alcove as an appropriate place to compose the message, along with his preliminary report to Star Fleet, reciting them into the tricorder for subspace transmission at the first opportunity. It was best to record the message to Remington's family now, he told himself, when he still could not be certain the boy had been murdered. If he knew for sure, he would be obligated to inform them—and it would be better if they never knew that the young man had been the victim of someone's unbalanced mind.

It was the Klingons' fault, anyway, that he had been critically injured. They *deserved* the blame for his death.

As Kirk finished the routine phrases and sought to personalize his message with his own memories of the boy, he found himself more and more determined to find out who had robbed Star Fleet of a fine young officer and the *Enterprise* of a valuable crew member. He would have to find out how to check out Sendet's alibi, but meanwhile he was eager to interview his other suspects.

Just as he finished his message, the lights went out. So even Vulcan had power failures. He wondered if too much air-conditioning had overloaded the system in the heat of midday.

The fire-pot's dim flicker threw enough light, once Kirk's eyes adjusted, to allow him to find the door—but instead of being lit by emergency lighting, the hall outside was pitch black.

There was a soft thud, and then a familiar voice said, "Damn!"

"Bones—over here."

"Jim?" Shuffling steps.

"This way." He turned on the tricorder, and waved the bright but empty screen end toward McCoy.

The doctor found his way into the alcove, and looked at the fire-pot. "One of *those* things."

"Don't complain—it seems to be the only light fixture working." He left the door open, and joined McCoy on the bench. "I'm beginning to think we should have come to Vulcan with full emergency gear."

"Yeah. There's something mighty peculiar going on. You think this power outage is coincidence?"

"What else?" asked Kirk.

"Your murderer," replied the doctor. "Jim, I just found a crazy error in the medical diagnostic programming. Spock and Sarek agree that it means someone's been tampering with the computer. You realize what that means?"

"Yes. I was right, Bones. We are dealing with murder. I'll tell you something—I have seldom been less pleased to be proved right."

McCoy nodded. "And *now* look at this place. One thing you gotta give Vulcans: they're efficient. They don't build power systems without emergency backup."

"And still we're sitting here in the dark," said Kirk. "Bones—have you ever seen what happens to a computer when *all* power to it is shut off? I mean, when even the temporary battery or whatever secondary power source it has goes dead?"

"Everything that has not been placed in permanent memory gets erased," replied the doctor. "And you can bet whoever's been playing games with the Academy computer hasn't put anything in the permanent memory."

"So the evidence Spock and Sarek were looking for has now been destroyed," Kirk said grimly. Then he saw a light sweep across the doorway. "Hey—somebody finally found the flashlights!"

"Jim?"

It was Spock's voice, and as Kirk and McCoy went into the corridor they recognized Sarek as well in the shadows behind the light beams. Both Vulcans carried extra torches, and passed one each to Kirk and McCoy.

"We are going to power central," Spock explained. "We may not be engineers, but Storn needs everyone who knows anything about power systems."

"I'll help," said Kirk. "I know how to do basic repairs—and if they're beyond my knowledge, I can always hold a flashlight for someone else."

"I'm going to the emergency room," said McCoy. "You can bet with a blackout like this, people are going to get hurt. And if the power stays off long enough, there'll be cases of heat prostration. It's already getting stuffy in here. Why'd they build this place with no natural ventilation?"

"So as to control the climate for the comfort of offworlders," Sarek replied.

When McCoy turned off down the corridor toward the emergency room, Kirk said to Spock, "Have you realized what this total power failure means to your search for evidence in the computer?"

"Yes," Spock replied flatly, "it has all been erased. Did Dr. McCoy tell you what he has found?"

"He did. Dammit, Spock, I just cannot think that this power failure is a coincidence!"

"I am certain it is not," said Sarek. "However, the Academy computer has a safeguard not built into most systems. We deal with students under pressure, and upon occasion, even though very rarely, there have been instances of . . . cheating."

"Of course!" said Kirk. "Star Fleet Academy has the same thing! There's a separate log, constantly going into permanent memory, of all entries from student terminals! But Sarek—do you think a student could be capable of this level of tampering? It's not just changing records to improve a grade, or having an early look at an exam, or borrowing another student's project. This is overriding safeguards and changing main programming without triggering alarms. Can any student do that?"

"A student about to graduate? Certainly. I could have, Spock could have, as students in our final training. But such students need not restrict themselves to student terminals. My assistant, for example, uses my terminal for her dissertation because it does not limit her access to information. For that reason, the special memory storage unit records activity from all faculty terminals as well. Obviously, there is work both faculty and graduate students must keep private. The record will not tell us what was *done* on each terminal, but it *will* tell us what programs were accessed from it in the past few days."

"What good is that?" Kirk asked.

"If one student were found to be accessing another student's work," Spock explained, "the second student could be asked whether he had given permission. What we will look for in this instance is accessing of the power system program. It will tell us what terminal was used—of course, we will then have to discover who used that terminal."

"Probably impossible if he had the sense to use manual input rather than vocal," Kirk said glumly.

"True, but still a place to start," Sarek agreed. "Meanwhile, Jim, your investigation as to motive and opportunity will help to narrow the search. Whoever programmed the computer to cut power to those stasis chambers must have sent that power surge through this morning, and cut both main and emergency power just now. Other patients, on other kinds of life-support, have had their lives placed in jeopardy. If surgery is in progress, it is now being performed by the light of torches and with equipment that will run on batteries."

"Whoever did this is concerned only with covering

his tracks," said Kirk. "He obviously doesn't care how many people are hurt in the process."

"We are dealing with an unbalanced mind," Spock agreed. "Motive is very important, Jim. We do not know if the victims have anything to do with the crime—considering all the tampering with highly sophisticated equipment, it could be some mad protest against technology, against the Academy, against the medical program, or against Sorel and/or Corrigan."

"And in any of those cases," Sarek said flatly, "Amanda could be the next victim."

CHAPTER **18**

When McCoy arrived at the emergency room, he was quickly pressed into service. Doors had been opened into an outer hallway with windows, where the blinds were opened despite the penetrating heat of Vulcan's midday sun.

The first injuries were minor cuts and bruises from floundering in the dark to find battery-powered light sources. Then people with more serious problems began being brought out of the dark depths of the buildings: a workman who had been under antigrav supported equipment when it collapsed; a girl who was crushed when a fire door snapped shut, her fellow students having somehow pried it open with sheer physical strength; several children who had fallen down a staircase when the darkness caught them between classes.

Two human students were brought in with chemical

burns; they had been working in the botany lab with a portable sprayer, and in the darkness had not been able to turn it off before both were soaked with nutrients of flora from Arcturus Seven.

Two Vulcan healers worked on the Vulcan patients, while McCoy took the humans and an Andorian who had broken an arm helping to rescue the girl caught in the fire door. As more patients arrived, Dr. M'Benga joined the Vulcans, while Daniel Corrigan came to aid McCoy.

They were using all battery-powered equipment. "Forty years at the Academy, and I've never seen anything like this," said Corrigan.

"Never a power outage?" asked McCoy.

"Oh, of course—there's no machinery that doesn't break down sometime. But I've never known the backup system to be off at the same time. It's got its own generator, which should have cut in the moment power from the city was interrupted."

"Is power off all over town?" asked McCoy.

"No," replied a Vulcan nurse who had just joined them. "I did not know there was a problem until I came in for my duty shift."

Corrigan paused between patients to wipe the sweat out of his eyes. "Then are offworlders who cannot take this heat being instructed to go into town for shelter?"

"I will see to it, Daniel," said the nurse.

They were working on the last patients now, and McCoy was glad. The heat was building steadily. He was drenched in sweat and was beginning to feel queasy.

Dr. M'Benga finished his last patient, and came over to McCoy. "You are not accustomed to Vulcan's heat, Doctor," he said in his deep, cultured voice. "Your help is greatly appreciated, but you should rest now."

M'Benga was black, but McCoy saw the telltale grayness of his skin beneath the sheen of perspiration, indicating that this man, too, had been pushing himself to work despite growing discomfort. "I will if you will," he replied, and M'Benga gave him a nod and a small, contained smile.

"We should remain on call," said Corrigan as the nurses and orderlies took the last patients away. "The room where medications are stored has a cooling system—if it's not tied in with the regular emergency power."

All three doctors quickened their pace at that thought, despite the heat. Precious drugs would have to be moved quickly to a cool place if their protective refrigeration system were not working.

But it was. The humans slumped against the wall of the small tiled room in blessed relief, letting the coolness penetrate their soggy scrubs. "I may stay here the rest of the day!" said McCoy.

"Indeed," replied M'Benga.

But just as they relaxed into the comfort, a strange, distant howling siren sounded, drifting in and out of human audial range. "What the hell is *that?*" demanded McCoy.

When he looked at Corrigan, though, he knew that it was bad news—the man tensed, his blue eyes wide, then jumped to his feet. "Oh, God—no!" he exclaimed. "That's the fire alarm!"

And both Corrigan's and M'Benga's pagers began beeping wildly.

CHAPTER 19

*I*n the Vulcan Academy's central power unit, James T. Kirk was indeed holding a battery-powered torch, so that Storn could see the circuits he was tracing in the emergency generator. "Here it is," the Vulcan said at last, pressing a circuit breaker into place. But the lights did not come on.

Kirk tried to remember how often he had wished for Scotty since he had arrived on Vulcan.

"I've found another one," came the voice of one of the other Vulcan engineers from the darkness penetrated only by the slowly moving torch beams. There was another click as the circuit breaker was reset.

"If we had computer power, we could locate all the breaks easily," said Storn.

"This has to be sabotage," said Spock as a third click resounded in the chamber, "and its main purpose is to *prevent* us from having computer power."

"There seems to be no permanent damage," Storn said as his hands moved along the circuit until he found another breaker. Another click. Still no power.

"Do you think every circuit breaker has been shorted out?" asked Kirk.

"We will proceed on that theory," Storn replied.

It took time. Kirk did not know whether they reset all the circuit breakers there were, but after about the twentieth click the lights came on.

"Now to find out what's wrong with the main power source!" said Storn, climbing to his feet.

Blinking in the brightness, Kirk asked, "This is only emergency lighting?"

"It's concentrated here, because here is where we must work on the main power source when the Academy is on emergency power. There is now relatively dim emergency lighting in the rest of the Academy buildings, but this small generator cannot provide energy for the ventilation or cooling systems, except to the hospital areas. I suggest that we begin at the connection with ShiKahr's main solar power generator."

Kirk followed Storn, although there was no longer any need for him to hold the light. From the small machine in the center of the room, Storn proceeded to the wall units—much larger than the ones aboard the *Enterprise*.

They found the same pattern—the unit had completely shut itself down, circuit after circuit, including the main connection. Storn's engineers began removing wall panels to expose the breakers.

Sarek said, "Now that some power has been restored, Spock and I will attempt to find out how badly the computer has been affected. Perhaps we can have it restore the circuits without your having to locate all the breakers manually."

"Excellent," said Storn. "There is a terminal just outside the door."

Kirk wished the ventilators would come on—he was sweating and beginning to feel dizzy. It was ungodly hot in here; even the Vulcans were starting to look pale.

As Storn began pressing circuit breakers into place, a high-pitched distant whistling sound barely penetrated through the walls. "That sounds like—" one of the engineers began.

Storn hit another breaker—and suddenly the room was filled with howling, shrieking noise.

"Fire!" exclaimed half the people in the chamber.

"But where—?" Storn began.

Spock ran back into the room. "Fire in the hallway—hurry! Everybody out before it traps you!"

They pounded out of the power unit, just as flames roared toward them from the left. There was now light in the hallway, but how long would that last if the fire got to the generator?

Flames leaped after them as they fled down the hall and through a fire door into a stairwell. Emergency power allowed them to open the door, and the lighting held as they swarmed up to the floor above—and came out in the hall leading to the stasis chambers. Kirk saw both Spock and Sarek look down that hallway, and realized that the flames were just below the room where Amanda lay helplessly in stasis!

Father and son scanned the walls—yes, there were fire extinguishers. Each grabbed one and started toward the chambers.

"Sarek! Spock!" Storn shouted against the wail of the alarm. "We must get out of the building!"

"Amanda is trapped down there," Kirk reminded

him—and ran down the hall to where he saw a third extinguisher hanging on the wall.

It was heavy, slowing him in his chase, but there were no flames yet. Perhaps the Academy's structure was good enough. . . .

They ran past the chamber, to where the floor was hot beneath their feet, and grimly waited.

It got hotter, but the flames seemed to be contained below. The wailing siren continued—surely ShiKahr had some kind of fire department that would be here soon!

They didn't try to talk. Both Vulcans were controlling their fears, and Kirk was having enough trouble containing his own.

Fire was the worst fear of those who traveled in space. A starship was selfcontained and alone—there was no place else to run. Kirk determinedly reminded himself that this was not a starship, and that help would come from outside . . . but there would be no help for Amanda if the flames approached that stasis chamber.

And she could not be moved, or she would die.

Looking back along the corridor, checking that there was still an exit, Kirk saw Storn and his engineers at the far end, helping the medical staff evacuate patients and personnel.

Then, at their end of the long hallway, flames broke through another stairwell door!

All three grasped their fire extinguishers and attacked the blaze.

Kirk struggled with his equipment, but soon had it spraying. He, Spock, and Sarek fought the flames, but they were fed from below by a strong updraft, and when they had eaten the door they began on the walls.

Nonetheless, the three men kept at it—they could *not* give Amanda over to the fire!

Kirk's extinguisher ran out of chemical solution. He started back along the hallway to find another.

People in protective suits were coming toward them —Academy security personnel with more extinguishers.

"Get out of the building!" one of them shouted at him, voice muffled under a breathing mask.

Kirk realized that he was coughing and choking only when he could not get any words out. He pointed down the hall to where he had come from, where Spock and Sarek were silhouetted against the flames.

The security man nodded, and insisted, "Go!"

But Kirk could not. His friends were in trouble.

He picked up a fresh extinguisher from the pile the security people had brought, and followed them.

The flames were now only a few paces from Amanda's chamber.

Suddenly the ceiling was ablaze!

As the flames leaped over their heads, Spock and Sarek tried to douse them—but Sarek's extinguisher fizzled out.

Kirk dragged his new one along to the scene as the security people tried to pull Spock and Sarek away. Understanding, he handed the extinguisher over to Sarek and went back for another.

Eyes burning, breath rasping, Kirk returned again, doggedly determined to add what strength he had to protecting Amanda.

Half a dozen extinguishers now staved off the flames. They could not contain them, but they slowed their progress. It could be only a matter of time. . . .

Kirk felt his skin burning. The lightweight clothes he wore were little protection; his thighs stung as much as his exposed face and arms.

He backed off behind the Vulcans in protective suits, but there were still flames to fight, creeping closer and closer to Amanda's chamber.

They were almost surrounded by flames now.

With a crashing roar, the ceiling collapsed!

Kirk was far enough back to leap out of the way, but he saw Spock go down under the flaming material.

Sarek struggled out from under one edge—Kirk saw that his shirt was aflame, leaped on him, and rolled him back onto the relatively cooler floor tiles, smothering the blaze. "Spock!" Sarek rasped.

Kirk's throat would not open to let him answer, but he turned back to where the figures in protective gear were lifting the burning material off Spock. He saw a foot, grabbed it, hauled. . . .

Sarek grasped Spock's other foot, and together they pulled him out from under the collapsed ceiling, slapping out the flames clinging to his clothes and hair.

Other people were arriving—firemen in much heavier protective gear, with a hose that spewed fire-fighting chemical ten times faster than any extinguisher.

Other emergency workers followed, lifting Spock onto a stretcher and carrying him quickly off toward the emergency room.

Sarek looked after them, but shook off the medics who wanted to take him, too. "My wife," he said, his voice a harsh croak.

The firemen were beating back the blaze now, pushing it step by step back along its own path. The door to the stasis chamber was black with smoke and dripping with chemicals, but it had held.

It was safe to leave.

Kirk's burns began to sting in earnest. He could hardly breathe. Tears were running down his face.

Unresisting, he allowed the medics to lead him toward a stretcher—

Then flames broke out at the far end of the hall! It had traveled under them and broken through again!

Kirk reached for a fresh extinguisher and started to haul it toward the flames.

The medics tried to stop him. "Leave it to the fire patrol," one woman told him—for even as she spoke a fresh troop of firefighters were charging out of the stairwell with another hose. "There are no patients left here except Amanda. They will protect her. There is no use risking your life protecting property which can be rebuilt."

The fire, though, as if renewed in strength now that it had the firefighters surrounded, roared louder from both ends of the hall, making the people fall back toward one another. Vile smoke poured from something the flames were consuming in their new attack. Kirk coughed and choked.

Renewed heat drove Kirk, Sarek, and the medics back toward the only stairs remaining as an avenue of escape. Blindly, Kirk groped his way, felt someone fall against him, and was driven down with the dead weight. He forced streaming eyes open, and saw that it was Sarek—unconscious? Or dead?

Through tear-glazed eyes, Kirk could not tell, but he feared it didn't matter. If those flames above had penetrated Amanda's stasis chamber, she was dying—and so was her husband. Spock was injured and unconscious, too—he could not save his father.

The medics carried Sarek down the stairs. Kirk stumbled after, and gratefully allowed himself to be placed on a stretcher by people waiting at the bottom.

Smoke and exhaustion took their toll at last as an oxygen mask gave him relief from coughing. Although he wanted desperately to stay conscious, to know whether the people he cared about were going to survive, no strength of will could accomplish it. Fighting all the way, he sank into oblivion.

CHAPTER 20

*L*eonard McCoy worked furiously in the emergency room, not allowing himself to think or worry, just concentrate on healing as he did on board the *Enterprise* in the midst of battle. The only difference, it seemed, was that instead of being thrown about by the blasts of photon torpedoes, here the hospital was inundated by the foul smells of smoke and fire-fighting chemicals. It was also still miserably hot, but whether it was from the fire or from the sun's beating down on the building he did not know.

No one had time to ask where the fire was and whether it was approaching them. All medical personnel were too busy taking the injured as they arrived, and trying to keep them alive.

At least they had lights now—lighting had already been on when he and the other two human doctors had emerged from their cool refuge in the pharmaceutical storage room.

Their first job had been to help all ambulatory patients outside. Volunteers quickly transferred them to other buildings where the cooling systems were working.

Then had come patients who should not have been moved, but had to be, on gurneys, or in their own beds with all sorts of equipment still attached. Vulcan efficiency moved them, equipment and all—Vulcan strength also coming to aid the cause, McCoy noted when a patient in traction was passed through with pieces of torn-out wall still clinging to the frame he was fastened to.

There was not enough portable life-support equipment for every patient; several on respirators had to make do with oxygen masks, a volunteer pumping to be sure air regularly entered their lungs. Those who were conscious and could ask for help, if needed, had to be temporarily disconnected from some forms of life-support, and share the portable equipment.

Then fire victims began arriving, so covered with grime that it was hard to see their wounds. Smoke and chemical inhalation was the most prevalent injury, but there were also burns, often irritated by chemicals from the fire extinguishers.

As time passed, the injured grew in number and in the seriousness of their injuries. Firefighters brought out people who had been trapped, some unconscious, some badly burned, some with broken bones or internal injuries, for parts of the building had collapsed. Even a huge Lemnorian, almost three meters tall and bulky to match, had been felled by collapsing architecture. To make a stretcher large enough to carry him, someone had fastened a gymnasium mat to a pair of vaulting poles.

McCoy worked in steady concentration, ignoring his own growing exhaustion as he labored to save lives, knowing the satisfaction of seeing most patients quickly relieved of their pain and set on the road to recovery.

Sorel and Corrigan were performing triage. M'Benga and T'Par were handling simple fractures, superficial burns, and smoke inhalation, which were all being treated in the emergency room itself. McCoy had been delegated surgeon for humans, it appeared; he moved from one O.R. to another as directed, always, it seemed, with a new patient waiting, scanners showing some new atrocity performed by fire, smoke, chemicals, or collapsed rooms. As a starship surgeon he saw a wide variety of injuries; experience somehow did not make him any less surprised and angered at what could be done to destroy a humanoid body.

Leaving a nurse to close after removing a ruptured spleen, McCoy stepped out of the O.R. to find Sorel directing two orderlies to take a patient into one of the O.R.'s set up for Vulcans. But McCoy knew that patient. "Spock! Sorel, let me take this one—I know those crazy insides better than any of your Vulcan surgeons could."

"He is your friend," said the Vulcan healer.

"All the more reason I'll be sure he survives. I've done it before."

"He will survive; his injuries are not critical, but his internal bleeding must be stopped."

"And fast," McCoy responded. "How's your stock of T-Negative blood with human factors?"

The healer's black eyes gave no indication of his feelings. "Pure T-Negative will do, but you are correct that our supply is limited. You probably are the best qualified surgeon for this particular patient. Take him to O.R. 4, T'Mir." Only then did McCoy realize that

Sorel's daughter had been pressed into service as an orderly.

McCoy stayed in the hallway for a moment as Spock was taken to be prepared for surgery. Someone had set up a table with food and drinks—he suddenly realized he was very thirsty, and went to investigate. A very lovely blond human woman was dispensing tea and fruit juice. "Not that, Doctor," she said as he started to pick up a cup of what looked like orange juice. "You must be new on Vulcan. Here, have some kasa juice."

"Thank you," he replied, realizing how pretty she was but having no energy to devote to any thought beyond that. His mind was on his patient as he gulped down the juice and started for what was still called the scrub room, although he would actually be bathed in disinfecting rays.

Suddenly there was a roar of pain, as gutteral and incoherent as the cry of a wounded buffalo.

McCoy turned to see the huge Lemnorian leap up from the improvised stretcher on which he had been dragged in. Corrigan, closest to the man, hurried toward him, saying, "Don't move! You'll injure yourself further!"

But the mountainous being lifted the arm someone had splinted by tying a small ladder to it, and swung it toward the human doctor. Corrigan instinctively leaped back, but the giant followed through on his swing, sweeping a Vulcan off a gurney and sending the wheeled cart careening into several others, causing more cries of pain as injured people were jolted.

The medical staff scrambled to protect the wounded, while the towering Lemnorian gabbled something McCoy's translator could not handle.

"He's delirious!" said Corrigan, staying just outside the injured giant's reach. "Get a sedative!"

"Which sedative?" asked a Vulcan nurse.

"Traxadine, 10cc. Hurry!" said Corrigan, and the nurse moved off toward the pharmaceutical room.

The Lemnorian was still watching Corrigan, as if the human doctor were the cause of his distress. Since he had his attention, Corrigan soothed, "It's all right. We're going to help you. Settle down, now—"

The giant roared again, and swung his broken arm against the wall, splintering the ladder. The arm bent where there was no joint, even in a Lemnorian. His hoarse roars changed to screams of agony. He swung the arm as if to throw away the source of pain.

"My God—he'll compound the fracture!" gasped Corrigan, making a leap for the thrashing giant.

With his good arm, the Lemnorian swatted the human doctor like some annoying insect. As Corrigan went down, six Vulcans converged on the huge being and—no easy task even with their combined strength— wrestled him to the floor.

The nurse was back with the hypo. Sorel grabbed it and dived into the mass of writhing bodies. McCoy heard the hiss, and hoped it had hit its target, but he was making his way toward Corrigan now that the path was clear.

T'Mir was there before him, calling, "Daniel! Are you injured?"

"Don't move him!" warned McCoy, and the girl turned huge, worried eyes to him.

But Corrigan was already struggling to sit up. "Lie still!" McCoy ordered, running his medscanner over him. "Nothing broken," he announced.

"I just—had the breath—knocked—out of me!" Corrigan gasped.

"Damn lucky that's all it was!" McCoy growled.

"How's the—Lemnorian?" Corrigan struggled to peer past McCoy.

"Subdued," replied Sorel, joining them. "He was in shock, and we must treat that first, as it is much more serious than the injury to his arm. Daniel, you were foolish to try to handle him when there were Vulcans here."

"They weren't doing much—to stop him—were they?" the human replied. "Other people were getting hurt."

"But he could have killed you," said T'Mir.

"Well, he didn't," said Corrigan, climbing heavily to his feet. "Come on—the excitement's over. We've got patients to care for!"

McCoy remembered that Spock was waiting for him, but on his way he stopped to get another cup of kasa juice from the pretty blonde.

Even as he was turning away from the table, the young woman, who had remained calm as any Vulcan during the altercation with the Lemnorian, gasped and jumped to her feet, jogging the table and sloshing juice out of the cups.

"Sarek!" she cried, and McCoy turned to see not one, but two people he knew being carried in: Sarek and Captain Kirk. Both were covered with grime, both were wearing charred clothing, and both were unconscious.

Corrigan was already running his scanner over Kirk. "Smoke inhalation; superficial burns; possible shock. Emergency room."

Sorel was examining Sarek, his face revealing nothing. The blond woman stood beside him with her eyes wide, demanding, "Tell me he's not dead! He *can't* be dead!"

McCoy started toward them, but behind him a Vulcan nurse called, "Dr. McCoy! Come quickly, please. The scan shows Spock's bleeding growing worse —you must operate immediately!"

CHAPTER **21**

James T. Kirk came to in the emergency room. There was a breathing mask over his face, and his body felt numb.

He pulled one arm out from under the sheet that covered him, and saw shiny ointment in a protective layer over burn-red skin. But the skin was there, though blistered in places; it was no more than a bad sunburn.

When Kirk sat up, Daniel Corrigan came over to him. "Lie down and rest, Jim. You'll be fine. I'm going to send you home as soon as you have your turn under the healing rays."

"Home?" It hurt his throat to talk, but he managed, pulling the mask off. "Spock? Sarek?"

"Spock is out of surgery and in healing trance," Corrigan told him as he put the breathing apparatus aside and ran his scanner over Kirk. T'Mir, who was passing out fruit juice, brought some to Kirk. "Leonard stopped Spock's internal bleeding," Corrigan continued. "It was not extensive surgery, and if I know Vulcans, Spock will be ready for release in the morning."

"Sarek?" Kirk insisted, his throat relieved by the juice. "Amanda? They're not both—?"

"They are both alive," Corrigan assured him. "The fire is out, and it did not penetrate the stasis chamber. Sarek suffered less physical damage than you did—he came to while Sorel was examining him. He, too, is in healing trance. Sorel or T'Par will wake him when you are ready to go home—and Jim, I'm leaving it up to you to *make* Sarek go home. He will have no physical pain after healing, but he must rest. Repairs on that computer can wait until tomorrow."

"I've noticed that Sarek is just as stubborn as his son," said Kirk. "Perhaps I can exercise some of the techniques I use on Spock."

"And what techniques are useful in persuading stubborn *humans* to rest?" It was Sorel, coming up behind Corrigan. "Daniel, I recall that you were supposed to go home this morning."

"You didn't complain when I was here to help with the emergency," Corrigan pointed out.

"Any protest at that time would have been pointless. However, the emergency is now over."

"How bad is the damage?" Kirk asked.

"The fire was confined to the emergency generator area and one wing of the hospital complex," Sorel answered. "Storn could tell you more precisely, but he is already busy making repairs."

"The important thing," Corrigan added, "is that no one died. It's a nuisance that the computer's down, but we've got power back, and our patients are being moved back to their rooms."

"And that is where you belong, Daniel," said Sorel, "in your room—asleep. T'Mir!" he called.

Kirk saw the healer's daughter leave a patient to whom she had just given a drink, and come to Sorel's side. "Yes, Father?"

"Take Daniel home to his apartment. Make him something to eat, and put him to bed."

"Sorel—" Corrigan protested.

"Daniel, you are operating on adrenaline. Now that the emergency is over it will subside—and if I did not see that you were cared for, you would eat nothing, fall asleep on the couch in your office, and tomorrow morning force yourself to do your duties on coffee and a sense of responsibility."

Kirk grinned. Sorel had just given a perfect description of another doctor he knew. "That reminds me," he said, "where *is* Dr. McCoy?"

Both Sorel and Corrigan turned at the apparent nonsequitur, but while Corrigan looked puzzled, for the first time Kirk was able to read the expression on the face of the Vulcan healer: perfect mutual understanding. "Leonard is in post-op," Sorel replied. "It will probably be several hours before he completes his work. I will see that he gets home, Jim. You do all you can to make Sarek rest . . . and, T'Mir, I have given you instructions. Is this the obedience of a dutiful daughter?"

The girl's eyes were velvet-brown and highly expressive—the one feature she could not control. Kirk saw them flare a moment's indignation—but she caught herself before she spoke. He could see her realize as he did that Sorel was teasing—but with a serious undertone.

The healer wanted his daughter and his partner alone together—face to face with the accusation T'Mir had made in the empty stasis chamber . . . was it only this morning?

For the first time since the fire, Kirk remembered that he was investigating murder. Had the murderer started the fire? It didn't fit. Would someone who toyed with other people's lives from a distance, playing with designs on a computer screen, be capable of getting his hands dirty by setting an explosive device or actually pouring out some flammable substance and lighting it? Ah, but if he were frightened enough that he had left evidence? One thing was certain: someone ought to examine the site where the fire had started for signs of arson.

As T'Mir and Corrigan left, Kirk asked, "Where's my tricorder?"

Sorel reached up to a shelf over Kirk's head, and handed it down, along with his Star Fleet ID, Federation credit voucher, Vulcan-set chronometer, and a few coins. "Your clothes were badly scorched," the healer told him. "We will find something for you to go home in."

"Can you get a message to Storn for me? That fire could have been arson."

"You are not the only one to suspect that, Jim," Sorel replied. "It is already being investigated."

But Kirk could not rest. His mind reverberated with possibilities, the most obvious of which was that whoever had set the fire had meant to kill Amanda and destroy the evidence at the same time. And that put him back to motives: whose motive could possibly connect T'Zan, Remington, and Amanda?

The more he thought about it, the more certain he was that either one of the three was the intended victim, with the other two as camouflage . . . or that the deaths were intended to discredit Corrigan, and possibly all humans on Vulcan.

By the time Kirk's turn came to go under the healing rays, the anesthetic effect of the ointment was starting to wear off. His skin began to burn and itch as much as his curiosity.

But finally McCoy, now working with Sorel's son Soton, placed him on a treatment bench much like the ones in the *Enterprise* sickbay. The burning and itching were replaced by a pleasant warm tingling as his cells were encouraged to speed up their healing process. It made him relax so deeply that he fell asleep, but woke when Soton came to tell him to turn over.

For a moment he mistook the younger man for his father, until he saw the warm brown eyes so like his sister's. Half asleep, Kirk blurted out the personal question he would never under ordinary circumstances have asked a Vulcan, "Soton, would you approve of a marriage between T'Mir and Dr. Corrigan?"

The young Vulcan retained his composure, not taking refuge in a lecture on Vulcan proprieties as Spock might have. To Kirk's surprise, he answered, "I know of the human expression, 'Some of my best friends are aliens, but I would not want my sister to marry one.' Such sentiments are foreign to Vulcans. Daniel Corrigan has been what humans would term a 'best friend' to my whole family since I was a child. How, then, could any of us possibly object to his becoming a member of our family?" The brown eyes studied Kirk curiously before the young healer continued. "I am not merely adhering to form; it would please me greatly if Daniel and my sister resolved their difficulties. It would formalize a relationship between Daniel and our family that has existed for many years."

Finding Soton willing to talk, and knowing he would

never dare ask Sorel, Kirk probed further. "What about your father?"

"My father has no brother by blood. When he met Daniel, he found someone to fill that role. I do not think T'Mir could have done anything else in her life to please Father as much as when she told him she wished to marry Daniel. That she caused Daniel pain today disappointed Father greatly. And . . . I fear it is unresolved anger toward my sister for accusing Daniel that has made me speak so openly to you. Please forgive me. I have not had opportunity to meditate and clear such negative thoughts from my mind. I beg your indulgence in not allowing them to go further."

"I haven't heard a word you said," Kirk assured him, recalling the time he had said the same words to Spock. And he had never breathed a word to anyone, although he knew that the Vulcans' unspoken secret was even now in Star Fleet records, placed there by sources unknown.

Soton went on about his duties. Kirk turned onto his stomach and drowsed under the healing rays until a soft hand on his shoulder woke him. He raised his head from his folded arms, and found Eleyna Miller standing beside him. It took him a moment to recall that he was stark naked—in time, fortunately, to restrain the automatic impulse to turn over onto his back and sit up. The healing rays had been turned off, but he felt his skin tingle just as much with blushing. *Maybe she'll think it's redness from the burns.*

"I brought you some clothes," she said, laying a bundle of cloth on the bench near his arms. "Sorel has wakened Sarek, and he is waiting for you in the lobby."

"Thank you," said Kirk, making no move.

"Do you need help getting dressed, Jim?" Eleyna asked.

"No—just a little privacy."

"Of course," she replied as if humoring a child. "I will be back for you in five minutes."

Kirk scrambled into the outfit provided, a sort of one-size-fits-all pants with a drawstring waist and a tunic with a belt—probably something borrowed from the Academy gymnasium. Decently covered, he stretched, and found that the painful burns were reduced to a very minor stinging. If it had actually been sunburn, he would have awakened the next day with a golden tan. As it was, he saw, dry skin was already flaking in patches off his arms, where the blisters had been. Well, a sonic shower would rid him of the terminal-dandruff effect.

Eleyna returned. "Ready to go? You know, you really do look good in *anything*, Jim."

"Uh, thanks. Which way to the lobby?"

"I'll take you. This part of the hospital is pretty much of a labyrinth."

It was also quite empty. "Everybody's gone home?"

"Everybody we could send. There are some cases that will keep the doctors and healers up all night. I've got a whole stack of exercises to grade yet—the fire alarm disrupted just about everything." She looked over at him, eyeing the tricorder slung on his hip. "I don't suppose you're in the mood to go out to dinner tonight," she said. "I'll just get something in the cafeteria. But perhaps tomorrow night—"

"It's a date," he replied, eager for something pleasant to look forward to after a day he knew he would spend in an investigation that could turn unpleasant indeed. But the moment his thoughts returned to his investigation, his mind went straight into detective-mode. "Eleyna, you've lived on Vulcan for years. How do the Vulcans treat you?"

"Treat me? What do you mean? I am accepted as an equal in the community of scholars at the Academy."

"But what about— That is, do you, um . . . date only humans? What if a Vulcan showed an interest in you—what would people think then?"

She frowned. "Vulcans do not worry about what 'people think.' They are concerned with tradition—but when an offworlder conforms to tradition, they accept him as one of their own. At least most of them do. You are not making the error of trying to fit all Vulcans into one mold, are you, Jim?"

He recalled T'Pring with her secret lover, Stonn. That certainly did not fit the Vulcan mold, yet both parties were pure Vulcan. "No—but I don't know very many. I was just wondering what would happen to Dr. Corrigan if he did marry T'Mir."

"T'Mir? Oh—Sorel's daughter. Are they getting married? I think that's wonderful!"

"You do?"

"Daniel has completely adapted to life on Vulcan. How likely is it that he will find a human woman compatible with him in other ways, who is also at home on Vulcan? There is no reason for him to live alone when he has found a compatible Vulcan woman." She paused as they approached the lobby where Sarek waited, to add out of the Vulcan's hearing, "While hardly common, marriages between Vulcans and offworlders have become much more accepted since Sarek broke tradition by marrying Amanda. He is an amazing man, Jim. Other Vulcans could do worse than follow his example."

CHAPTER **22**

It was a long, long time since Daniel Corrigan had felt restraint with a member of Sorel's family, but he felt a similar hesitancy in T'Mir. It was a most uncomfortable, silent walk to his apartment through the hot evening air. It was midsummer, the sun still up although the hour grew late.

Once home, T'Mir made Corrigan sit on the sofa while she dialed up soup from his kitchen computer and brought it to him in a mug. By this time, his body was reacting to the tiring day; the hot soup was pleasant despite the fact that his apartment cooling system was set for Vulcan, not human, comfort.

If his body temperature was low with exhaustion, his mind was feverish with anguished anticipation. Was there any way he could keep T'Mir's friendship in spite of their embarrassing faux pas? Would he ever get over the memory of last night's hope and joy, now forever shattered? She would marry another, a Vulcan. Had he learned enough of mental discipline to face T'Mir and her husband without pain?

It was T'Mir who broke the unbearable silence. "Daniel—I brought dishonor upon my family today."

Her words were so far from anything he might have expected that all he could do was blurt out, "Oh, no—never! T'Mir, we were not bonded or married. There is no dishonor in changing your mind when you find you have chosen wrongly."

"I did not choose wrongly," she said, bringing all her Vulcan disciplines to bear so that even her lovely eyes were unreadable. "Perhaps you did, for I proved unworthy at the very first test."

"No Vulcan can be expected to cope with human emotions," he said flatly.

"Then how can I be expected to cope with Vulcan ones?" she asked, her voice starkly devoid of feeling, harsh contrast to the words she spoke.

"Vulcan emotions?" Corrigan asked in total confusion.

If anything, T'Mir became even more controlled. "This morning . . . my father asked me if I would disgrace my family by invoking the challenge, rather than accept a Vulcan husband in his Time of Mating."

"Good God!" Corrigan exclaimed. "I thought I knew Sorel! That cold-hearted—! His own daughter—! How *dare* he—?"

He was on his feet, ready to go back to the hospital to find Sorel.

"Daniel."

T'Mir's soft voice stopped him. "My father was correct to ask me that question. I have been seeking the answer within myself all day."

"It's not a fair question," he insisted. "You have never been bonded; you have only fear to judge by, no experience of caring for someone you— Someone you are married to."

"Someone you love?" she asked.

"Humans would put it that way," he acknowledged. "The word doesn't matter—the experience does. And you have no experience at all of living with and caring for a husband, let alone sharing a mental bond . . . so how can you possibly answer the question your father asked? You have insufficient data. All it can do is frighten you to contemplate the Time of Mating as an abstract concept. Sorel was criminally irresponsible to put such an idea into your mind. If T'Zan were here—"

"My mother would see that my father was right. Daniel, I *have* sufficient data. I know the answer to Father's question."

Corrigan sat down again, facing her, aching to help her with the terrible burden Sorel had placed on her. "And what is your answer? Could you accept the violent emotions of a husband in pon farr?" He deliberately used the Vulcan term, rather than the usual euphemisms.

"Yes," she replied serenely, ". . . and no."

"That is not an answer."

"Daniel, what I had to understand, what Father made me face today, is that I can and will accept a man's harsh and painful emotions, learn to look beyond them to the strength and honor at the core of his being . . . so long as that man is you."

". . . what?" He could not believe he had heard her correctly.

"I watched you and Father working together today, saving the lives of the fire victims. My father is alive because you were able to accept his pain—the greatest anguish a Vulcan can know, the agony of a broken bond. And for the first time I examined my own . . . feelings. You are aware that I could have had several different motives for deciding to marry you if you would have me?"

"I know it was not gratitude for saving Sorel's life," Corrigan said. "I also know that, much as Sorel might approve of your marrying me, he would never suggest it to you. And he has the control not to give you subliminal signals."

"You are correct. I had no idea that Father would approve so readily, although I knew he could have no logical objections. But today he made me face my own reasons. I deeply regret having hurt you and dishonored my heritage—but I have no shame. Shame would be appropriate only if I had found that I had sought a human husband to avoid the . . . pon farr."

It had been in the back of his mind all day, too, but he had not allowed the accusation to surface. Now he asked, as gently as he could manage, "Can you ever be certain of that, T'Mir? You did say your answer to your father's question was both yes and no."

"The answer is no . . . I could not accept a husband in pon farr because that husband could not possibly be you, Daniel. It is you I want to touch me, never and always, and no other. When Father left me in his office this morning, to meditate on his question, I was ashamed at first—for I could not picture myself able to accept a stranger, burning with illogic, needing me— Over and over I turned from the scene, disgraced, dishonored, cast out from all that is Vulcan."

"Oh . . . T'Mir." He wanted to take her in his arms, but she was sitting stiffly erect, reciting without passion the journey of her soul.

"Then the fire alarm sounded. I ran to help—anyone would, but to be needed for physical work was a welcome escape from my meditations. Father set me to work moving patients—and you were there, concerned, your face and voice showing your compassion for those who suffered, while you did not allow your feelings to affect your work. And I thought, *That is what I have lost.*

"When the Lemnorian attacked you, and I saw your courage—I knew again that I had chosen well, if only I could have deserved you."

"T'Mir—"

"Let me finish. When he hit you, I thought you were dead. And I had never known your mind, Daniel—never except for that one foolish moment in which I destroyed our hopes."

"Humans are tougher than Vulcans realize," Corrigan reassured her. "It would take a lot more than one delirious Lemnorian to kill me."

"Your . . . toughness . . . is in your mind and heart. For a moment today I wanted to gather you up and take you away from that emergency room, lest something else threaten you. But that was a moment's fancy—I knew you belonged there, that like my father you will always put your patients' welfare before your own. I have always known that, Daniel—it is one reason I desired to bond with you. It is, also, the very reason for your guilt over my mother's death, although I could not understand that until I had time to meditate and find the logical connection."

"T'Mir, human emotions cannot be analyzed logically."

"Perhaps, in time, I will come to understand how you *do* deal with them. But I have analyzed *my* feelings, Daniel—my father's question made me search out the true reason I chose you rather than a Vulcan husband. I was not seeking to escape pon farr.

"I came *to* you, not away from something else. When

the fire was out and all the patients cared for, I had a moment to meditate again. This time I pictured you needing me—you with all your strange illogical guilt and pain and fear—and I did not back off. I wished only to ease your pain, as you ease the pain of others."

Her eyes left his face. She looked down at her hands, clasped in her lap, as she said, "Sometimes a woman hesitates to go to her husband in his Time of Mating—but if she overcomes her fears and joins with him, both are rewarded with a stronger and deeper bond, such as my father and mother knew. I am not a healer; I have never touched another mind except within the family, until you. If you cannot accept me, I understand—I have already hurt you too badly for you to risk joining your destiny with mine. I can only ask that you forgive me for this morning's illogical reaction."

"The cause was sufficient," he quoted Surak, and was rewarded with her startled eyes meeting his.

"You do understand."

"Enough to know we can make a marriage if we are always willing to be as open with one another as we have been today. If you will understand that my first reactions to stress are not always logical, and give me time to think things out—"

"I will—joyfully," she replied. "Can you accept that I may sometimes misinterpret your feelings, and help me to understand?"

"Gladly," he replied, "if you will do the same for me."

"Then . . . let us bond, Daniel."

He smiled wryly. "It was supposed to be tonight, wasn't it? I don't have a Vulcan time sense. Yesterday evening seems a hundred years ago. It will seem like another century until—"

"No," she said, "now. Just as we planned."

"But it was supposed to be a family ceremony."

"Father and Soton will be at the hospital until late into the night. It does not matter—we are adults, and can have a witnessing after the bonding. I want to be one with you now, Daniel."

"Sorel would never forgive me—"

"He would never forgive *me* if I did not follow through on my decision. Why do you think he sent us home together? It is impossible to hide much from a healer's ESP; he knew the conclusion I had come to."

"But you are not a healer, T'Mir, and I am close to psi-null."

"If we try and fail, Father will help to bond us tomorrow. But I do not think we will fail, Daniel—at anything we attempt together."

Her warm fingertips touched the side of his face. He knew the pattern of psi-points, found them on her face—and she was with him. He had no apprehension, for he had now experienced what a mind-touch could be outside of the coldly restricted healing meld. In some ways, this bonding meld was the same as the family healing meld he had experienced with Sorel. It had the same deep-seated acceptance, the same warmth of recognition and ultimate trust.

But it was more. There was the exquisite awareness of male and female, opposites drawn to one another deeply and strongly in the eternal plan of nature. And as each found what he or she sought, there was a new sense formed— *I think your thoughts!* Corrigan realized, and felt the delighted laughter T'Mir would never utter aloud vibrating like the song of a silverbird.

She was as exquisite mentally as she was physically, all Vulcan logic overlaid with her own charming thought patterns—and he could perceive himself in her mind, exotic yet familiar, alien without being foreign. She saw him as strong, sensitive, reliable, intriguing— but he laughed aloud at her mental visual image of him as a rugged sea captain at the helm of a sailing ship. *You know that is fantasy, T'Mir.*

And your image of me is not? She reflected back to him an elfin creature of the Irish woodlands of his boyhood, dancing in a fairy circle in the moonlight, wearing filmy garments that seemed almost gossamer wings. *I had shared my fantasy with you, Daniel, but you had never told me yours.*

I never dared to recognize it, he discovered—and she found the thought along with him.

Tenderly, they explored one another's consciousness, entwining thoughts as they sat touching only through their fingertips on one another's faces. Corrigan wanted it to go on forever. *It will,* T'Mir told him, her mind unfolding to him like a rosebud, inviting him into the depths of her being while at the same time she seemed to be everywhere in his mind, never prying, just there as a sweet presence, until—

T'Mir dropped her hand. "No!" Corrigan gasped involuntarily, but she took his hand and insistently pulled it from her face. The intensity of contact lessened—but it was not gone. She was still with him! He had never known anything like it—and it seemed he had been searching for this feeling all his life. "Never and always," he whispered, and realized that there were tears rolling down his face. "Forgive me," he murmured, fumbling for his handkerchief.

T'Mir took it from him and wiped his face. "No," she said, "I will not forgive you for being human. It is what you are, Daniel. Would you forgive me for being Vulcan?" And he felt her sweet acceptance in his mind, saw his own joy reflected in her eyes.

And this time when he kissed her, she responded, the bond intensifying again at the contact. When he released her, still leaving his arms about her, she very definitely smiled up at him and said, "Now I know what this form of touching means . . . my husband."

CHAPTER **23**

*I*t was almost midnight when Leonard McCoy felt it was safe to leave his last patient in the care of the nursing staff. T'Par, Soton, and M'Benga would remain on duty anyway, but he always felt a certain responsibility toward patients he had seen through a crisis, and would not leave until all were stable.

Sorel was in his office, filling out forms by hand as the computer was still down. "Reports, reports, reports. Looks as bad as Star Fleet," McCoy observed.

The healer put down his stylus. "It can all wait until morning. Come—I will drive you to Sarek's house on my way home."

But when they stepped outside, McCoy could not believe his eyes. Hanging in the sky was a moon, huge and glowing—brighter than the harvest moon over Georgia.

"But—Vulcan doesn't have a moon!" McCoy exclaimed.

Sorel looked up at the brilliant object. "It is not a satellite of Vulcan, Leonard. That is T'Kuht, sister planet to ours. It has an eccentric orbit which brings it close enough to Vulcan approximately once in each seven years to appear in the sky as you see it. Fourteen years from now it will approach as closely as it ever does, perhaps once in three centuries; at that time the disk fills half the sky, and when T'Kuht is in the night sky it is as bright as day."

"It's beautiful!" McCoy said, the brightness and beauty overcoming his weariness.

"It is a . . . tourist attraction," said Sorel. "Perhaps during your stay on Vulcan you may take one of the desert night tours for offworlders."

"I'm not sure I'm up to walkin' in the desert, just for the fun of it."

"No, Leonard, no one walks! It is far too dangerous to be afoot in the desert at this time of year—when T'Kuht is shining at the height of summer the le-matya are at their most active."

"Le-matya?"

"Predators, larger than sehlats, with poisoned fangs and claws. At midsummer they roam widely, seeking water as the desert watering holes dry up. When they find prey, they will kill to drink blood, even when they are not hungry."

"Vulcans certainly have peculiar ideas about what constitutes a tourist attraction!" observed McCoy. They had reached Sorel's ground car, and even the short walk in the hot night air had added to his impatience.

The Vulcan laid his hand on the latchplate and the doors slid open as he explained patiently, "The le-matya are not the attraction; the beauty of the desert night under T'Kuht's light is what people go to see. The tours are conducted in vehicles with protective transparent shells—they will all have left town by now, so as to be on the desert at the rising of T'Kuht."

"Yeah, I guess that would be a pretty sight," McCoy agreed as the car's cooling system relieved his feverish feeling, "from an air-conditioned car and with a mint julep in hand."

"A . . . mint julep?" the healer asked.

McCoy grinned to himself—perhaps you couldn't catch Vulcans with honey, but you sure could with curiosity. "It's a cool drink—probably the best damn drink in the galaxy. Tell you what—if Sarek and Amanda have any mint in that fancy greenhouse, I think we can scare up the rest of the ingredients in ShiKahr. When Amanda's home again, maybe we'll have a nice little party—and I'll introduce you Vulcans to mint juleps. Great drink for a hot summer night!"

"It is strange that Daniel has never mentioned this drink to me," Sorel mused. "Humans are very much concerned with food and drink . . . but Daniel's preference is for Irish whiskey, neat."

"That's because he grew up in Ireland, where it never gets very hot, even in the summer."

"Ah, yes. You are also from Earth, Leonard?"

"Yes—Georgia, which is in the southern part of North America. Much warmer climate than Ireland, though I suppose you Vulcans would find it cool."

"Such varieties of climate on a single planet," mused Sorel. "Perhaps that is why you humans are so adaptable. I would like to visit this Earth of yours someday. My daughter has returned from her apprenticeship with tales of a great variety of cultures on many different planets. I, myself, have never been off Vulcan."

"What—never?" McCoy was surprised. The healer was so cosmopolitan compared to people like T'Pau that McCoy could not believe his only exposure to other customs and cultures came from the offworlders he met at the Academy. "You know—your kids are grown, and you're still young enough—why don't you sign up for a five-year tour in Star Fleet? See the galaxy. We've got enough Vulcans in the Fleet now to need healers badly—only we can't get them. You have experience in both Vulcan and human medicine. You would be a tremendous asset to a starship."

"An interesting notion, Leonard. It never occurred to me, although I have helped train some of the Star Fleet doctors here at the Academy. Five years is not so long a time that Daniel could not cover our practice and research with the aid of some of our colleagues. I will give the idea serious consideration."

Again McCoy was surprised; he had expected the healer to dismiss the suggestion out of hand. But then, to a man who could expect to live for another century, five years probably did *not* seem much to give to a worthy cause . . . and at the same time satisfy his curiosity about other worlds. McCoy wondered if it was possible for a Vulcan to know the wanderlust that had kept him in space after his own first tour of duty.

Sorel had just lost his wife. That gave him a certain freedom, as well as a reason to get away from home. Recalling how frightening it was to treat Spock for anything more complex than the tying off of bleeders he had done today—and the abject terror he had wrestled down like some mad dragon in order to perform surgery on Sarek—McCoy pressed his advantage. The example of a healer of Sorel's stature might well draw other healers into Star Fleet.

"Now is the perfect time," he said. "Forgive me for reminding you, but you've just had a major change in your life. Getting off-planet for a while might be just the thing to, uh, give you a new perspective."

"Leonard, that is precisely why I cannot go at this time." Sorel pulled the car to a stop before Sarek's gate. "I am not yet prepared to seek another wife . . . but I cannot wait five years to do so. Therefore I can give your suggestion consideration only at a later date."

"Oh," McCoy said flatly, embarrassed at not having realized the healer's problem. For a moment there he had had hopes of getting Jim to pull some strings, and get someone who really understood Vulcan medicine to fill an upcoming vacancy on the *Enterprise* medical staff.

The light of T'Kuht seemed even brighter away from the center of the city. McCoy said good night to Sorel and entered Sarek's gate. Funny how Vulcans kept walls around their gardens, but no locks on gates or doors. The walls probably kept kids and sehlats out of the gardens, he decided, trying to picture Spock with a live teddy bear . . . with six-inch fangs. He hadn't seen one of the beasties yet—must be sure to before he left Vulcan.

Even in T'Kuht's soft light, the front garden appeared dry and withered. The ground retained the day's heat, which came up through McCoy's shoes. The night air was still suffocatingly hot, and he was glad to get into the house.

A light was shining in the main room. McCoy thought it had been left on for him until soft strains of music met him when he quietly opened the door. In the main room he found Kirk lying on the couch, possibly asleep, and Sarek sitting in a large oak rocking chair, obviously another of Amanda's heirlooms. *How many times was Spock rocked to sleep in that chair, I wonder?*

Sarek was playing a lytherette, a Vulcan harp like the one Spock played on board the *Enterprise* except that this one appeared older, worn where generations of players had rested their hands.

As Spock did when he joined his colleagues in the rec room, Sarek had tuned the versatile instrument to tones that were pleasing to human ears. At the moment he was playing a waltz—one McCoy had heard many times before, but did not know the name of.

When McCoy entered the room, Sarek nodded to him but kept on playing. Kirk opened one sleepy eye, took in the fact that McCoy was not eagerly waiting to deliver a message, and closed it again.

McCoy took the chair opposite Sarek's—a chair of Vulcan design, but with several pillows that could be placed for human comfort. Amanda's touch again.

Sarek finished playing, and said, "Good morning, Leonard. Is all well at the hospital?"

"Spock is fine, all the other fire victims are still alive, and you and Jim were both supposed to be asleep hours ago."

"Jim *is* asleep, I believe," said Sarek, looking toward the couch where the starship captain now snored softly. "He did go to bed soon after we arrived home, but did not stay there. He said he could not sleep, and I was still up—"

"So you decided to try a lullaby."

"As it were. However, I do not believe he allowed himself to fall completely asleep until you returned; even off-duty the captain appears to be most conscientious about the members of his crew."

"He knows I'd have interrupted if there were anything wrong. I'm glad I didn't have to; that was a lovely tune you were playing. I know I've heard it before; what's it called?"

"I do not know," Sarek replied. "Amanda calls it the Ubiquitous Waltz."

"The—what?"

"When I was Ambassador to Earth, where I met my wife, I was called upon to attend many formal functions where there was dancing. According to protocol, I was required to learn one dance, the waltz, and to dance it with the hostess of each occasion. Every humanoid ambassador was expected to do the same, and I learned that it was permissible to avoid any further dancing once I had fulfilled that obligation."

"Well, you've got to give those hostesses credit for fulfilling *their* obligations, too," said McCoy. "Imagine having to dance with the ambassador from Tellar."

"I do not understand," Sarek said in that totally flat tone which McCoy had come to understand was a diplomatic way of saying, "I am refusing to understand so that you will not be embarrassed when you realize that you have said something gauche."

"Never mind," McCoy said. "Go on with your story."

"The reason a Vulcan would prefer not to dance with another man's wife is that according to our customs it is not appropriate for a man to hold in his arms a woman who is not his."

"But you were on Earth, and when in Rome—"

"Precisely. Religious prohibitions are accepted in an ambassador, it seems, but not those stemming from mere custom. I had been on Earth for some time when Amanda first came to the Embassy. You know her now as a teacher of languages and a well-established linguistic scholar. At that time, however, she was quite young, just beginning her career. She had recently learned Vulcan, and during a summer vacation from her first teaching job she obtained permission to spend her days among the Vulcans in the Embassy to perfect her accent in our language.

"The Embassy was located in a relatively cold climate, and summer seemed to bring on an excessive number of balls and garden parties. As I watched Amanda listening to the constant plans, I realized that what to me was a duty bordering on an annoyance, was to her a potential pleasure. Therefore I invited her to accompany me to one of the balls."

That lady must know her body language as well, thought McCoy, *because I'm sure she'd never have dared come right out and ask you.*

"At the ball," continued Sarek, "I danced my obligatory waltz with the hostess at the first opportunity, and retired to one of the anterooms to discuss some diplomatic problems with several other ambassadors. Several times, though, when I had occasion to pass through the ballroom, I saw Amanda dancing, each time with a different partner. Our human protocol officer at the Embassy had rather apologetically reminded me that if I escorted a woman to the ball, I was obligated to dance the last dance of the evening with her. I was glad that he had told me, for I had not known the human custom and would not have wanted to offend Amanda out of ignorance.

"When the last dance came, I found Amanda surrounded by young human men—but she, of course, knew the custom, and was waiting for me. For the first time, I took into my arms a woman who belonged to no other man."

"Is that when you decided it would be logical to marry her?" McCoy inquired.

"No. That decision came at the end of the summer, after I had gotten to know her much better. And," the tiny hint of a smile turned up the corners of Sarek's mouth, "it *was* a logical decision, although I would never attempt to explain even to my son its true logic. But that first dance with Amanda led to our discovery of how much our minds work alike. The musicians were playing that waltz, one of the staples in the dance musicians' repertoire.

"I invited Amanda to other balls, and the journalists quickly began to link our names. She was concerned that that would embarrass me, but I explained that there was no offense if I took none. At every ball, that same waltz would be played at some time in the evening, and I would seek out Amanda to dance with her. I suppose humans would call our behavior sentimental, but in reality it was quite logical: we both knew that when that music played, we would meet one another on the dance floor. We did not have to make any advance plans, or concern ourselves with finding one another."

Oh, yeah, totally logical, thought McCoy. *In a pig's eye!* But he kept his face expressionless as he listened in fascination to the tale of Spock's parents' first acquaintance.

Sarek went on, "Somehow we never did find out the title of that piece of music. Amanda began calling it the Ubiquitous Waltz, and I am afraid we both think of it by that title to this day. And I have learned over the years, that if Amanda is unhappy with a problem she cannot overcome with the logic she has learned here, it often helps if I play that waltz for her."

"And you were thinking about her tonight," added McCoy, "so you naturally started playing it. But she'll be out of stasis tomorrow—no, today, since it's morning already."

"Tomorrow," Sarek corrected.

"Hmm? Daniel Corrigan said two days."

"Rough human estimate. Actually, the removal process takes two days, six hours, and fourteen minutes, Vulcan time. It was begun yesterday morning, and will end tomorrow afternoon."

"Well, today's not gonna feel like today till I get some sleep," said McCoy, stretching and yawning. He glanced at Kirk. "Guess we'd better put the captain to bed—at least for once I don't have to try to get his boots off."

"You . . . frequently have to put your commanding officer to bed?" asked Sarek.

"Oh, we've seen a few shore leaves together . . . ! Well, at least this time neither one of us is drunk, either. In fact, I haven't had a drink all day."

"Would you like something, Leonard? We have some brandy—"

"No, thanks—tired as I am, I couldn't appreciate it, and I certainly don't need anything to help me relax."

As they helped Kirk down the hall to bed, McCoy saw through the open door to Sarek and Amanda's bedroom the holograph of the young Amanda with the baby Spock. He still could not believe that that smiling baby had grown up into the stiff first officer of the *Enterprise,* but Amanda as he remembered her still had those big blue eyes and that sweet smile. At the age she was in that portrait—how could any man not be charmed by her, even a logical Vulcan?

But he knew that look, too. While it melted his heart looking out of the holograph, McCoy knew who must have taken the picture. That particular look was reserved for only one person: her husband. He had seen her look at Sarek that way aboard the *Enterprise.* God willing, he would soon again see them touch fingers, shut out the whole world, and share that look once more.

CHAPTER *24*

James T. Kirk awoke the next morning at dawn. He didn't remember going to bed—the last time *that* had happened was after a shore leave on Wrigley's!

He felt much better than he usually did when returning from shore leave, although he saw that more skin had flaked off his arms and face while he slept. A sonic shower left his skin tingling more than usual. He saw in the mirror that he was still slightly pink. His eyebrows and the front of his sandy hair were scorched, but not burnt away. For the first time, he opened the medicine cabinet in the guest bathroom—and found everything he could have asked for.

A couple of snips with small, sharp scissors, and the scorched hairs were gone. There was an odorless skin oil labeled, RECOMMENDED FOR HUMANS, LEMNORIANS, AND ANDORIANS; NONTOXIC TO VULCANS, which he slathered over the burned areas of his skin, and was surprised to see it soaked right up. Perhaps he should have been using it every day in this climate. Sure enough, the fine print told him it contained a powerful sunscreen; he must remember to tell McCoy about it.

The door to the doctor's room was still closed, however. Kirk went to the kitchen, but it was empty. For the first time, no coffee was made or fruit juice set out.

"You are still unable to sleep, Jim?"

It was Sarek, just entering the kitchen.

"I slept fine," Kirk replied. "The naps I took under the healing rays and on your couch, plus the time in bed, probably add up to more sleep than I usually get. So I'm ready for the day."

"Perhaps you should rest longer. You are still healing."

"No—I've got to get on with my investigation. Did I hear you tell Bones that Amanda won't be out of stasis till tomorrow?"

"That is correct."

"Then if she is a target, she is only too vulnerable for the time being. I plan to be very visible at the Academy today, questioning suspects. If the murderer just wanted to discredit the stasis research, he's done enough. My investigation may keep him from risking exposure by attacking Amanda."

"That is logical," said Sarek. "Unfortunately, the perpetrator may not be acting logically. Yesterday's fire was not the same efficient attack, aimed at one specific person, that we have seen before. However, it may be that the fire was unrelated to the previous incidents."

"And what would you estimate is the probability that they are unrelated?" Kirk asked.

"I have insufficient evidence to estimate the probability," Sarek replied. "Perhaps when I see the results of the investigation into the source of the fire—"

But the results of that investigation were inconclusive. "What is obvious," Storn pointed out to Sarek and Kirk when they joined him after leaving McCoy at the hospital, "is that a power surge was sent through the permanent memory storage unit of the central computer."

"To destroy evidence," said Kirk.

"Possibly," Storn replied stiffly, clearly holding back irritation at Kirk's interruption. The man had been up all night directing repairs, and had obviously gone directly into his arson investigation from there. His eyes were sunk into deep olive circles, and he had the harsh formality of someone refusing to let himself be pushed too far.

It dawned on Kirk that Storn probably felt the attack on the computer and power systems of the Academy the same way Scotty felt an attack on his precious engines. So he remained silent, waiting for the Vulcan to continue.

"The fire was not set with foreign material," Storn explained. "The permanent memory storage unit is physically the least vulnerable part of the computer. Therefore, the Academy's heat, smoke, and chemical sensing units are connected directly into it—if other parts of the system fail, this unit will sound the alarm.

"What seems to have happened is that power from all the rest of the Academy was rerouted into the permanent storage unit—hence the power failure yesterday. If it was done deliberately, whoever did it used many times the power necessary to wipe the memory."

"Overkill," Kirk commented before he remembered he had meant to avoid interrupting Storn again.

However, the engineer merely replied, "Indeed. The

intent could have been to burn out the unit in the figurative sense—wipe its memory. But it was also burned out literally: the power surge overloaded the circuits so rapidly that the breakers could not react. The unit overheated and caught fire. When the power was released into the system, the overload released all *those* circuit breakers. That is why power did not immediately return to the rest of the Academy—and why no fire alarm sounded until the smoke reached a battery-powered detection unit."

"And by that time it had spread dangerously," Kirk concluded. "Storn, is there any way power could have been diverted to the memory unit by accident—the way tampering with the stasis program accidentally affected the medical diagnostic program?"

"No," the engineer replied. "The permanent memory storage unit has nine-fold safeguards. Had," he corrected himself, sounding ever more like Mr. Scott. "Those safeguards had to be deliberately removed. I have ordered a new unit, which will arrive this afternoon. Computer access will be available tomorrow morning, although everything that is not in data storage units owned by the Academy, staff, or students, will have to be reprogrammed."

Kirk remembered Eleyna Miller saying last night that she had student work to grade—she must not have realized that there was no active terminal available. Oh, well—he had been far too tired to take advantage of her free time then. He just hoped that she would not have to cancel their plans for this evening.

If I don't have to cancel them myself, he amended.

Sarek said, "Storn, I think we now have such an obvious pattern of computer tampering that we must admit that someone has deliberately used the computer to kill two people, and then destroy the evidence."

"I agree," said Storn. "Since we now have no way of

determining the identity of that person, your wife must be protected at all costs—and I would say that the first safeguard is simply not to reconnect her stasis chamber to the computer. The independent backup systems can continue to monitor her."

"That's right," said Kirk. "Since the fire turned out to be unintentional, we have as the murderer someone who doesn't get his hands dirty, who kills at a distance by pushing buttons. If we don't cause that person to panic again, we can protect Amanda by making it impossible to reach her that way. Meanwhile, I have suspects to interview. I would still feel much better if we knew who the murderer was and had him in custody."

"I agree, Jim," said Sarek. "Meanwhile, Storn, my classes are canceled until the computer is operational. My son is due to be released from the hospital this morning. Let us take over the repairs here, while you and your assistant rest."

So Kirk left Sarek to supervise the fresh engineering crew preparing the room to receive its new computer unit, and went to work on his list of suspects. He had already eliminated Sorel and Corrigan, he knew *he* hadn't done it, and McCoy had an alibi for yesterday even if he had had the computer skills to overcome the safeguards—which he hadn't. Sorel's son, Soton, had turned out to have no motive Kirk could discern—he was positive the boy had been totally honest last night. T'Mir had neither a motive Kirk could discern, nor an opportunity in her mother's case. Only Sendet was still suspect, until his alibi was confirmed.

Kirk was startled to discover that he had only one person left on his list that he had had no chance to investigate: T'Pau. Wondering what one actually used to gird one's loins, he set out to beard the lion in her den.

CHAPTER **25**

T'Pau's office was located in a part of the Academy Kirk had not yet visited. The signposts took him away from the tall modern buildings surrounded by sunburned grass, across a deserted playing field, also dry and scorched, to where a cluster of old stone buildings surrounded a green glade, watered by a natural spring and overhung by the first trees he had seen on Vulcan.

It was a relief to reach shade after his long walk. His skin stung despite the sun-shielding oil, and he breathed heavily in the heat and gravity.

A bench beside the spring looked most inviting, and Kirk sat down to compose himself before facing T'Pau. A stone plaque bore an inscription in Vulcan. Kirk stared at it for a while before he realized that there were buttons along the side, unobtrusively designed to blend with the ancient-appearing stone. One of the buttons was labeled ENGLISH. Kirk pressed it, and a cultured female voice—he recognized it after a moment as Amanda's—began to recite.

"To this oasis in the desert, Surak came five thousand years ago with a small band of followers, to practice a new philosophy of nonviolence. It is said that when warrior bands approached, seeking to seize control of the precious source of water, Surak welcomed them and bid them drink their fill while he spoke to them of logic, and the peace found through emotional control.

"The small community was frequently attacked, but refused to fight back—an attitude the warriors could not comprehend. Since their code of honor did not permit killing unarmed people, they tried instead to enslave Surak and his followers. They, however, went without resistance, spoke eloquently of Surak's teachings at every opportunity . . . and then disappeared out of the warrior camps despite chains or other restraints, to rejoin their fellows here at the oasis of ShiKahr.

"Over a period of several centuries, Surak's philosophy of nonviolence and emotional control gained the respect of all of Vulcan, until eventually it became the prevailing way of life of the Vulcan people.

"The Academy grew up around the philosophers who followed Surak. Disciples came here to learn from them, and the first buildings were built of desert stone. Those ancient buildings are the ones clustered here about the spring. Over many centuries the Vulcan Academy of Sciences grew from this center into the huge complex you see today.

"Most modern Vulcans adhere to Surak's original philosophy of emotional control. However, some time after Surak's philosophy had spread planet-wide, certain philosophers felt it necessary to refine his teachings to include total rejection of emotion, rather than emotional control. Followers of this stricter philosophy still exist today, practicing a discipline known as Kolinahr. They removed themselves from ShiKahr to a harsh volcanic area of the planet, which is forbidden to offworlders, and even to Vulcan curiosity seekers. The practitioners of Kolinahr are known as the Masters of Gol.

"Very few Vulcans, however, attempt to purge away all emotion. Surak's philosophy has been enough to keep peace on this planet for five thousand years. You are now visiting the very spot at which he began the teachings which were to have such influence that today he is known as the father of Vulcan philosophy."

The recitation ended. Kirk pulled himself out of Vulcan's past, and prepared to meet its present—all Vulcan in one package.

He entered the oldest Academy building. The outside, weathered by thousands of years of desert winds, was eroded and pockmarked. Inside, the stone was smooth and polished: Centuries of academic feet had worn paths in the stone parquet floor. Here and there new paving stones, perfectly cut to match but lacking the patina of the originals, showed where careful repairs had been made when the unevenness threatened to become an obstacle.

Everything else appeared to be preserved as it had stood thousands of years ago. Unashamedly naked insulated cables brought power to modern lights set in fixtures once meant for torches; obviously no modern holes were to be drilled in these ancient walls. There were no ventilator grilles—yet it was naturally cool inside the stone building. Kirk realized in relief that he would not have to face T'Pau drenched in sweat.

There were few people in the halls, as this was not a

classroom building. It housed the Academy archives, and a few offices . . . including T'Pau's. The doors to rooms open to the public, such as the tiny museum housing the few personal effects attributed to Surak, were labeled in several languages. All the other doors bore only Vulcan symbols.

Kirk had a good memory—but he certainly hoped that this time it would be good enough! He had looked up the location of T'Pau's office in Sarek's directory. The Vulcan symbols for her name had been there, but he had not expected to have to locate her by them. He hoped he remembered them accurately.

Finally he located a door bearing the markings he thought he remembered. Pushing it open, he found a woman at a desk—not T'Pau, but just as old and dignified. There was a computer terminal, but the screen was blank. The woman had an ancient book open on the stone desk, and directly in front of her a facsimile copy of the page it was open to. She was making marginal notes on the facsimile.

When Kirk entered, the woman finished the note she was making in a bold hand. Then she looked up, not allowing herself to show surprise at finding a human intruder.

This was the second Vulcan Kirk had seen with blue eyes. The first had been Stonn, whose eyes had blazed anger when T'Pring denied him the right to be her champion. This woman's eyes were devoid of any expression. "Are you lost?" she asked coldly.

Her pause to finish her work before addressing him had given Kirk a chance to assess the place. Another door led out of this room, opposite Kirk. The woman's desk did not quite block it, but was positioned as the desks of secretaries were the galaxy over, so that the boss's privacy could be protected.

"I have come to speak with T'Pau," Kirk said.

"T'Pau has nothing to discuss with outworlders."

So, he was in the right place and his quarry was behind that closed door.

"Tell T'Pau that James T. Kirk wishes to speak with her," he said firmly.

"The wishes of outworlders are of no concern to T'Pau," the woman replied flatly.

"*T'Pau* will wish to know," Kirk said loudly, "that you are preventing her from learning that two murders have been committed here at the Academy."

He was rewarded with one scornfully raised eyebrow. "You are mistaken. Had such an event occurred, T'Pau would have been informed by proper authorities."

"As I understand it," Kirk said, keeping his voice at an intensity he hoped would penetrate the heavy inner door, "Vulcan *has* no proper authority for investigating violent crimes, since they so rarely occur here."

"There are never—" the woman began . . . but the door opened behind her.

"I will speak with thee, James Kirk," T'Pau said, and turned and walked back into her office. Kirk followed her and closed the door—but not before he had the pleasure of seeing her secretary's jaw drop a millimeter. *Probably the first visible sign of emotion she's given in the past century.*

T'Pau's office was lined with shelves holding scrolls and books. A skylight poured intense Vulcan sunlight onto a desk piled with more scrolls and books. There was no computer terminal here, no sign of cassettes or storage units for computer data. The only modern touches were a lamp, now unlit, set where it would illuminate the desk when sunlight was unavailable, and an electronic tablet like the one that had fouled up the beginning of Kirk's investigation.

Without those two anachronisms, Kirk could have believed he had stepped a thousand years or more into

Vulcan's past. T'Pau was dressed in loose robes of brown and gray cloth that could have come from any era. The shelves, like everything else in this building, were carved stone. The documents on them . . .

He recognized a sigil carved beneath a shelf space draped with a dark brown cloth. He had seen that mark on the plaque by the spring: *Surak*. Instinctively he put out a hand toward the drape, but dared not touch it. "You have documents actually written by . . . Surak?" he asked in awed reverence.

T'Pau did not reply. Instead, she walked slowly around him until she stood facing him, peering up into his eyes. "What dost thou know of Surak?" she asked finally—but her voice spoke more of perplexity than challenge.

"What everyone knows: he was the founder of Vulcan philosophy. I know he is a personal hero to my friend Spock, the way Abraham Lincoln, from human history, is to me. That alone tells me he's worth knowing much more about than I do." He looked from her face back to the scrolls. "Please tell me. Are there actual manuscripts in there that Surak wrote?"

He looked back at T'Pau, and found her bright black eyes studying his face intently. Suddenly, decisively, she turned, lifted the protective covering, and took a scroll from its holder with greatest care. To Kirk's astonishment, she held it out to him.

Kirk accepted it as if it were some incredibly delicate living thing. It smelled of history. A braided cord was tied about it in a loose slip knot; Kirk recognized that no pressure was now required to keep the scroll rolled, and the cord was too frayed, the parchment too brittle, to chance tying tightly.

Kirk held the scroll by the bamboolike sticks it was wrapped on, swallowing hard at the thought that five thousand years ago Surak's own hands had held this scroll as he prepared to read his latest discoveries on logic to his followers. It was as if the philosopher's quiet courage flowed down the centuries to guide him.

Watching T'Pau carefully for any negative reaction, he loosened the cord and gently unrolled the scroll, just enough to see a portion of the writing. He could not read the symbols, but the bold, firm, square hand spoke to him of an ordered mind, a firm purpose, and a strong sense of leadership. *No wonder Spock seeks to emulate him.*

Carefully, he let the scroll roll up to its original shape, and retied the cord loosely. "Thank you," he said as he handed it back to T'Pau.

She did not say, "One does not thank logic." They both knew that what had just happened was not logical.

T'Pau put the scroll gently back into its holder, pulled the protective cloth over it, and turned to Kirk once more. "You do comprehend tradition, James Kirk."

"Humans also have traditions, T'Pau."

"I misjudged you. When you first came to Vulcan, to stand as friend to Spock at his marriage, I thought he was flaunting his mixed heritage by bringing out-worlders to our most sacred and secret rituals. Until her confession afterward, I truly thought that this grave insult was the reason T'Pring challenged."

"Spock would never deliberately give offense."

"I see now that he chose well. You have not only the physical courage you displayed at that time—which a ruffian may have as well as a warrior—but also a reverence for tradition . . . even that which is not your own. You were worthy of the honor Spock accorded you. I regret that I did not trust his judgment."

"I understand why you could not. You don't really know Spock, do you?"

"No—but I shall remedy that situation. But James—

tell me of the other man, McCoy. He profaned the ritual. How did Spock come to choose such a man to accompany him?"

"McCoy is a doctor—a healer. It's true: he lied to you, to me, and to Spock—but it was to save a life. That will always be his priority; you may be certain of it."

The Vulcan matriarch nodded regally. "So McCoy shares our reverence for life. I thought perhaps it was so; that is why I did not oppose his return to Vulcan when I was told you were bringing your injured crewman here to the Academy. Now—you claim this Carl Remington was murdered?"

Kirk noticed she had all her facts. "Yes, and the Lady T'Zan also."

"I understood that they died because of equipment failure."

"Equipment designed by a human?"

"Possibly I easily assumed that it could fail because an outworlder had a part in its design. I did not consciously think so, and I must take care not to allow such assumptions to influence my thinking about Daniel Corrigan in the future. He is now a member of my family."

"When did *that* happen?" Kirk asked in astonishment.

"Last night. He is bonded to Sorel's daughter, T'Mir. But explain to me why you think the deaths of two of Sorel and Daniel's patients were murder rather than accident."

Kirk laid out his facts: the computer tampering, the destruction of evidence. "The problem is, neither person who died has any known enemies on Vulcan. Thus I am proceeding on two possible assumptions. Either the target is Corrigan and/or Sorel—the idea being to discredit their work—or one of the three patients is the target, with the other murders strictly as red herrings. Uh, that means they are committed to confuse investigators as to what motive could possibly account for killing three people with no connections with one another at all. That way the stasis equipment gets the blame."

T'Pau was sitting with her elbows on the desk, her chin resting on her folded hands, as Spock did when he concentrated. "Fascinating," she said at last. "Then the reason you came here to question me this morning . . . is that you believe me to be the one person with access to Academy equipment, who also has a motive to do away with all three occupants of the stasis chambers?"

CHAPTER **26**

Kirk had never been so embarrassed in his life. He had, in fact, totally forgotten that T'Pau was on his list of suspects, and was intent on using her sharp mind to help him solve the murders and protect Amanda. Yet, after the unexpected rapport they had established, he could not lie to her—not even a tactful lie.

"I'm afraid . . . you *were* on my list of suspects."

"And now?"

"No, of course not."

"And why not?" she asked. "James—be logical. Nothing said here today is sufficient to clear me of suspicion. However, you may verify with T'Nie, my assistant, that I do not have the computer expertise necessary to perform the complex functions you describe. I do not have a computer terminal in my home, and the one in the outer office is of the simplest library type, used only to store and catalogue data, and to access information from the archives. Someone who is truly efficient with computers, like Sarek, would hardly consider my computer programmable. I do not think it possible to access medical or engineering programming from that terminal.

"There is also no way in or out of this office without going past T'Nie. She can tell you that I remained in this room all yesterday morning, leaving only when the fire alarm sounded. Once we verified that our building was in no danger, and that we were not needed to help at the hospital, we returned here and worked the rest of the day. If I understood you correctly, would not the person who caused the power surge which started the fire have had to do it at the time? Or could it have been programmed in earlier?"

"Storn and Sarek seem to think it was done right at the time, unlike the other tampering, which may have been preprogrammed. I can use a computer for anything *I* need, but compared to Spock or his father I'm working at a schoolboy level. So I trust their word. And I trust yours, T'Pau."

Her regal head tilted slightly to one side. "It is many years," she said, "since I have had to *earn* anyone's trust. But now, James, you seem to have cleared all your suspects."

"Making them all equally suspect again," he agreed. "No—those without opportunity are still clear. That leaves you in the clear, I'm relieved to see."

"What if the true murderer is not on your list? James, you are questioning many people—even if the murderer is not among them, he may fear your investigation. Given someone capable of taking the lives of two other people, why should he hesitate to take yours?"

"If he tries, I'll know who he is. I can defend myself,

T'Pau; Amanda cannot. If the killer were after either T'Zan or Remington, he has achieved his end. Perhaps I can prevent him from risking exposure by attacking Amanda. The same is true if his intent were to discredit the stasis project—in fact, we want him to know it would be futile to strike again, since we already know the failures were not in the equipment."

"You are speaking as if the murderer will act logically."

"He has so far. Too *damned* logically. Our only clue to his identity is that he is a computer expert—on a campus full of computer experts."

"It is Vulcan belief," T'Pau said, "that the ability to commit murder is a form of mental illness."

"Do all Vulcans believe that? When Sarek was aboard the *Enterprise* there was a murder—a Tellarite Sarek had had a disagreement with. I asked Spock whether his father were capable of murder, and he told me that if the circumstances warranted it, Sarek could kill, logically and efficiently."

"Kill," said T'Pau. "Not murder. What he meant was that a Vulcan may kill in defense of himself or of the lives of others—or in racial survival as at the Koon-ut Kali-fi. But murder for personal gain is not possible to a logical mind. If this killer is Vulcan, his mind is not working logically—to our way of thinking, he is very ill. I do not know how he can prevent giving himself away through other illogical acts.

"If the murderer is not Vulcan, however, his day-to-day actions may be what we would term illogical—and if you have been questioning Vulcans about him, what to a member of his race might appear out of the ordinary could seem to us not unexpected of an outworlder."

"You're right," Kirk said. "Chances are, then, the murderer is not Vulcan. Yet, Vulcans can come to understand members of other races very well, you know. Spock can always tell when I'm not acting normally."

"But Spock is half human. And if he can 'always' tell . . . are you not suggesting that such episodes are frequent enough not to cause the suspicion that they indicate a mental breakdown?"

Kirk smothered a grin. "I think he may worry about that sometimes—except that worry is illogical, as he would quickly remind me. At any rate, he went on record as testifying that *I* am not capable of murder one time, when all the evidence was stacked against me. And went on to help prove me innocent, too." He frowned. "That was also a case of computer tampering, but it seems obvious and easy now compared to the present situation. No damn evidence—except the fact that there must have been some if it was worth the effort to wipe the computer's permanent memory!"

"And so, like an ancient warrior protecting his flock from the le-matya, you set yourself up as a target, hoping to lure the killer to strike at you instead of at Amanda."

"I wasn't thinking of it that way—but you're right!" he agreed. "It just might work!"

He got up. "Thank you, T'Pau—for everything."

"James." Her imperious tones stopped him before he reached the door. "Take every precaution," she said when he turned to her. "Tell Sarek and Spock of your plan, and let them protect you. The ways of an unbalanced mind cannot be predicted. Live long and prosper, James Kirk. I do not wish to learn that it was fated that your human blood would water Vulcan's desert sands."

CHAPTER 27

Sarek looked around the central memory storage room. It seemed a different place from this morning. All the debris was gone; the scorched panels had been replaced by new ones, the circuitry behind them repaired and renewed. The center of the room stood empty now, awaiting the arrival of the new memory unit.

Spock came over to him. "Everything is in order, Father. We can do nothing more until the unit arrives."

"That will be several hours yet. I am going to look in on your mother. Will you join me?"

"I am honored," Spock replied.

Why that particular reply? Sarek still did not understand his son's responses. He did not know why Spock had not *asked* to see his mother—afraid that his father would consider it an illogical request, or truly satisfied that since there was nothing a nonhealer could do for her there was no point in entering the stasis chamber?

They climbed the stairs and walked along the smoke-blackened hallway. A burly, athletic Vulcan with a phaser strapped to his hip stood guard outside the door, despite the fact that it would open only to preprogrammed voices. The guard recognized Sarek and Spock and stepped aside. Sarek spoke into the voice-lock, and the door opened.

When he stood with his son under the sterilizing rays, Sarek noted, "Your mother will say you are too thin."

"Mother *always* says I am too thin," Spock replied, and pulled on the sterile gown. The inner door opened, and the two men entered the chamber.

Spock went to the wall of gauges—because that was what interested him, or to give Sarek a moment alone with Amanda? Would he ever know what his son was thinking?

He found out one thing on Spock's mind when he came to join him beside the stasis tank. Looking down into the swirling blue mist veiling its mysterious occupant, Spock asked, "Why *did* you marry her, Father?"

"At the time—"

"No. You are not teasing Mother now. I wish to know, truly, why you chose an Earthwoman."

"I did not. I chose Amanda, who happens to *be* an Earthwoman."

"You were not . . . instructed . . . for diplomatic purposes—"

"No. Nor can I explain to you how your mother and I chose one another, except to say that it was a mutual choice. One day, Spock, when you choose your own life's mate, you will understand."

"You do not intend to arrange another marriage for me?"

"It is illogical to repeat an error," Sarek replied.

"Your mother strongly opposed your being bonded in childhood. She was proved right. The old ways are not always the best ways, Spock, although they should not be rejected simply because they are old. When you are a father, you will understand how difficult it is to decide what is right for your children. You *will* make mistakes. Perhaps then you will be able to forgive mine."

"I made no accusations, Father. There is nothing to forgive."

"There is an eighteen-year silence, for which I now find it very difficult to find a logical reason—although at the time I thought I was acting quite reasonably." He looked at his son, and caught a slight upturn of his lips. "You find it amusing?"

"Dr. McCoy or Captain Kirk will sometimes say to me, 'You are a stubborn man, Mr. Spock,' and I always reply, 'Thank you.' I come by it honestly, from both you and Mother."

"And if you are thereby twice as stubborn as I am, you may one day have twice as many regrets. Spock, I made an error with you that I somehow avoided with your mother: I created an image, and expected you to live up to it. In doing so, I drove you away, into Star Fleet."

"No, Father—I think if you had not given me a single path, the Vulcan Way, I would not have known what to try to be . . . and I would have ended up in Star Fleet anyway. For there I can be myself . . . whatever that may be."

"Perhaps," said Sarek. "But at least there would not have been the silence." He waited . . . but it seemed his son was not ready to forgive. Perhaps he never would be.

The door swooshed open—and palpable joy penetrated Sarek's telepathic barriers to light the tiny room like a beacon.

Spock did not react; he obviously had his mental shields up against the intensity of the conversation with his father. Sarek turned, though, as Daniel Corrigan paused just inside the chamber, looking as happy as he felt.

Sarek felt the human control clumsily, and was reminded strongly of Amanda in the first days of their bonding. She had had the advantage of spending most of her time those first weeks among nontelepathic humans while the Vulcans at the Embassy taught her to avoid projecting the feelings intensified by her bond with Sarek. By the time she came to Vulcan, Amanda was well able to control, despite being mind-blind to anyone but her husband.

Daniel was walking around in a world of telepaths— even total strangers would know his new status today.

"Forgive me," he said to Spock and Sarek, not sounding the least bit contrite. "I didn't know there were any Vulcans in here—should have looked in before releasing control."

"You gave no offense, Daniel," Sarek replied. "May I offer congratulations on your bonding?"

Daniel blushed. "Did Sorel tell you, or was I that wide open?"

"It was not . . . unexpected," Sarek explained.

"It was to me!" the human doctor replied. "Please tell me if I slip up again—I really don't *intend* to project my feelings all over the place, but it only goes one way. I don't get any feedback except for raised eyebrows and a few disapproving stares."

Spock said, "No one disapproves once he realizes the reason for your condition. Control will soon become habitual. Please allow me to offer my congratulations, too, Daniel."

"Thanks. I still don't quite believe it, except that I

can, uh, sense T'Mir with me somehow. And I have to try not to think about it, which is easier while I'm working." He went to the wall of gauges. "Everything is proceeding normally here. We will remove Amanda from stasis tomorrow afternoon."

"Should not a technician be monitoring those gauges?" asked Spock. "Since the chamber is now independent of the Academy's systems—"

"Storn installed a radio signal," Daniel replied. "If anything should go wrong, Sorel, T'Par, and I will all be alerted. Since we are dealing with sabotage, we are letting as few people as possible into the chamber. The door is not keyed to open for the guard, for example. He is simply a precaution against anyone who might attempt to break in the door, unlikely as that seems."

"Do not discount any possibility," said Spock. "It is better to take precautions which may prove redundant than to risk another life."

"Your mother is going to come out of this just fine," Daniel assured him with a smile. "The stasis equipment and all the monitors have been left on the independent power supply, and will not be reconnected to computer control. Only the lights are on the Academy system, and it can't hurt Amanda to be in the dark."

"Excellent," said Sarek. "I hope the precautions will prove unnecessary—but I am gratified that you have taken them."

Daniel looked at his chronometer. "I have to get back to my other patients—humans, thank goodness, so I can stop worrying about sending off signals for the next couple of hours."

But he wasn't really worrying, Sarek could see.

And tomorrow I shall touch Amanda's consciousness once more, and know that vital link renewed, he thought as he watched the human doctor depart.

As the airlock door closed behind Daniel, Sarek became aware that his son was studying him . . . and that he had relaxed his telepathic barriers.

Spock's ESP was much stronger than Sarek's—he could have taken healer's training if he had chosen to do so. Sarek's ability was at the lower level for Vulcans; he remembered fearing when Spock was a small child that his son, with a psi-null mother, would not have even the minimal abilities to be considered a true Vulcan. Instead, the boy had turned out unusually sensitive—not a welcome gift when it exposed him so young to the crude, unshielded thoughts of his schoolmates.

And to the occasional lapses of his parents. Sarek's lack of the strong ESP that ran in his family had sent him in unusual career directions: computers, which required no sensitivity of that nature, and diplomacy, in which insensitivity to other people's unshielded emotions was a distinct advantage. He understood perfectly well why someone like T'Pau could not accept a seat on the Federation Council. Even the light mental shielding which was all he required to avoid being bombarded by alien emotions became a strain in the midst of a long, heated debate. Someone with strong ESP would have to hold the tightest of barriers all that time.

Yet Spock, with his great sensitivity, had chosen to spend his life among the mixture of peoples in Star Fleet. The result, Sarek noticed, was even stronger telepathic barriers than he had developed before he left home.

But those barriers were down now, and Spock's deep-set eyes studied Sarek with ferocious Vulcan curiosity.

"What is it, Spock? Surely there is no question you cannot ask your father."

Spock looked away from Sarek, at Amanda floating

in the blue mist. "You and Mother—" he began, but did not continue.

Sarek let his own shields drop completely—something he had never done since Spock's growing telepathic talent had been diagnosed when he was five years old. He would not touch his son and invade his privacy, but he was determined to be open to anything Spock might project, no matter how painful.

Spock turned with a start, eyes locked with Sarek's. "It is the same," he said in a hoarse whisper. "I sense Mother through you, even though she is unconscious."

"Of course," said Sarek. "We are bonded." He wondered why Spock seemed surprised.

"I . . . could never sense that bonding when I was a child," Spock explained.

"It is a private thing," said Sarek. "Your mother learned long before we had you to shield those feelings —as Daniel will learn to do."

Spock swallowed hard, externally controlled, although Sarek could sense that there were questions in his mind. "Is it . . . is it thus only when an emotional human is in the bonding?"

". . . thus?"

"So strong and . . . joyful," Spock clarified in flat, scholastic tones.

"I should think it would be even stronger between two Vulcans," Sarek replied, "although I cannot speak from experience. As to joy . . . I have long suspected that the differences your mother and I rejoice in, have much more to do with being male and female than with being Vulcan and human."

"Father . . . I never knew such rapport with T'Pring. When . . . the pon farr came upon me, I sought her presence in my mind—and found less than you now perceive while Mother is unconscious."

Sarek reinstituted his shields to cover his shock. The woman had rejected his son to that degree—!

Spock continued bleakly, "I looked at her picture, and tried to reach her." He turned again to Sarek. "I thought the bonding was inadequate because I am only half Vulcan."

"You are not *only* anything, Spock. You are more, not less, because of your dual heritage. It is fruitless to wish now that I had made that clearer to you when you were a child."

"You wanted me to be Vulcan."

"That is true," Sarek agreed. "And you *are* Vulcan, representative of IDIC in its fullest sense."

Spock studied his father. "You never put it to me that way. The last time you and I spoke as father and son, before I went to Star Fleet Academy, you reminded me of how important it was that I think of myself as Vulcan. Do you remember your words, Father?"

Sarek remembered. "I am Vulcan by birth. Your mother is Vulcan by choice. You are Vulcan by both birth and choice."

"And then I disappointed you by making a different choice."

Sarek searched his memory, trying to recover the logical reasons for what now seemed completely irrational. Finally he said simply, "I was wrong."

Spock's eyebrows disappeared under his bangs. Sarek continued, "You knew that you were right. It was time for you to leave home. I wanted you here, at the Science Academy, because you are my son. I did not want you far away, facing the dangers of the military life. It was not the reaction of a Vulcan, Spock. It was the reaction of a father."

"One day I shall return home," Spock said evenly.

"If you choose," Sarek told him. "I left, and chose to return. But your mother left *her* home, and has never returned except for temporary visits. She has made her home here. You may make your home elsewhere, Spock, but you will never cease to be Vulcan. Nor will you ever disappoint me, no matter what you choose."

Sarek felt Spock's understanding and acceptance at last—a permanent version of the momentary rapport they had known in the *Enterprise* sickbay, after McCoy's surgery and Spock's blood had saved Sarek's life. Through teasing Amanda they had found one another for a fleeting moment then; now their mutual concern for her welfare had brought father and son together permanently.

At least Sarek hoped it was permanently. *It will be,* he thought, *if I can learn to understand my son as well as his human friends seem to do.*

CHAPTER *28*

James T. Kirk found Sarek and Spock just emerging from Amanda's stasis chamber. "I've talked with T'Pau," he informed them.

"She agreed to speak with you?" Spock asked.

"Of course," Kirk replied casually. "That is some lady, Spock. Anyway, she's off my list of suspects, and I'm about to start over. Motive, method, and opportunity—I'll start by eliminating everyone without the opportunity for at least one of the two murders."

He called up the list of names on his tricorder screen:

KIRK
SPOCK
McCOY
SAREK
SOREL

CORRIGAN
SOTON
T'MIR
SENDET
ELEYNA MILLER
T'PAU

"Why do you have yourself on the list?" Spock asked.

"*I* know I didn't do it, but *you* don't," Kirk replied. "Either Remington or Amanda could be my target, with T'Zan's death to make it appear to be equipment failure."

"I do not understand," said Sarek. "Why would you want to kill my wife?"

"You can't prove a negative," Kirk replied.

"Ah, I see," said Sarek. "Simply because I do not *know* you have a motive, I cannot dismiss the possibility that you could have one."

"Right," Kirk said. "I started with motives, and eliminated all my suspects. That means either the murderer is not on my list, or I have not been able to discover his motive."

"What motive did you ascribe to my assistant?" Sarek asked.

"Could be out to get you, through Amanda, if you were flunking her."

Sarek had obviously taught long enough to recognize the human slang term. "Eleyna's work is exemplary; she has no reason to expect any but the highest recommendations from me."

"Good," said Kirk. "I really don't think she has a thing to do with it, but I am proceeding logically," he added with a glance at Spock, "and she had plenty of opportunity to play games with the computer."

"Then my father and his assistant would be your most likely suspects," said Spock, "along with myself. We have the highest degree of computer skills."

"Actually," said Kirk, "I think you and I alibi one another for the day we arrived, Spock. Were we ever apart long enough for either of us to set up T'Zan's death?"

Spock ran the question through his computerlike memory and replied, "No. The times we were separated that day were too brief to allow you, as someone unfamiliar with the Academy's computer, both to familiarize yourself with it and to set up the malfunction."

"Furthermore," said Sarek, "Jim was with me when he was not with you, Spock. And were you not with Leonard, Daniel, and Sorel?"

"And McCoy was with Sorel and Corrigan all day, till we met for dinner," said Kirk. "Look, Spock, Sarek, you understand that I don't really suspect either of you—but by eliminating suspects *this* way, we're certain they're really clear." He deleted the first four names from his list.

"T'Mir cannot be the murderer for the same reason you three cannot," Sarek pointed out. "She was off-planet at the time the first instructions must have been programmed into the computer."

"Sendet has an alibi I have yet to verify—but he seemed very certain he would be cleared. And T'Pau's assistant confirms that she spent yesterday in her office, where there is no computer terminal," said Kirk. "She could not have started the fire."

"Nor could my father," added Spock. "He was with either you or me every moment before the fire yesterday."

"True," said Kirk, looking at the dwindling list, *unless he had an accomplice.*

An icy shiver went down his spine as he studied the names left:

> SOREL
> CORRIGAN
> SOTON
> SENDET
> ELEYNA

"Well, I guess the next step is to check alibis on the rest of these people," he said, snapping off the tricorder.

"Jim," said Spock, "Sorel and Corrigan alibi one another because of the healing meld. If either were guilty of T'Zan's death, the other could not have helped discovering it. Opportunity is irrelevant . . . unless you think they were working together. And in that case you must also assume that Daniel Corrigan has the control no Vulcan would have, to be able to hide such guilt when he bonded with T'Mir."

"Yesterday she thought he *was* guilty," Kirk recalled. "But then she wouldn't have bonded with him if she hadn't been convinced otherwise."

"The news of their bonding does not seem to surprise you, Jim," said Spock.

"No—T'Pau told me."

"Then if Sorel should need an alibi for this morning," Sarek observed, "we know what he has been doing: notifying the family."

Kirk caught himself before suggesting that he would have his secretary or nurse or whatever do such a job—it might well be Vulcan custom that he had to do it himself. And Kirk did not want to mention assistants before Sarek just now. In fact, he wanted desperately to get away from Spock's father before he felt compelled to accuse him of murder for a second time.

Surely I'm wrong again! But he has suddenly become my most likely suspect!

"Let me go find out what Soton was doing just before yesterday's power failure," Kirk said. "And I want to talk to Storn later, too—what if the murderer is not on my list at all?"

He hurried away, feeling Spock's curious stare between his shoulder blades. His friend undoubtedly knew he was lying—but he hoped he would never have to tell Spock what was truly on his mind.

Eleyna Miller was Sarek's assistant; Spock's father said she knew nearly as much about computers as he did. That meant she had method, and with all those hours spent unobserved at Sarek's computer terminal, she also had opportunity. Yesterday . . . yesterday he had told her they suspected computer tampering rather than equipment failure—and not long after she had gone back to Sarek's office had come the power failure and the fire!

Oh, damn, why did it have to be so logical? She had method and opportunity, but no motive. Sarek said she was an exemplary student. How exemplary? So much so that he wanted her around permanently—as his wife? Would he discard one human for another? Why not, if he had chosen that way once?

It was illogical. But Vulcans were capable of such illogic—T'Pring had rejected Spock, and been willing to see him die at the hands of her lover. Then, when the opportunity arose, she had protected Stonn by choosing Kirk as her champion.

He remembered Sarek and Amanda boarding the *Enterprise.* Sarek had introduced Amanda as "She who is my wife," rather than by name. Had they been fighting? Made up, as people do, over Sarek's brush with death? Later, as people do, found their differences still irreconcilable after the immediate concern for Sarek's life had subsided?

It all fit. If they had been as close as married couples normally are, how could Amanda have been ignorant of Sarek's previous heart attacks? He had not told her—had, indeed, taken on a mission guaranteed to put a strain on his heart. Had his life at that point been so unpleasant that he risked it casually? Could it be his wife who made life that unpleasant? And did Vulcan law allow the husband no way to end his marriage?

If Sarek had wanted to be rid of Amanda, her illness would have been a relief—and then Sorel and Corrigan came up with their treatment. Not only would it save her life, but it would rejuvenate her; he would be stuck with her for many more years beyond the human lifespan.

The unwanted husband or wife. It had to be the oldest motive for murder in galactic history.

But a clever—logical—murderer would find a way to avert suspicion, and what better way than by using someone else to do his dirty work? First, arrange to blame Sorel and Corrigan, who had invented the very treatment that caused him to take the drastic step of murder. Second, use an accomplice to do the actual programming, so that just in case the computer tampering were discovered, Eleyna would be blamed instead of Sarek.

But why would Eleyna do it? *Sarek* said she was a brilliant student—but what if she wasn't quite good enough? He could have provided her with the other programs—but yesterday she had acted on her own, in panic, and had done far more than wipe the permanent memory bank as she had intended.

Sarek could have promised Eleyna recommendations she didn't truly deserve if she helped him. Or . . . he could have promised her himself. He could actually want her, or he could simply be using her. Kirk recalled overhearing two of his female crew members discussing Spock's father one time, agreeing that they found him quite compelling—even more so than Spock. And Kirk was quite aware that his First Officer was attractive to women.

Furthermore, Sarek was a very wealthy, powerful man. There were plenty of women, and men, too, who placed considerations of money and power above physical or mental attractions. No, there was little doubt that Sarek had the requisites to persuade a vulnerable young person to do what he wanted—one way or another.

Oh, it was logical—only too marvelously logical.

And what would it do to Spock if Kirk were right? If after eighteen years of silence he made up with his father only to find out that he was trying to murder his mother—and in the process had casually dispatched two other people?

Kirk was walking toward the central hospital area. He had started in this direction to lend credence to his statement that he wanted to determine Soton's whereabouts before the fire. Actually, Soton was low on his list of priorities. He would call Eleyna, try to talk to her now—

"No! No! You have no right!" The voice was hoarse, Vulcan, filled with outrage.

It was followed by a cry of surprise from a second voice—and then a scream of pain!

Kirk rounded the corner at a dead run, and came upon a startling scene. Sendet, who had apparently just come out of his laboratory, had Daniel Corrigan backed against the corridor wall, his hand covering the human doctor's face in some kind of mind meld.

Corrigan was fighting, trying to tear Sendet's hand

away, but he was no match for the strong young Vulcan.

"You flaunt your bonding, but you won't keep her!" Sendet spoke softly, but threat grated through his words.

Kirk saw Corrigan's mouth form a grotesque square of utter agony—the worse because no sound came forth!

The human struggled even more violently. Kirk saw Sendet's free hand move toward Corrigan's shoulder.

He would use the nerve pinch, then do whatever he wanted to the helpless human!

Kirk leaped!

He caught Sendet's arm and dragged it down—but like a claw, the man's other hand kept its grip on Corrigan's face.

Sendet flung Kirk against the wall. "Stay out of this!" he ordered. "It is not your affair, outworlder!"

But Corrigan's struggles were growing feebler— could Sendet kill him through a mind meld? Kirk bounced back, this time tackling Sendet at knee level.

Both Kirk and Sendet went sprawling, and Corrigan slid down the wall to collapse in a heap—free of Sendet's grip.

Kirk was aware of other people in the hallway now. As Sendet kicked free and turned to lunge at him, two other Vulcans, a man and a woman, caught him from behind. T'Ra and Skep, his fellow workers in the neurophysics laboratory.

From behind Kirk, Spock and Sarek came running around the corner.

Sendet was trying to break free of his colleagues, insisting, "Let me go! He has dishonored me! He dishonors all of Vulcan. He cannot have her!" But T'Ra and Skep held him firmly.

Kirk climbed to his feet, unhurt. Spock glanced at

him, saw that he was all right, and went to kneel beside Corrigan as Sarek asked, the voice of authority, "What happened here?"

T'Ra and Skep looked at one another uneasily as Sendet ceased struggling at last, staring defiantly at Sarek. "You!" he spat. "You started it with your outworlder wife and your half-breed son! Vulcan is being contaminated—and this one offends even further. He dares to bond with the woman who should have been mine. She *will* be mine!"

Corrigan gave a low moan. Spock, whose hand touched his face gently, in a position different from the one Sendet had used, looked up. "Get a healer!" he said. "And Daniel's bondmate—quickly!"

But even as Skep was eyeing Sendet as if to decide whether he dared let go of him, Sorel and T'Mir came running from the direction Kirk had been headed.

T'Mir was so pale Kirk wondered how she kept from fainting, her eyes huge and dazed. She said nothing, falling to her knees beside Corrigan as Spock relinquished his place to Sorel.

Father and daughter placed their hands on either side of Corrigan's face. Both Corrigan and T'Mir gasped once, then fell silent.

Silence seemed to stretch endlessly through the corridor, the watchers hardly breathing as Sorel and his daughter attempted to heal whatever damage Sendet had done to Corrigan. Kirk didn't understand what had happened—but he knew pain when he saw it, and Sendet had had Corrigan in agony.

Time dragged on, but Kirk curbed his curiosity until, at last, Sorel raised his head and lifted his hand from Corrigan's face. Corrigan opened his eyes, looked into T'Mir's with a smile, then sat up—obviously startled to find a varied audience watching. "We're all right," he said. "Sendet did not succeed."

"Thanks to Captain Kirk," said T'Ra. "I fear Skep and I would not have been in time to stop his attempt to. . . ." She let the words trail away, as if she could not credit the possibility of whatever it was Sendet had been trying to do.

Kill Corrigan, Kirk was certain. "You were caught in the act this time, Sendet. You said it yourself: it would take an unbalanced mind. Did you really think people would stand by and let you commit murder?"

"Murder?" Sendet asked blankly.

"Worse than murder, Jim," said Sorel. "Sendet was trying to break an established bonding. That is . . . unthinkable."

Kirk realized that Sorel spoke from recent, excruciating experience. He marveled at the healer's restraint— wouldn't even Vulcan law excuse him if he promptly executed the man who had murdered his wife?

Sendet said implacably, "The outworlder is unworthy of bonding with T'Mir. He is not Vulcan. I was merely righting an offense against tradition."

"And what wrong were you redressing when you murdered the Lady T'Zan?" Kirk demanded.

"T'Zan? No!" Sendet stared around at the circle of people studying him menacingly. "No—I had nothing to do with her death, or that of the outworlder."

"We'll see about that when I check out your so-called alibi," said Kirk.

"Alibi?" Sarek asked.

"I questioned Sendet yesterday," Kirk explained. "He claims that he could not have programmed the failure to T'Zan's stasis chamber, because it would have had to be done after he found out which chamber she was placed in."

"That is correct," said Sarek. "However, Sendet learned advanced computer techniques from me, and was an excellent student. He is quite capable of the

213

necessary manipulations. I would estimate that locating the programming, overriding the safeguards, and re-programming would be the work of four to seven hours—not necessarily all at one time. It was almost a full day between the time T'Zan was placed in stasis until the failure to her stasis chamber. Can you account for all that time, Sendet?"

"I do not have to account to you," Sendet replied.

"T'Ra and Skep were with him all day," said Kirk. "He was still in the laboratory when they received the news that there was a malfunction—and we saw him then at the hospital."

"But he had the night before," said Spock. "Just after T'Zan was placed in stasis."

As Sendet remained stubbornly silent, Kirk said, "He claims he took public transport across the desert to the—the Shrine of T'Vet, and remained there all night, meditating. I haven't had time yet to find out if the tram operator or anyone at the shrine can verify his story."

"The story is a lie," said Sorel, his voice softly hoarse the way Spock's was when he was struggling to main-tain control. "You would not know it, Jim—but any Vulcan would. When T'Kuht is shining, the Shrine of T'Vet is closed to visitors. It is a time of solitary meditation for the keepers of the shrine. The trams do not run to and from the shrine during these nights."

The healer walked over to Sendet and stood facing him. "Sendet, I accuse you of murdering my wife, thus breaking my bonding. There are eight witnesses here to your attempt to break the bonding of Daniel and T'Mir. This is the greatest crime any Vulcan can commit."

"No!" Sendet protested, unsuccessfully trying to shrug out of T'Ra and Skep's grip. "No—I lied to the

outworlder, it's true. I was not at the Shrine of T'Vet—
but I did not spend the time programming the computer
to kill T'Zan. I swear it, Sorel—I did nothing to
interrupt a true Vulcan bonding!"

"We will see," replied the healer. "There must be a
Verification . . . before it is decided what your fate will
be. Bring him," he said to T'Ra and Skep, and turned
to walk regally away, T'Mir and Corrigan following.

"What's going to happen to Sendet?" Kirk asked
Spock. "Tal-shaya?"

"Possibly," his friend replied, "if he is found to be
guilty."

"You doubt it?" Kirk asked in amazement.

Spock looked at him reprovingly. "Long before
Vulcan joined the Federation our law agreed that a
person is innocent until proven guilty. I believe you
have a similar law on Earth?"

"Yes, of course," said Kirk. "But what is a Verification? Should we go along, as witnesses? I have Sendet's
testimony on my tricorder—"

"Sendet will be his own witness," Sarek said softly.
"A circle of healers will seek the truth from his own
mind. If he resists . . . there are good reasons why
tal-shaya, the quick, painless breaking of the neck, is
considered a merciful form of execution."

"You mean . . . this Verification could kill him, uh,
less mercifully?"

"Only if he tries to hide shameful thoughts and acts,"
said Spock. "Considering the act in which we caught
him, I fear that he does indeed have things he will wish
to hide." He turned to Sarek. "The law is to be
respected, Father, but . . . I do believe we may now
rest easily concerning Mother's safety."

Kirk saw the open relief in Sarek's eyes, and suddenly was consumed with guilt for the terrible things he had

been thinking about Spock's father just before he came upon Sendet and Corrigan. Thank goodness *he* wasn't facing a Verification!

And, he thought more cheerfully, *I can stop being suspicious of Eleyna—and go out tonight and have a good time!*

CHAPTER **29**

Daniel Corrigan ignored the dull, throbbing ache behind his eyes, and watched Sorel efficiently contact T'Pau, explain the situation, and begin arrangements for a Verification. He knew the technique—hypothetically. A group of healers would meld with Sendet, forcing his mind open layer by layer until they found the truth or falsity of his claims.

Vulcans do not lie.

It was a myth, Corrigan well knew—or rather, an ideal. The casual lie was unknown here, the diplomatic lie rare but occasionally to be found. The lie for gain or to avoid the consequences of one's actions was what Vulcans tried to breed out of their children. For the most part, they were successful—their society as a whole practiced honesty as naturally as breathing. Hence the virtual absence of crime.

Yet it was possible, as with any society, to find those who did not live up to the ideals. The pressures of Vulcan society usually made such people keep themselves under enough control to live comfortably with other Vulcans—unless they erupted as Sendet had today.

Corrigan fought down shudders at the memory of the attack, the hand on his face, the searing pain of the forced meld, the even greater pain of interference with his bond with T'Mir, her presence growing faint. . . .

He reached mentally, as was beginning to become natural, and she was there, a sweet, cool presence easing his tension, reassuring him that she would always be there. And he could feel her welcoming his touch—for she had suffered just as much at the tearing pressures Sendet had placed on their bonding. *She needs me,* Corrigan thought contentedly. The deep certainty relieved the last of his physical tension, and his headache disappeared.

Deliberately, he stopped concentrating on T'Mir, telling himself he should not distract her from her work. For T'Mir was taking up her new duties in the xenobiology department, which would include teaching a class when the next term began. As soon as she and Daniel had made certain that their bond was intact and neither had suffered neurological damage, T'Mir had returned to her work.

Now Sorel looked up from his latest call, and said, "The Verification is set for this afternoon at the fourteenth hour. I must prepare. Please take my patients or have T'Sel make other arrangements for them, Daniel."

"Then when am *I* supposed to prepare?" Corrigan asked.

Sorel stared at him. "Daniel, a Verification is a difficult and dangerous procedure. Only Vulcans—"

"Sorel, you have never, even once in all the years we have known one another, pulled the 'You are not Vulcan, so you cannot understand' routine on me. I am not going to take it from you now."

"Forgive me," said his partner. "I should have said only trained telepaths may participate. The clearest, most disciplined minds must act with total objectivity."

"Objectivity? Sorel, the man murdered your wife. How can *you* be objective?" He waited, watching the impassive face as Sorel thought that over. Corrigan knew what Sorel had suffered at T'Zan's death—perhaps it would be best if his friend did not expose himself to the emotions of her murderer.

"I am the one injured," Sorel said finally. "It is my right to participate."

"I have the same right," Corrigan insisted.

"Daniel—"

"Is it not the law?"

Sorel's black eyes held his for two deep breaths. Then, "It is the law," he conceded.

But when Corrigan joined the assembled healers around the table in a small conference room later that day, he was challenged again.

T'Par was one of the healers who would participate; the others were Sev and Suvel, apparently chosen as neutral parties because they rarely worked closely with Sorel and Corrigan. Sev, in fact, was frequently off-planet, as he was the physician usually assigned to Sarek's diplomatic missions. However, it would be impossible to assemble a group of healers who did not know one another at all.

T'Pau was there, too. Although not a healer, as arbiter and guardian of the law she was supposed to prevent the Verification from straying into areas of Sendet's privacy which were irrelevant to the investigation at hand.

It was Suvel who said, "Daniel, this proceeding requires a healer's training."

"I've participated in mind melds before," Corrigan told him. "Besides, the law says that the injured party may participate, healer or no."

"Daniel."

It was T'Pau. Corrigan steeled himself to be told again that he was not Vulcan, before it dawned on him that it was the first time T'Pau had ever granted him the Vulcan courtesy of addressing him by first name only.

The Vulcan matriarch said, "There is no need to Verify what Sendet did to you. You have no reason to undergo a painful experience. Be assured, your interests will be protected."

"I never doubted that, T'Pau."

"Sendet attacked your mind once," said Sev. "He might attempt to do so again."

"Sev," said Sorel, "Daniel has a true bonding. Sendet did not succeed in breaking it—the most he could do was interfere, although I believe the Verification will show that his intent was to break it. I can also attest to the discipline of Daniel's mind . . . although I, too, have discouraged him from subjecting himself to this proceeding."

T'Pau was studying Corrigan so intently that he almost believed he was reading her curiosity directly, although he knew full well that he was sensitive to no one but T'Mir.

The matriarch rose. "Daniel, I believe there is another motive in you . . . and if I am correct, then it is imperative that you participate."

Now what in the world could she mean by that? Corrigan had no hidden motives that he was aware of.

"Come to me," T'Pau beckoned. "Give your thoughts to me," she said when he approached and, leaning heavily on his bond with T'Mir to allay his fears, knelt before her.

Her fingers spidered over the side of his face, and he felt her mind—as disciplined as Sorel's, but overlaid with many more decades of experience—touch lightly on the confusion of his surface thoughts and lay them gently open to him.

Well, I'll be damned, he thought, and felt a tolerant amusement in T'Pau's mind which would never reach her face.

T'Pau withdrew her hand. "Tell them," she instructed Corrigan.

"In a way," he explained as he returned to his place at the table, "I identify with Sendet. That is . . . I understand why he does not understand the seriousness of his offense."

He looked out at a circle of raised eyebrows. "Sendet has never been bonded," he explained.

Again the curiosity.

"Look," said Corrigan, "I know I've probably slipped up several times since I got here, and you all know by now that I'm newly bonded. I'm still learning how to avoid broadcasting my feelings—if I had had better control this morning, Sendet would probably not have felt my merely walking down the hall as a provocation. But . . . I don't think he had any idea of the pain he meant to inflict on me. He does not know what he tried to take from me. Until yesterday, I did not know.

"I know, from having helped to heal Sorel, what agony there is in a severed bonding . . . but even that I knew only second hand. Sendet is no healer. He has never experienced what a bonding means . . . even secondhand. That does not excuse him, but it makes his act comprehensible."

"And we are here to comprehend," said T'Pau. "Daniel, you are needed at this Verification."

At her word, there could be no further protest. "Bring in the accused," said T'Pau, "and let the Verification begin."

CHAPTER **30**

James T. Kirk was alone at Sarek's house when Eleyna Miller arrived . . . with a picnic basket. She smiled in appreciation of the outfit he had chosen for a night on the town, but suggested, "That's good for dancing, but not exactly the thing for walking in the desert."

"The desert?" he asked blankly.

"T'Kuht will rise in two hours—by then we will be far enough from ShiKahr that the city lights will not dim the view. The rising of T'Kuht is one of the most beautiful sights in the galaxy."

"Are you sure it's worth a two-hour walk in this heat?"

"The desert cools when darkness falls. Please, Jim—I know you will be glad if you come along."

I never could resist a beautiful woman, he thought. Besides, if Eleyna could stand the walk, he certainly

223

could now that he had had a few days to acclimate. A little moonlight romance. . . .

He went back to his room—Spock's room, really. Kirk had brought with him a sturdy suit and boots, for Spock had suggested they might go camping in the mountains after the summer heat abated. He put on the boots and the trousers to the suit, but decided the heavy shirt would be far too hot, and chose a short-sleeved light shirt instead.

As he turned to leave the room, his eye fell on a display of weapons on the wall. Spock had a collection of spears and swords in his quarters aboard the *Enterprise*. These were knives of various shapes and sizes. He had always thought it strange that his gentle friend should collect weapons.

Remembering Sarek saying something about flesh-eating plants in the desert at this time of year, he considered that there might be other dangers as well. He wished he had a phaser, but of course he had not come armed to visit Spock's family.

This is not an exploration mission, he told himself. *It's a walk with a pretty girl in the moonlight!*

Nonetheless, he picked from Spock's collection a knife with a sheath—one that looked more like a modern utility blade than a classic antique—and slipped it into his boot.

Kirk and Eleyna went out through the back gate in the garden wall, straight into the desert. There was still a good bit of lingering daylight, and Kirk's eyes adjusted as that faded away. Eleyna pointed out the jagged black line of the L-Langon Mountains in the distance, explaining that if they headed straight toward one particularly formidable peak, they would come to the place she had in mind to watch T'Kuht rise.

It was still hot, but the way was smooth, a thin layer

of sand over rock. Without the sun beating down, Kirk was not too uncomfortable . . . and perhaps it was wishful thinking, but the temperature did seem to be getting a little more tolerable. The gravity, though, made him start to feel tired long before he would have on Earth.

Eleyna pointed out a rock formation ahead. "That's where we're going—we'll climb up onto that flat-topped rock and have a marvelous view of the country-side." Kirk glanced at her and saw that *she* remained cool and collected, not a hair out of place.

As they approached the foot of the outcropping, Kirk looked up at a steep cliff some eight or ten meters high. "We can't climb up there!" he said.

"There is a way up on the other side," Eleyna explained. "Come around this way."

In the shade of the rocks, some vegetation survived even the heat of midsummer. As their footsteps vibrated through the rock layer, Kirk thought he saw long, snakey leaves move. He looked closer, but all was still. Curious, he stamped his foot. Sure enough, the branches snaked across the sand in his direction.

"Look at that!" he said to Eleyna. "Is that one of those man-eating plants?"

"Hardly *man*-eating," she said with a laugh. "They catch animals that take shelter in the shade of the rocks. Besides, they probably wouldn't care for the taste of humans."

Saying, "Let's not find out," Kirk skirted around the plant, not liking the way its branches slithered as far as they could in his direction as he circled it. Sure enough, the other side of the rock provided hand- and foot-holds, not an easy climb, but perfectly accessible to two humans in good condition.

Perfectly accessible, were it not for Vulcan's high gravity. Half-way up, Kirk found his arms and legs leaden, his chest heaving as he gasped for more oxygen than Vulcan's air had to offer. His heart pounded in his ears. But Eleyna was still climbing. He forced himself to continue upward.

At the top, Kirk stood still to catch his breath while he looked around. Eleyna was right—the view was worth the climb!

The light had shifted to blues and purples, so that for the first time in Kirk's experience Vulcan actually *looked* cool.

Overhead a few bright stars glowed, but most of the densely-packed stars of this part of the galaxy could not compete with the growing glow in the sky. Kirk, realizing that it was getting brighter, concentrated at one point on the horizon, where T'Kuht would soon show itself. Herself. Hot Vulcan's cool sister.

The L-Langon Mountains maintained their jagged black march across the far horizon. "What is the shrine of T'Vet?" Kirk asked suddenly.

"T'Vet was the patron saint or goddess—it's not clear whether she was a real person or not—of the warrior clans," Eleyna explained. "Her worship was already old when Surak lived—and the attacks on his community were done in her name."

"But there's supposed to be an active shrine to her in the mountains," said Kirk.

"There is. Although Surak's philosophy prevailed, it did not seek to destroy the old ways. T'Vet is the female force toward racial survival. In the ancient days she was perceived as protecting the warriors in their battles for food and water to keep the women and children of a clan alive through the summer.

"Once Surak's philosophy spread, and people began to cooperate instead of making war, they learned irrigation, and the more profitable use of arable land for vegetable crops rather than meat animals. As war and famine were eliminated, worship of T'Vet dwindled away. Today there is only that one shrine left."

"Preserved as a historical curiosity?" Kirk asked.

"No—it's an active shrine," Eleyna told him. "The worship of T'Vet and the philosophy of Surak exist side by side here. In fact, some of the ceremonies practiced by today's Vulcans have been adapted from rituals of T'Vet. There are . . . things I have heard rumored, but that offworlders cannot get a straight answer about— such as a ritual apparently permitted but never practiced, whereby a marriage can end with two men actually duelling over the bride!"

Kirk smothered a grim smile at the incredulity in her voice. "I suppose a warrior goddess *would* approve of such things. But are there still worshipers of T'Vet who don't practice Surak's philosophy?"

"I don't know, but I doubt it," Eleyna replied. "Why do you ask?"

"I was just wondering if that would account for Sendet."

Eleyna had heard from Sarek about Sendet's attack on Corrigan, and the Verification, Kirk had learned on the way here. "I don't want to talk about Sendet," she said now. "What he did was horrible. Come—let's have some wine and toast T'Kuht's rising."

They spread a cloth atop the rock, which was still warm from the day's sun. Eleyna had brought wine, fruit, and kreyla—delicious crisp biscuits in a variety of flavors, one Vulcan food humans took to happily.

The wine was Rigellian—the sort exported throughout the galaxy, inexpensive but quite a good bargain. The flavor took Kirk back to his own student days, when this very wine had marked occasions too special for beer. He sat in a hollow atop the warm rock, leaning back against an outcropping that seemed designed to support him, and wondered how many generations of courting students had climbed this rock to watch T'Kuht rise. Should he be surprised that he and Eleyna had it to themselves tonight?

Then Vulcan's sister planet peeked over the horizon, and he forgot everything but the beauty of the night and the presence of Eleyna. She moved closer to him, and he put an arm about her, breathing in the fragrance wafting from her warm skin.

T'Kuht rose slightly golden, like Earth's harvest moon, but much larger—the optical illusion as it poised on the horizon made it seem too close. Surely Vulcan and T'Kuht must fall toward one another and collide!

Kirk smiled to himself at his spaceman's fancy. Eleyna was probably thinking it was close enough to touch. He looked down, intending to ask her thoughts, and found her eyes looking into his, drowning in the light.

It seemed the most natural thing in the world to kiss her, and she responded eagerly. For a long time, they kissed and caressed one another while T'Kuht climbed the sky, ignored.

The time for a decision came. Kirk released Eleyna and sat back, waiting for her move that would tell him exactly what she wanted tonight.

She poured them each some more wine, then got up, carrying her cup to the edge of the precipice.

T'Kuht had turned silver, and lit Vulcan's desert with a strange, deceptive light, turning Eleyna's blond hair almost white and casting her shadow long and black.

Kirk drained his cup, set it down, and went to Eleyna. Saying nothing, he put his hand over hers on her wine cup, took a sip, then guided the cup to her lips. Eyes locked with his, she drank, tossed the unbreakable cup aside, and put her arms about him.

Kirk's back was to T'Kuht, and to the edge of the precipice. He started to guide Eleyna gently back toward their picnic area, but she tripped as she took a step backward, and almost fell.

As her knees gave way, Kirk bent to catch her, putting himself off balance as in awkward ballet in the high gravity, Eleyna lurched against him. She tried to straighten, her arms going up—and she hit Kirk's shoulder, sending him stumbling toward the edge.

"No!" Eleyna cried, reaching out toward Kirk, but he felt the wine throwing his reflexes out of kilter in the gravity, saw her stumble again, felt her flailing hands hit him—and fell.

The drop was so fast in the high gravity that Kirk could not get his body into the best position to absorb the impact without injury. His left foot hit the ground first, and although he tried to roll, pain stabbed from his ankle up the outside of his leg to his knee. He gave an involuntary yelp, but Star Fleet training took over despite the pain, and although he felt the hard rock under the sand bruising him as he rolled, he knew he sustained no serious injuries.

Except to his ankle. As he came to a stop and slowly straightened his body, waves of pain shot up from the injury.

Eleyna was kneeling at the edge of the precipice, the light of T'Kuht distorting her features weirdly. "Jim! Are you all right?"

He sat up. "I'm okay except for my pride. And my left ankle. Can't tell if it's sprained or broken."

"I'll be right down!"

While Eleyna was working her way down the far side of the rock formation, Kirk took off his boot. The ankle was already starting to swell, the throbbing pain exacerbated by the act of pulling the boot off. He could not feel any broken bones, but even if it was a sprain he wouldn't be able to walk on it.

Some damn fine romantic moonlit night!

Eleyna came running around the rock formation. "Can you walk?"

"No . . . but I guess I'll have to," Kirk replied. "Nothing around here to make a crutch. I'll have to lean on you."

Her gentle hands peeled away his sock, fingers prodding at the rapidly-swelling flesh. "Oh, no," she said, "you *can't* walk on that! But it's all right. I'll go back up and get the food and wine for you, then I'll walk back to ShiKahr. By this time Sarek will be home—we'll bring his ground car for you."

Chagrined, Kirk had to agree that her plan made sense. "Sorry I was so clumsy."

"Oh, but it was my fault, tripping like that!" she said. "Jim, I'm so sorry—you could have been killed!"

"Not from a little fall like that," he reassured her. But he had seldom had a date end so inauspiciously.

Eleyna brought the picnic things down from the top of the rock and made Kirk as comfortable as possible. . . not very. He leaned against the bottom of the cliff, his injured foot propped up on the picnic basket. There was less than a cup of wine left in the bottle—*no wonder we were clumsy,* thought Kirk, not remembering having drunk that much. "I wish you had brought some water," he said, realizing that after climbing down, up, and down the rock again, Eleyna was probably thirsty herself. Maybe she had drunk some more wine.

"I didn't expect any problems," she said. "You're right, though—I *should* have thought to bring water. Well, I have a long, lonely walk now in which to kick myself for not bringing water and for deciding we should walk instead of borrowing a ground car."

Kirk hoped the effect of the wine she had drunk would not hinder that long walk. At least she wouldn't get lost: the path of their footprints was plain under T'Kuht's bright light.

"I'll be as quick as I can," Eleyna said when she had done everything she could for Kirk. "Now don't you worry. It's possible Sarek won't be home yet—you know how Vulcans are. If he and Spock are still working at installing the new computer, they won't think about eating or sleeping. In that case I'll walk back to the Academy and find someone with a car to come and get you. You just rest till I get back—and don't move that ankle!"

Kirk watched until Eleyna's form disappeared, then took a sip of wine. He wanted to drink it all down in his pain-thirst, but reminded himself that it was a two-hour walk for Eleyna, and then probably the better part of another hour before she could return with a car.

He wished for water again. Dumb move to go into the desert—any desert—without a canteen. Basic survival training for first-year cadets. Why hadn't he thought to ask Eleyna if there was water in the basket he had carried for her? And a first-aid kit? He was certain a quick search of Sarek's well-equipped kitchen would have turned up both a first-aid kit and a canteen.

To the throb of his aching ankle, Kirk lifted his foot from the insulated basket and took a piece of fruit to ease his thirst. It was some help . . . but from the corner of his eye he saw something else move as he did.

The plant! It was off to his left, but its snakey limbs were stretching in his direction.

Could the thing actually grow toward him? Maybe pull up its roots and move to where a good meal was available? There were plants on Cygnus 15 that could do so.

Even so, he could crawl out of its reach, he told himself. Still, it made him uneasy to sit here helplessly while that thing contemplated having him for its next meal! He took the knife out of his boot, ready to hand . . . and wished for a phaser.

The beauty of the Vulcan night had turned alien. The harsh, black-and-white contrast of T'Kuht's light distorted shadows into fearsome shapes.

And off somewhere in the direction of the L-Langon Mountains, where from up above Kirk had seen other rock formations rising from the desert floor, there rose the distant but hair-raising caterwauling of some beast he could not name. A howling at the light challenging its nighttime dominance of the desert? A mating call? Or the hunting cry of a predator who sensed injured prey waiting, his for the taking?

CHAPTER **31**

Daniel Corrigan could not have told who he was, where he was, or how long he had been in the strange group-mind conducting the Verification of Sendet's guilt or innocence. It seemed they had been struggling forever against the barriers the man held—until slowly, before the implacable constancy, they began to crumble one by one.

Like all Vulcans, Sendet was trained in the mental techniques that had first been developed by Surak, but improved over the centuries by generations of philosophers and healers. The first barrier to crumble, however, displayed the man's contempt for the philosophy of peace and nonviolence.

When the struggle is removed from life, the weak survive to propagate and racial strength is diluted!

Corrigan recognized it along with everyone else as

the basic argument of the followers of T'Vet. Since Vulcan had complete religious and political freedom, proponents of her violent philosophy were not silenced. Why should Sendet feel it necessary to hide so carefully his affiliation with a group which, if not approved by most Vulcans, was certainly tolerated? It would make no difference to his advancement at the Academy. If he wished to sit on the High Council, a few followers of T'Vet were elected every session, and their opinions received the same hearing as anyone else's.

The group saw, though, that Sendet's perceptions of Vulcan life as most of them lived it, were distorted; he saw physical weakness as encouraged—and apparently he had completely forgotten:

Every Vulcan child must survive the test of the Kahs-wan. Those who do not pass either die in the attempt or are not permitted to marry.

Corrigan could not tell whose mind guided the thought; the knowledge came from all of them, but somehow it was presented coherently.

All barriers suddenly crumbled.

What of outworlders?!

Sendet's focus was on Corrigan. *He passed no test of manhood, yet Sorel gives an outworlder his daughter! It was bad enough when Vulcan men diluted our blood by bringing in females of other races. It is the right of the warrior to win the females of other clans in battle or by trickery, but to consider their offspring full members of the clan—*

It was clearly T'Pau's mind that answered, *All children of outworld marriages have been subject to the Kahs-wan, and none have failed. None, Sendet. The same cannot be said of all children of pure Vulcan blood. You, yourself, as I recall—*

Suddenly the group-mind was plunged into agonized memory—Sendet, a boy of seven in the L-Langon

Mountains, filled with family pride as he hurried through the survival course, determined to reach his destination in the least time. The course was laid out to take ten days. It had been done occasionally in nine. He was determined to make it in eight days—no one had ever done it so fast before.

To have a chance of completing the course faster than anyone before, Sendet had chosen the shorter but more difficult high trail through this part of the mountains. By evening he would join the main trail again, but today he would cut at least four hours off his time by clambering over the rocks with his rope.

He was five days into the course, far ahead of all the other children. And then he stumbled upon a wild sehlat cub on the trail. A four-year-old knew better than to go near such a baby animal, lest the mother think he was attacking it. But it was right in his way!

If he sat here on the narrow mountain trail and waited for the cub to wander away, he could lose hours of his lead time. But there was no way around it—nor did he know where the mother was. If he came between her and her baby, he was in grave danger. But how was he to get past?

The course here led along a ledge, on which the cub sat eating some berries growing along the rock wall. The ledge was wide enough to walk very easily so long as one had no fear of heights. For to the left was a sheer drop, far into the valley below.

Sendet peered over the edge, and saw another ledge below. But it was only a few paces wide, not leading anywhere. He could use his rope to get down to it, but it would not take him past the sehlat cub.

Then he looked up. Far above, a narrower ledge led right past the sehlat—wide enough for a small Vulcan boy, but not for a full-grown sehlat. There was no chance he would meet the mother up there.

The cub showed no sign of moving. Sendet took a small sip of water from his canteen, and made his decision.

He went back along the path he was on until he came to a place where he could climb up to the higher ledge. It was indeed narrow—narrower than it had looked from below. He looked down on the cub, but it had finished off the berries and was now stretching out in the sun for a nap. Why wouldn't it go away?!

He got out his climbing rope, and began looping it about supports above him as he edged his way along the narrow ledge. It was hard—maybe too dangerous. Judgment was one of the things the Kahs-wan tested. Yet each time he got another firm support and looked down, that cub was still there. He thought of dropping pebbles on it, to frighten it away—but if the mother smelled fear-scent on her cub, she might come looking for what had frightened it.

Slowly, he worked his way along the narrow ledge, often having only a toe hold. His pride increased at negotiating such a difficult trail to keep ahead of the rest of the children. Finally he reached a spot where he could not find a firm enough purchase for his feet to allow him to stand while he moved the rope. But by craning his neck he could see a wide spot a few paces ahead. Perhaps he could swing over to it.

Preparing to swing across, Sendet gave a good tug on the rope to test its purchase—

The support gave!

The rope fell on Sendet, who tumbled off the ledge, bounced once near the startled sehlat cub, and fell further yet—onto the small ledge below!

He fell on something hard, with sickening pain—and fluid trickled from under him. He was bleeding to death!

Above him he heard the wails of the sehlat cub as it

ran in terror—but what would it matter if it did bring its mother? She could not reach Sendet down here . . . and he was dying anyway.

Yet he could move—enough to get off the piece of rock he had fallen on, which was stabbing him in the side. . . .

It wasn't a rock. It was his canteen that he had fallen on, and it was not blood trickling away, but his precious supply of water!

The stabbing when he breathed told him he had broken ribs. He also hurt everywhere in his body there was a place to hurt.

He had failed.

That pain was far greater than any pain of bruises or broken bones.

Other children would pass by him on the ledge above, but all were forbidden to speak with any other Kahs-wan child—this was a test of individual survival, and teamwork was forbidden. Those who saw him trapped here would report him when they reached the end of the survival course . . . but it would be tomorrow before any of the other children even reached this point, and five days before the first could possibly reach the end of the course.

And by that time, without water, he would be dead.

Sendet tried to reassure himself that he would die like a warrior, without whimpering—even though no one would ever know.

Time passed slowly. By midafternoon, Sendet had given up trying to place himself in healing trance—a skill he was not expected to master for another few years, but which might have saved his life had he been able to do it now—and had fallen into a drowsy stupor.

Pebbles falling on him woke him with a start. He automatically started to sit up, and the pain of his broken ribs stabbing him drew forth an involuntary cry.

A young Vulcan face peered down at him from the ledge above. Someone had been that close behind him—and to add further to his humiliation, it was the half-breed Spock!

Spock represented everything Sendet's family stood against. At his age Sendet understood little more than that it was acceptable to call the outworlder names. That this boy would now be the first one to complete his Kahs-wan was agony to Sendet. He turned his face away from the one looking down at him.

And saw the green bloodstains on the rock. He *had* bled, if only slightly.

But Spock saw the stains, too. When Sendet looked up at him again he saw plainly on the half-breed's face the indecision as to whether to break his own Kahs-wan by speaking to Sendet. He saw the other boy's eyes go to the smashed canteen . . . and determination settle over the young features.

"Life must be preserved," Spock said. "How badly are you hurt, Sendet?"

Failed already, Sendet had no reason not to answer. "You have spoken to me in vain, Spock, son of Sarek. I will die despite your failing your Kahs-wan."

"You're bleeding," Spock said, "but not very much. If I let down my rope, can you climb up?"

"No. My ribs are broken."

"Then I will come down to you," said Spock. "Others will be along. Several of us together can pull you up to the trail."

"How many others will take this trail?"

"I think two or three more will," said Spock. "You need water, and I have some. If no one will stop and help us, they *will* report us to the judges at the end. We won't be working. The water in my canteen will last until someone comes for us."

And Spock fastened his rope, and slid down to Sendet.

"You are a fool," Sendet told him. "No one will stop to help us. Only an Earther would fail his own Kahs-wan to help another."

"Then you are fortunate that my mother came from Earth," Spock replied and, despite Sendet's protests, began to inspect his wounds and try to make him comfortable.

Sendet was right that the other two children who chose to save time by taking the harder trail would refuse to stop. Spock shouted to them, even threatening to climb up and throw them down to the ledge, but each one merely hurried on without speaking.

Eventually, ravaging thirst drove Sendet to accept water from Spock's canteen, and the two boys survived until, five days later, an antigrav mountain-hopper appeared, and they were lifted off the ledge. Two fathers waited, Sendet's telling him, "You have disappointed me gravely," Spock's telling him, "You did well, my son. You saved another's life, which is much more important than passing a test you can take again."

But Spock did not have to take the test again—and Sendet and the two boys who had passed by, refusing to help, did.

Sendet's father challenged the judges' decision, claiming that Spock had not finished his test, any more than Sendet had. The judges, however, declared that Spock had showed proper maturity in giving up his own Kahs-wan to save a life—and pointed out that if Spock had hurried on as the other two boys had done, Sendet would certainly have died.

Sendet passed his Kahs-wan on the second try, of course, but all the meditation techniques he learned as he grew up succeeded only in allowing him to hide his resentment of Spock—and by extension all out-worlders. His father had blamed his failure of Kahs-wan on the first attempt for Sorel's refusal to bond his daughter to Sendet—even though Sorel did not bond either of his children to anyone else.

Sendet had tried time and again to win favor with T'Mir, his father's choice for him, but she was never more than tolerant of him—and then she insulted both Sendet and all of Vulcan by choosing an outworlder as husband!

And that was why, when he had had that bonding thrown in his face—into his very mind—by the braggart Earther—

The Vulcans in the meld stopped the scene short before they were bombarded again by the pain Sendet had caused Corrigan. But while his mind was open and volatile they went after the other information:

Did you kill T'Zan?

Did you kill Carl Remington?

No! Sendet's mind immediately replied. *No! No! I killed no one!*

Then where were you the night you lied about, the night someone programmed the failure to T'Zan's stasis chamber?

At . . . a meeting . . .

He could not, would not, verbalize it, but as the group meld opened his mind they were at the meeting—rabid Vulcan followers of T'Vet, planning to leave off the peaceful means they had been using for centuries in fruitless attempts to have the old ways restored—discussing the possibility of violent overthrow of the Vulcan High Council, raising the warrior clans again. . . .

No final plan was agreed upon at that all-night meeting . . . but all could see the danger in the midst of peaceful Vulcan—all the more dangerous *because* Vulcan was so peaceful that no one could conceive of the possibility of violence.

I killed no one! Sendet insisted. *I will kill in combat, openly, as a warrior—not by trickery!*

And the images in his mind showed himself and the others imagining themselves as ancient warriors, returning to the old clan system, ruling the planet—*a very small band of malcontents, thank God,* Corrigan's thought surfaced in the maelstrom. . . .

At T'Pau's guidance, the group meld dissolved, for their questions had been answered. Whatever else he might be, Sendet was not the murderer of T'Zan and Carl Remington.

Daniel Corrigan found himself once more inside his own head, Sendet staring at him from across the table, his eyes sick with revulsion. "You have won," the Vulcan said thickly. "You have made me a traitor!"

"Sendet," T'Pau said gently, "the violence in your mind is an illness. Yes, we have seen the identities of others suffering from this same illness . . . and we will cure you, not punish you."

"There is no cure for patriotism!" Sendet exclaimed —and slumped forward.

The healers were at him at once, medscanners whirring. "He stopped his heart!" said Sev. "We can—"

"Leave him," T'Pau said.

"He'll die!" said Sorel. "T'Pau, we have only minutes—"

"Allow Sendet his choice," she replied. "Is that not the Vulcan Way? We will contact the others who were planning with him . . . and give them a choice, also."

"Death—or having their minds reprogrammed?" Corrigan asked, suddenly very sick himself.

T'Pau stared at him. "They cannot be permitted to commit violence against others in the name of patriotism. But you represent the true Vulcan attitude, Daniel. Yes, there are always alternatives. I think the High Council will agree. Vulcan has planèts available for colonization that we have not yet begun to populate. If this group of people should choose not to be reabsorbed into Vulcan society, they may become colonists on one of those worlds, where they may develop their own society . . . until eventually they develop their own Surak. Unfortunately, some lessons must be learned many times. Sorel—can you still revive Sendet?"

The healer nodded, and Sev and Suvel brought a gurney while Sorel called for a resuscitation unit. Corrigan went with them as they took Sendet to meet the unit and attach it—Sendet began to breath again. Corrigan looked at his chronometer. Sendet would suffer no brain damage.

He did not envy the young Vulcan and his cohorts their fate—but was eternally glad that T'Mir would not be forced to be a part of it.

And then, finally, it penetrated that their troubles were not over. Sendet had *not* killed T'Zan and Remington.

There was still an unidentified murderer loose in the halls of the Vulcan Academy of Sciences.

CHAPTER 32

T'Kuht rode straight overhead, about to disappear from James T. Kirk's view behind the rock formation he leaned against. He pulled out his chronometer and studied the dimly-lit face. Almost five hours, Vulcan time. Eleyna should have been back here an hour ago.

He licked his lips, and considered drinking the last of the wine in the bottle. Surely at any moment he would see a ground car coming along that clear path. . . .

But what if he didn't? What if . . . Eleyna had abandoned him? He left the bottle inside the insulated picnic basket, telling himself he could wait for that last bit of moisture—and he wanted his head clear. It was beginning to spin out the strangest fancies.

For example: if this place were truly the common student rendezvous he had thought, why were his footprints and Eleyna's the only trail across the desert waste? Vulcans were tidy—there was no surprise in not finding empty bottles or food wrappings despoiling the picnic area—but if others came here, no one had since the last time there was a wind strong enough to erase the trail.

His mind went back to that morning, when he had almost accused Eleyna of being in conspiracy with Sarek to murder Amanda. *But then we caught the real murderer.*

Sendet certainly looked like a killer. He had never seen eyes so wild on a Vulcan—not even Spock the time he had been infected with the spores that released his emotions—and Kirk had deliberately provoked him to fury. Not in the pon farr, when he had intended to kill Kirk—that was survival, not killer instinct.

Of course they had caught the right man!

Unless Eleyna had deliberately pushed Kirk off the precipice, and left him here to die . . . because he knew too much. After all, he was the one with the tricorder full of evidence—the only one who had been systematically searching out *all* the evidence, *all* the suspects—

Come on, James T., Eleyna's just having trouble finding someone with a ground car.

Undoubtedly Sarek and Spock were still at the Academy, working on that blasted computer. So Eleyna would have had to walk from Sarek's house to the Academy, then find them, lure them from their work. . . .

Spock, he was sure, would drop his fascinating work with the new computer to rescue his captain.

So where were they?

Kirk's ankle was still throbbing with the beat of his heart. Contingency plan: if no one came in—say an hour—he must try to walk back to ShiKahr before the morning sun rose to broil him alive. He would meet anyone coming along the trail for him. Yes—that was a good plan.

Except—how was he to walk on his badly-swollen and painful ankle?

The swelling had stopped increasing some time ago. If he could support it, he would be able to walk on it if he had to—and it was beginning to look as if he might have to.

Another animal howl sent a shiver up Kirk's spine. That sounded close! God—what if Eleyna had never made it back to ShiKahr? What if some roaming beast had followed her—one of those things with the poisonous fangs and claws? Le-matya, he remembered from his studies about Vulcan. They normally stayed out in the mountains; wild animals on any planet did not come this close to a city the size of ShiKahr.

But there was drought now. If their watering holes had dried up; if their usual prey had died of thirst. . . .

Kirk thrust aside such morbid thoughts, and busied himself with the question of how to support his ankle should he have to try to walk on it.

His abandoned left boot was no use now; he would never get the swollen ankle back into it.

The picnic cloth! Thankful for having brought the knife, he began hacking the strong material into strips. Survival training came back again—those lessons about how to make a bandage out of anything available. It took a while, but he managed a secure wrap about his foot, coming up above the ankle bone.

Cautiously, he stood and tried his weight on it.

Pain shot up his leg, sending sweat springing through his pores. How far could he possibly get when every step was agony? Sick and shaking, he sat down again, heavily.

The flesh-eating plant moved again, its branches

rustling as they slithered toward him. Was it closer? Or was that his pain-drugged imagination?

Eleyna, dammit, where are you?!

A growling cough answered his thought.

Sheer primitive terror shot through his gut as he looked up and saw the beast on top of the rock formation, silhouetted against T'Kuht's light.

Le-matya!

The creature crouched like a cat, its pointed ears flicking forward, its nostrils twitching. Its tail swept back and forth behind it as it sniffed Kirk's scent.

I hope I don't smell like food to it!

Survival instinct held him perfectly still. He was in the shadows below the cliff. If the thing could not see his humanoid shape, and if his smell was wrong—

The le-matya shook its head and gave its coughing growl again. The light of T'Kuht glinted off its leathery hide.

Kirk saw it gather itself to spring—

He rolled tight against the bottom of the cliff.

The le-matya sprang over him, but whirled, reaching for him with its claws—poisonous claws!

Ignoring the stabs of pain from his ankle, Kirk crouched against the cliff, ducking from side to side as the thing tested him, catlike, playing with the prey it must know could not escape.

Behind it, the flesh-eating plant slithered—the le-matya was distracted by the sound, reaching out to the plant, which shot out a tentaclelike branch as if to grab the beast! The le-matya danced back, growling.

Then it was back to Kirk, the odd diamond-shaped markings on its hide dancing weirdly as it moved.

Kirk stared at the beast, holding his knife ready to defend himself, yet withholding the urge to slash at the paw reaching toward him again. He dared not anger it with pain from a slight wound—he had to get in a single fatal blow!

But where?

He didn't know where the thing's heart was. That left him only one choice—the one vulnerable spot on every creature with its brain in a head poised on a neck: he had to slit its throat!

That meant attacking from behind. How was he to circle the thing, jump onto its slippery back, and hang on out of reach of claws and fangs until he could get to the vulnerable throat? Never mind how—he *had* to!

Kirk heaved himself to his feet, gritting his teeth as his ankle screamed agony through his nerves. He tried to circle, but the catlike beast became more aggressive as its prey showed spirit. Its mouth opened, revealing rows of sharp teeth besides the poisoned fangs—it hissed, sending a foul stench into Kirk's face.

He side-stepped—and felt something grab his injured ankle!

The damn plant!

Furious, he bent and slashed the thin tendril— amazed at the strength it took to cut through only the tip. He realized as he clumsily flung himself away that if the thick main part of the branch had caught him, he would not have been able to cut through it!

Meanwhile the le-matya had decided it was time to stop playing games and eat—it sprang at Kirk, who held his knife at the ready, slashing for its throat. The leathery skin deflected his knife.

The creature's claws caught in his heavy trousers and it lifted him high before dropping him, ready to pounce again.

Again he tried to circle—but it was no use. His injury made him far too slow, and he doubted that even without it he could have outmaneuvered the le-matya.

As the creature crouched to spring again, he saw the plant behind it try again to grab, just missing the thrashing tail.

And then he saw his only chance.

Kirk continued to circle, no longer trying to get behind the le-matya. It followed him, tail thrashing, growling deep in its throat in annoyance. A paw flicked out toward him—he ducked just in time, and rolled right to the edges of the flesh-eating plant.

He stayed there, crouched, holding his knife as if to slash at the le-matya. "Come on, monster! I can take you!"

The beast crouched as well, answering the challenge with a roar. It sprang!

Kirk whirled to one side—skidding when his ankle gave way!

The le-matya barreled past where he had been, twisting in midair to slash once more at him, one claw gashing across the knuckles of his knife hand—

But the beast landed right on the flesh-eating plant!

The thing's branches closed up around the thrashing le-matya, tighter than an Aldebaran shell-mouth!

Ungodly yowlings accompanied the animal's death throes.

Kirk stared in disbelief as the plant's tendrils dug into the body of the catlike beast—he heard bones crunching! The tangle of plant and animal throbbed and shivered as the yowls turned to screams of pain . . . and finally died away.

The plant quivered for a while, and then was still. Digesting.

Kirk swallowed hard—and felt the burning in his hand where venom from the le-matya's claws was doing its work.

He was terribly thirsty—but that last bit of wine was

all he had to sterilize the knife—he had to cut into the wound, draw out the poison!

Shaking, he crawled to the picnic basket, had the presence of mind to pour the wine into its lined bottom. He soaked the knife blade in it, hoping, praying, the alcohol content was strong enough—but he could wait no longer. He steeled himself, cut into the gash on the back of his hand until blood flowed, then sucked it out, spitting blood and poison onto the sand, over and over and. . . .

He felt dizzy. Obviously some of the poison was in his system. Eleyna had pushed him off the precipice, left him here to die—prey to that plant, or to the le-matya. . . .

He had fooled her. He was alive. Alive!

His awkward left hand shook. He dropped the knife, tried to find it—how would he defend himself if—?

T'Kuht's light went out. Kirk slumped, unconscious.

CHAPTER **33**

*L*eonard McCoy awoke to find himself alone in Sarek's house. He had been alone when he got home last night, but that had not been surprising. Jim had been out on a date, and Sarek and Spock so busy installing the new computer that they had told him to go ahead and take Sarek's ground car.

Apparently none of them had come home at all.

He wasn't really surprised to find Jim's room empty, the bed unslept in. And, he supposed, he ought to expect like son, like father from Spock and Sarek when it came to playing with computers.

He went to the kitchen to make coffee. While it was brewing, he looked out into the back garden . . . and noticed a heavy, dry frond from one of the trees lying against the wall near the gate.

He could not have said what caused him to go out to investigate—but something "felt" funny. No one had been home to do anything in Sarek's garden, nor had there been any wind in the breathless heat of Vulcan's summer. Besides, the wind would not lay the branch so neatly beside the gate.

On impulse, McCoy opened the gate. There was nothing to see but desert. Except . . . neat side-to-side marks in the sand, as if someone had been out here sweeping it. Perhaps with that frond?

Feeling slightly ridiculous, McCoy walked out onto the freshly-swept sand. The heat sprang at him from the sun overhead, the sand below. He didn't know what he was looking for . . . until he saw it.

The sweeping marks—camouflage—continued as far from the gate as he had been able to see while standing in Sarek's garden. But from that point on there was a trail in the sand: footprints.

Sand did not hold a print well enough to show which direction the people had gone—to or from Sarek's house—but the camouflage told him someone had returned and swept clean the last of the trail, ending up on the path in the garden. Now who would want to obliterate such a trail—?

Good God!

Someone who had taken another person out into the dangers of the Vulcan night, and left him there!

He remembered Sorel saying no one walked in the Vulcan desert at this time of year—and that it was exceptionally dangerous now, with T'Kuht shining! Who didn't know that? He hadn't, until Sorel had told him. And . . . chances were, no one had mentioned it to James T. Kirk!

McCoy raced back to the house, grabbed his medikit, and ran to Sarek's ground car. He could not take it through the garden—the gate was not wide enough. He drove impatiently down the street, turned, came to a road that would take him into the desert, hoped he wasn't breaking the traffic laws as he turned off the road along the neat back fences until he came to where the trail moved off across the desert, and followed it.

The land lay flat and ugly, nothing breaking its surface except the distant mountains. The trail went straight on, definite and determined. Mirages showed waves of water across the trail, but McCoy knew there was none in this waste.

Off in the distance, he began to see rock formations which presaged the mountains to come. The trail led toward one of them—beneath which he could see a weirdly-engorged plant of some sort, and what looked like a heap of discarded rags!

McCoy jumped from the car and ran. He could see it was a man. Unconscious—or dead?

Jim Kirk.

His skin was blistered with sunburn, his right hand swollen, ugly purple, his left foot bandaged. . . .

Only the medscanner told McCoy that Kirk was alive. His breathing was too shallow to be seen. His heart was sluggish.

McCoy pumped antishock serum and a broad-spectrum antibiotic into Kirk, then hauled him to the ground car, wishing it were an ambulance with plasma to fight his obvious dehydration. At least he was now out of the vicious sun, in a cool, air-conditioned car!

The doctor jumped back into the car, and drove rapidly back along the trail to ShiKahr, shot over to the road, and raced for the hospital emergency entrance.

As soon as he started trying to haul Kirk out, two Vulcan orderlies were there to help.

McCoy ran inside. "I need someone who knows how Vulcan poisons affect humans," he told the nurse on duty. "Dr. Corrigan—"

"He is not in this morning," the nurse replied.

"Dammit, there's a man dying—"

"I can help you, Doctor," came a deep, rich voice, and McCoy turned to find Dr. M'Benga approaching.

"Thank God! It's Captain Kirk. My scanner can only tell me it's some sort of weird alkaloid—"

"Let me see."

The orderlies were wheeling Kirk into the emergency room. M'Benga held his own scanner close to Kirk's misshapen hand, getting the same readings McCoy had. "Le-matya venom," he said. "He must have drawn most of it out before he became unconscious. He is fortunate: it looks as if he was grazed by a claw. If the beast had sunk its fangs into him, he would have been dead in minutes."

"Is there an antidote?" McCoy asked.

"Yes," said M'Benga, and named some tongue-twisting Vulcan medication to the nurse.

Meanwhile, they set up an I.V. to alleviate Kirk's dehydration, and the orderlies stripped the unconscious man, cleansed his wounds, and covered the sunburn on his face and arms with soothing salve. His ankle was badly sprained—nothing to worry about compared to the poison in his system and the condition of his right hand.

McCoy found himself working side by side with M'Benga as if they were a practiced team.

They took Kirk into the intensive care unit, and hooked him up to the monitors. His heartbeat was still too slow and irregular.

It faded, returned, faded again.

"Come on, Jim!" said McCoy.

"You got him here just in time," said M'Benga. "How did he come to be clawed by a le-matya?"

"I don't know! I found him out in the damn desert.

He was supposed to be on a date. I don't know what happened!"

"You saved his life, then, by bringing him in," M'Benga assured him.

"And you did by knowing what medicine to give him. I'd have had to do a serum test . . . or try to make an educated guess."

Kirk's heartbeat picked up. The monitor rattled arhythmically for a long moment while McCoy felt his own heart pounding in his ears, and then settled into a steady beat.

"He's all right," McCoy whispered.

"He is going to be very sick for a day or two," M'Benga said, "but yes, he will live."

"What about permanent effects? His hand?"

"It will probably be paralyzed for as long as ten days," M'Benga replied. "Assure him when he wakens that it is temporary."

McCoy smiled in relief. "Thank you. That will be important to him. Dr. M'Benga," he added, "when will your training here on Vulcan be completed?"

"In just over a month."

"Has Star Fleet given you your next assignment?"

"No, not yet."

"Well, if you don't mind, I'm going to ask Captain Kirk to see what strings he can pull to get you assigned to the *Enterprise*. I've seen you treat both Vulcans and humans, and I'd like you on my medical team."

The black doctor gave him a small bow and a slight smile. "I would be honored to serve with you, Dr. McCoy."

When M'Benga had gone, McCoy read all the monitors again, decided Kirk was in no danger now, and let his mind worry at what Kirk had been doing out in the desert.

He was supposed to have spent last night with that

pretty blond girl, Eleyna Miller, Sarek's assistant. What had changed his plans?

Just as he was considering trying to find the girl to ask her, Daniel Corrigan entered the intensive care unit. "Dr. M'Benga told me you asked for me. I'm sorry I wasn't here. What happened to Jim?"

"He tangled with a le-matya out on the desert."

Corrigan frowned. "But . . . how? Why?"

"Beats me," McCoy said, "except that it looked as if somebody took him out there, and then tried to cover up the trail. If the murderer hadn't been caught yesterday—"

"He wasn't," said Corrigan.

"What?"

"Sendet did not kill either T'Zan or Carl Remington. I was at the Verification, Leonard. It ran late into the night, which is why I came in late this morning."

"Then the murderer's still loose!" exclaimed McCoy. "Of course he'd go after Jim—he deliberately let it be known he was investigating! That means Jim knows who it is—whoever took him out into the desert."

Just then Kirk's heart monitor increased its pace, and his breathing became more rapid. Suddenly he opened glazed eyes. "Eleyna!" he gasped, writhing as the pain indicator shot up.

"Jim—you're all right. You're safe!" McCoy told him.

Kirk stared wide-eyed at nothing in the room. "Le-matya! No! Man-eating plant! Eleyna! No! *Eleyna!*"

There was an electronic sleep inducing unit beside the bed—a better way to sedate a patient in Kirk's condition than drugs. But it took McCoy and Corrigan working together to get the headset onto Kirk. All the while he was off in some other place—apparently fighting le-matya and man-eating plants.

Then, just as they got the sleep unit into place and

Corrigan flicked on the switch, Kirk caught McCoy's arm with his good left hand. "Bones!"

"Turn that thing off," McCoy told Corrigan, looking into Kirk's feverish but lucid hazel eyes. "Yes, Jim, it's me. You're all right. You're in the hospital."

"Bones," Kirk insisted, "tell Sarek!"

"Sure, Jim. What should I tell him?"

"Tell . . . Sarek," Kirk repeated, his words slurring. He had no strength. "Tell him . . . Eleyna. Eleyna. She's—"

And he slipped into unconsciousness again.

A hideous sinking feeling clutched at McCoy as he recalled the scene in the desert where he had picked up Kirk. There *had* been a plant nearby, grotesque thing, obscenely swollen, its branches all wrapped up around—

"Oh, my God," he said, holding on to the bed, "the murderer got *both* of them!"

"What?" asked Corrigan.

"Eleyna—that pretty girl. She and Jim went out together last night. The murderer must have ambushed them, forced them out into the desert . . . oh, God. There was a plant thing, gorged with something, near where I found Jim.

"What he wants us to tell Sarek, I think . . . is that Eleyna is dead."

CHAPTER 34

When he arrived to prepare for his morning class, Sarek found Eleyna in his office, grading the last of the assignments that had had to wait. The computer was on line again, basic programming restored. It would take days to put in all the data faculty and staff were supplying from their private storage files, and certainly users would be discovering gaps in information for months to come.

But it was functional, and that ended the hiatus in Sarek's teaching schedule. He had left Spock helping Storn to test the programming.

Sarek was surprised to see that Eleyna had completed grading most of the assignments. "You must have come in very early," he said. "Did you not stay out late with Jim last night?"

Eleyna raised a disapproving eyebrow at his interest in her private affairs, but replied, "No, we did not go out. Jim . . . came to my apartment, and said he was very sorry, but something important had come up."

Sarek frowned. "What could that be?"

"I do not know, Sarek," Eleyna replied. "But he asked to reschedule for this evening. And he gave me his tricorder to return to T'Sey." She gestured toward the instrument propped up on the desk. "He said . . . the investigation was over now that Sendet was caught —and he had something else he needed to do."

"That is . . . peculiar," said Sarek.

"He is human," said Eleyna. "But you must be pleased, Sarek, that you need have no further fears about Amanda's safety. Has Storn reconnected her stasis chamber to the computer?"

"No," he told her. "Sorel brought us the results of the Verification. Sendet is innocent."

"What? But he was caught attacking Dr. Corrigan!" Her astonishment made her more animated than Sarek could recall ever seeing his calm assistant before.

"He is guilty of interfering with a bonding, but he had nothing to do with the deaths of T'Zan and Remington. So Amanda's chamber is still on independent power, and the guard is back before it. I will be . . . most gratified when my wife is released from stasis in seven hours," he admitted. "Meanwhile, I have a class to teach."

"Will you be working in your office after class?"

"No. I will go to see Amanda, as usual. Then I will probably continue aiding the restoration of full computer function until I am needed for Amanda's release. You may use my terminal today, if you wish."

"Thank you, Sarek."

It was almost time for class. Sarek was about to gather up the student cassettes when the communicator buzzed. He flipped the switch, saying, "Sarek here."

There was no reply—only a moment's soft hiss of an open line, and then silence.

"Wrong code," said Eleyna.

"Apparently," Sarek replied. As he went off to class he saw Eleyna pick up the tricorder and make some sort of adjustment to it—but his mind was on how best to restructure today's lesson to begin making up for lost time.

As was to be expected, having had a substitute teacher and then canceled lessons, his offworlder students were reluctant to settle down to the effort of progressing faster than usual. In fact, Mr. Watson's first question showed that he had forgotten a lesson from the early days of the term.

Sarek reminded him briefly, then began reviewing the lesson Eleyna had taught.

He had their full attention at last, and was leading them toward the next assignment when something flashed across the back of his mind, interrupting his train of thought without his being able to tell what it was.

His words stumbled to a halt. The faces before him returned, as if from a distance.

Picking up the lesson, he continued to speak, while part of his mind sought the source of that strange—

Again his concentration faltered as vague startlement assaulted him.

Several students were now staring at him curiously.

Fear pried at the back of his mind as he tried to pick up the threads of the lesson again. Amanda's presence was still quietly with him, an assurance that all was—

SAREK!

It was not really his name—it was a mental shriek of incoherent terror, directed at him as the sole source of help.

"Amanda!" he gasped, unaware that he had spoken

aloud until two of his Vulcan students ran forward to support him.

He had a moment's impression of the humans in the class staring in wide-eyed amazement—but the dislocated fear clutching at his mind overshadowed everything else.

Amanda's steady presence had changed. She was not conscious—yet somehow she was struggling for her very existence, her mind seeking Sarek's as an anchor.

Not even giving a thought to the curious students, Sarek shook off his would-be helpers and ran.

He passed through halls, out into blazing sunlight, and into endless corridors, running blindly in a physical world which seemed to have no connection to the world in his mind, where Amanda struggled against some force trying to drag her away from him into a directionless void.

People stared at him—two wearing the green badges of medical personnel tried to stop him. He knew them—could not put names to them now—understood they meant only to help, but—

"My wife!" he managed to bring out, speech feeling alien against the inner world in which he struggled.

They let him go, and he ran on, the corridors seeming to grow longer each time he turned a corner—

At last he stood before the door to Amanda's chamber. There were people behind him. Others came from a room across the hall—one was family—

"Amanda!" he raged at the door, which would not open. He pounded on it, not able to articulate the password.

One of the people spoke. "Corrigan."

The door slid open. Sarek stumbled in, wanting the inner door to open, too—

The outer door slid shut, leaving him in the airlock with two other people.

"Father—"

He could not answer, could not concentrate on anything but his hold on Amanda's mind—if he let go, he would lose her!

"Help me with him," one of the figures said to the other. "He's got to get in there!"

Then he was being stripped of his clothes, shoved into the beam of the sterile rays—

The lights went out!

The buzz of the sterile rays stopped. Blackness and silence enveloped them.

The door would not open!

They were trapped in the airlock while on the other side of that door Amanda was dying!

Sarek's fear communicated to Amanda.

Her mind was not coherent—separated from consciousness, she knew only primal terror. She fought Sarek, feeling his fear—

With an animal roar, he flung himself at the door. It was built to withstand normal Vulcan strength—but at that moment Sarek's strength came from desperation.

He wrenched the door open, revealing the stasis chamber lit by the blue glow of the mist and the dim light of the gauges.

"Sarek—don't!"

But he leaped for Amanda—and bounced off the stasis field!

The two other men were talking. Sarek heard the words, but they meant nothing to him.

"Daniel, something *is* wrong with Mother. I can feel it, too, although not so strongly as Father does."

"Good God! The timer's been changed, Spock—the stasis release sequence has begun. Stimulants are being applied before preliminaries are complete!"

"Can you stop it?"

"No—look. The sequence was triggered, then the mechanism smashed. Someone's been in here!"

"I can't repair this—not without tools and parts."

"There's no time anyway. The field will collapse in less than five minutes. I wish we had Sorel—but until they get the power back on, no one else can get through the outer door. Spock—help your father. If you two can bring Amanda's mind back, there's a chance to save her body."

"I understand, Daniel."

Sarek knelt beside the stasis box, staring into the blue mist. He had somehow forced calm into his mind, and kept his tenuous connection with Amanda.

A hand touched his face—a mind sought his.

Go away!

Father, let me help.

Kinship flowed—Sarek felt Amanda respond positively, a mother's instinctive rapport with her child.

Yes.

Instinct was all they had to work with until they could bring Amanda's mind back to consciousness. She could not think now—only respond.

The stasis field began to dissipate. It lost its box form, and its glow faded as Amanda settled slowly to the floor.

Sarek caught her limp body into his arms. She was as cold as death!

"That's right, Sarek—warm her. She's hypothermic —give her the warmth of your body."

But it was the cold emptiness in which Amanda's mind wandered that terrified Sarek. He laid his hand against her face, finding the appropriate contact points . . . and still did not find his wife's presence *there*.

She was distant, in some realm having nothing to do with the physical form Sarek held.

Daniel was running his medscanner over Amanda. "She's not breathing. Spock—can you help me?"

In his mind, Sarek felt his son's assurance that what he and the human doctor must do to Amanda was right. Keeping his touch on her, he let them stretch her pale form on the floor, manipulate, breathe into her mouth —it all had nothing to do with Amanda herself, to whom he had such a slender tie.

"Now," said Daniel. "Go ahead."

Spock's hand touched Sarek's face once more. Sarek gathered Amanda's body into his lap, feeling breaths come and go . . . feeling it begin to draw warmth from him.

But it was empty, still, unconscious. It was not Amanda.

Amanda. Come to me. Come to me, my wife.

Mother, Spock's mind added. *Mother, come back. All is well.*

The faint, irrational spark of Amanda's presence greeted them with fearful questioning.

Sarek projected warmth and welcome.

Spock, though, hesitated—and Amanda's fear returned.

She is your mother, Spock. You have the right to care about her.

Like a rusty piece of equipment too long unused, Spock's buried filial caring crept slowly from the restraints he kept on all his feelings.

Father and son together called Amanda with their hope and joy in her presence—and she came to them. . . .

Into her body, into her mind, and into a whirlwind of memories of the three of them. . . .

Of the day Sarek had taken the picture which sat on Amanda's dresser, when with such shared joy they had brought their healthy, thriving baby home from the hospital.

Of their combined horrified embarrassment and secret pride in the intellectual accomplishment of their son, when it was discovered that he had tampered with the classroom computer to sabotage the lessons of the boys who tormented him.

Of their joint pride—although Sarek would not admit to the term—when they learned that their son had sacrificed his determined effort to pass Kahs-wan on the first attempt, in order to save the life of another boy . . . one of the very boys who had taunted and teased him about not being fully Vulcan.

Of Amanda's agony when Spock had announced his intention to make a career in Star Fleet, and she had been helpless to prevent a silence that had stretched on into eighteen endless years.

Of her fury at Sarek when he refused to attend what was supposed to have been his son's marriage.

Of her fury at Spock, when on board the *Enterprise* he chose his duty to Star Fleet over his duty to save his father's life. She had hit him—Sarek experienced now both Amanda's anguish and Spock's bitter shame over a scene he had never before known had happened.

But Spock *had* saved his father's life—and now, at last, they were a family once more. Amanda's love suffused her husband and her son, drawing them tantalizingly deeper into the seductive meld—

Mother—Father—it is time to break the meld.

Spock's disciplined mind took over, ordering reality. He guided them into the withdrawal chant, first in unison:

"I am Sarek. I am Amanda. I am Spock. I am Sarek. I am Amanda. I am Spock. I am—"

"—Sarek."

"—Amanda."

"—Spock!"

Sarek was in his own mind, his own body, holding Amanda. The side of his face felt cool, where Spock had just removed his hand. His son knelt beside him, watching his mother.

Amanda's eyes fluttered open. She looked up into her husband's face, and smiled. "Sarek!" She threw her arms about him, hugging him tightly. "Oh, Sarek, I love you."

"Amanda," he murmured against her hair. "Beloved."

He felt Spock's start, and sharp stare, but their son said nothing.

Amanda released Sarek, and saw her son. "Spock. You *are* here. I thought I was dreaming."

And Sarek stifled a smile as he watched his stiff and proper son force himself to allow his mother to embrace him . . . before witnesses.

Sarek realized that the lights were on. Not only Daniel was in the small chamber with them, but Sorel—and behind him Storn.

As if on signal, when Amanda released Spock, everyone began to move. Sorel and Daniel bent over her with their scanners. Storn handed Sarek his clothes, and he dressed as he watched the doctor and the healer examine his wife.

He knew they would find nothing wrong. If she were in pain, he would have felt it in the meld. When they came out of it, Amanda had felt to him like her normal, cool self—not the cold, clammy creature he had held at the collapse of the stasis field.

Sorel stood. "Your wife appears to be in excellent condition, Sarek."

"Good," said Amanda. "Let's go home!"

"Oh, no, you don't," replied Daniel. "You're staying in the hospital for observation. All right—everybody out. Sarek and Spock, you may visit Amanda this evening. We'll move her to intensive care for the rest of the day, just as a precaution. Now go."

Sarek knelt and touched fingertips with Amanda, feeling as much as seeing her warm smile, the reassuring glow in her sapphire eyes, alive with promises.

Then he left with Spock, just as orderlies were wheeling in a gurney.

Spock put a hand on his arm. "Father, I—"

"Sarek!" A female voice interrupted what Spock had started to say.

Eleyna emerged from the open airlock to the chamber in which Carl Remington had died. She ran to Sarek, saying, "I'm so sorry. I grieve with thee. But it will be all right. Sarek, I will—"

She lifted her hand toward his face, Sarek staring at her in puzzlement, understanding only that she must think Amanda dead—

But even as he opened his mouth to tell her that his wife lived, another shout interrupted them.

"Stop that woman! She's the killer!"

Leonard McCoy came running breathlessly from the stairs.

"No!" Eleyna cried. "No—he's mine! You can't take him from me now—I've waited for him—"

As she reached toward Sarek again, Spock did not even bother to use the nerve pinch. He simply grasped both Eleyna's arms, and held her immobile with Vulcan strength.

"He needs me!" she cried. "Let me go, Spock! Do you want your father to die, too?"

"You are hysterical," Spock told her flatly. "Calm yourself. Dr. McCoy, you say that this woman—?"

"Killed T'Zan and Remington—and very nearly killed Jim Kirk."

"And Amanda," Sarek murmured, his eyes on the

tricorder slung over Eleyna's shoulder. He snatched it from her, switched it on—

"Sarek . . . to see Amanda," it said in his voice.

"That's how you got into the stasis chamber!" he realized. "That call this morning—it was not someone calling the wrong code. You programmed it in, to enable you to record me speaking my name—and you steered our conversation for the other words—"

"She also knows how to make a computer do what she wants," said Spock. "You taught her, Father."

As the blood rushed to his head, Sarek saw green. He reached for Eleyna, all the instinct of his warrior ancestors propelling him to break her neck—

"Father!"

Spock's voice brought him back to present-day Vulcan, to the control he maintained as a responsible citizen.

Deliberately, Sarek folded his hands behind his back and, forcing calm, asked Eleyna, "Why? Why did you kill the Lady T'Zan and Carl Remington? Why would you want to kill my wife?"

"For you—I love you, Sarek. I've waited patiently for you. When Amanda became ill, I knew you would need me when she was dead. Then came the treatment —it wasn't *fair!* She had already had you all those years! It's *my* turn!"

Sarek looked to Spock, who obviously found the woman's explanation as incomprehensible as he did. To seek a man who belonged to another? Unthinkable . . . although another man had sought the woman who had by right belonged to Spock, and only yesterday Sendet had tried to break the bonding between Daniel and T'Mir. Yes, he supposed all sorts of things were thinkable, to an illogical mind.

Still, "If you sought to kill Amanda, why did you kill two other people?"

"T'Zan was an accident," she replied. "I didn't even know about the Star Fleet officer—that was your fault, Sarek. You should have told me there would be some-one else in stasis! You told me your son was coming home—and I knew that was the time. You would need him to meld with you when your bond with Amanda was broken. So I programmed the computer to cut power to the stasis chamber."

"And it did," said Spock, "to the first chamber in the power sequence, which happened to be T'Zan's. And after that," Sarek saw his son's hands tighten on Eleyna's arms, "you killed Carl Remington just to make everyone think the stasis machinery was at fault. Logical."

"I am honored."

"That was not a compliment," he replied.

"Jim Kirk was coming too close to the answers, wasn't he?" Leonard McCoy put in. "So you lured him out into the desert, figuring to feed him to the le-matya. But you figured wrong—Jim just woke up and told me what you did to him. Damn—we'd have had you an hour ago if I'd understood what he was trying to tell me!"

"Is Jim all right?" Spock asked.

"Yeah—you know our captain, Spock. He always pulls through."

"Humans are like that," said Sarek, just as Amanda was wheeled by on the gurney. She smiled at him in passing, and both Spock and Leonard were silent, all in accord that she should not know the danger she had been in.

But Eleyna's silence was that of shock. "She's—she's alive!" she gasped when Amanda had been taken around the corner. "No—it's not *fair!*"

"Was it fair that you killed two innocent people,

almost killed a third—and burned down half the hospital?" Leonard demanded.

"I didn't mean to start the fire!" Eleyna protested. "All I did was wipe the records—"

"With a power surge that started the fire," said Spock. "Father, this woman is an offworlder, not a Vulcan citizen. She admits murdering a Vulcan citizen and a citizen of Verinius Four. Her *attempted* murders are against a citizen of Vulcan and a citizen of Earth. The property damage she caused occurred on Vulcan. There may be questions of jurisdiction."

Sorel joined them. "This is the person who—?"

Eleyna stared at him, then dropped her eyes as she realized who he was. "I'm sorry," she said. "I didn't mean to kill your wife. You've got to believe me—it was an accident—it was Amanda I meant to kill!"

Sorel stared at her. "She is not sane," he said. "I cannot treat her myself, but she must be admitted for treatment at once. I will take her. Perhaps T'Par can arrange her schedule to see her today."

"Hey—wait a minute!" said Leonard McCoy. "That's a murderer you've got there. You can't just—"

Spock said, "Doctor, the Academy can give her better treatment than she would receive at any Federation penal colony. Since all her hostile acts occured on Vulcan, Vulcan law takes precedence—and by our law, since she has admitted her crime, she may choose death or treatment. Under Federation law, treatment at a penal colony would be her only choice."

"It isn't fair," said Eleyna. "After everything I did for you, Sarek—I don't care what happens to me anymore."

As Sorel took the woman away, Leonard said, "Damn! Why do I feel sorry for *her?* Wait till you see what she did to Jim."

"He *will* recover, though?" asked Spock.

"Yeah—you can see him later, Spock," said the doctor. "He's gonna be in considerable pain—you're probably the only person he'll be able to stand. Your son would've made a good doctor," he added to Sarek. "I don't know how he does it, but he's really good with people in pain."

Spock's eyebrows shot up at the unexpected compliment from the man Sarek usually saw him trade barbs with. Then Leonard left them to go back to his patient, and Spock turned to Sarek. "May I ask you something, Father?"

"What is it, Spock?"

"When Mother became conscious, you called her . . . ?"

"Beloved."

"I do not understand," his son said flatly. "Like all Vulcans, you deny understanding any such feeling, and yet—"

"It is simply her name, Spock."

"What?"

"My son," Sarek said, "surely in all your studies of Federation languages, you cannot have missed encountering the literal translation of 'Amanda'?"

CHAPTER **35**

*T*hree days later, both Amanda and James T. Kirk were released from the hospital. Kirk felt like himself at last, the poison finally all out of his system. McCoy had to help him dress, though; his right hand and arm, to the elbow, were completely paralyzed.

But that was a temporary nuisance—and the wounded hero with his arm in a sling would meanwhile cut a dashing figure around the Academy.

Since yesterday afternoon, when the pain had finally faded to annoyance, he had had a series of visitors, a surprising number of them female. Not that he would consider flirting with T'Pau, T'Mir, or Amanda . . . but word of his adventures had spread considerably further, since it was carried along with the shocking story of the murders. Several human women tenuously associated with the hospital had found excuses to stop in to meet him. If he wished, he could fill his evenings with a variety of female companionship for the rest of his stay on Vulcan.

For the moment, though, he was satisfied with the company of Spock's family and friends. Amanda was lovely and charming as he remembered her . . . almost *exactly* as he remembered her, physically.

He had rather expected her to come out of the stasis treatment looking like her own daughter. Instead, her hair was still silver, her movements still sedate . . . she merely looked thoroughly healthy and rested.

When she had visited last evening, she had caught him surreptitiously studying her, and laughed. "It's all inside," she told him. "No more nerve degeneration. Also—look." She held out her hands, bent and stretched them. "No more stiff joints—and no age spots. Daniel says the cosmetic effects will increase for about six months yet. But it's not going to turn me into a twenty-year-old, Jim."

"You couldn't possibly have been as lovely at twenty as you are now," he told her gallantly.

"That's what my husband says," she agreed, blue eyes twinkling, "only Sarek *means* it. Vulcans do not value youth for its own sake. But I'm human, and I have my vanities—so I must admit that I enjoy looking younger almost as much as feeling that way. And I'm having my hair left silver—to keep the respect of my students," she explained deadpan, then added with a smile, "and because in my mid-thirties, which is the approximate age the treatments are supposed to leave me, my hair had just enough gray in it to look faded, and not enough to be a pretty silver. I have informed Daniel that I refuse to go through that stage again!"

Amanda might feel young and strong, but Kirk noted that Sarek treated her like breakable porcelain as he helped her into the ground car for the ride home.

It was only after they were all gathered at Sarek's house that Amanda began to demand answers to her questions. At her husband's insistence, she was lying on the couch. Sarek sat in the antique rocker that seemed to be his favorite chair, and Kirk sat in the comfortable armchair opposite, that he assumed was normally Amanda's. Spock and McCoy had drawn up other chairs to form a circle—it felt as if they were all part of a single family group.

"Now," said Amanda, "I want the whole story."

"What story?" Sarek asked, picking his harp up off the mantel over the empty fireplace.

"Don't give me that innocent look—or you either, Spock. I know something went wrong while I was in stasis. Your injury was somehow a part of it, Jim—and I would really like to know what your getting mauled by a le-matya could possibly have to do with there being no healer in the meld to bring me out of stasis!"

The four men looked at one another, and then Sarek looked down at the tuning controls of his harp, adjusting them as he said, "My wife, how could two such disparate events possibly be logically connected?"

"That's what I'd like to know!" she insisted. "In the hospital, once I was allowed out of bed I heard a lot of very interesting silences suddenly start, the moment I entered a room. I was told what happened to Jim—but somehow nobody had an answer for what anyone with common sense was doing out on Vulcan's Forge when T'Kuht was shining."

"I'm afraid my common sense got a little bit blurred for a while there," Kirk admitted.

"By what?" Amanda wanted to know. "What is it all of you men are keeping from me?"

"Why would we keep anything from you, Mother?" Spock asked.

"Spock, when you were four years old you began

copying your father's trick of avoiding answering a question by asking another. I didn't stand for it then, and I won't stand for it now. Tell me, my son, what were *you* doing in the meld with Sarek to bring me out of stasis? Sorel should have been there, or T'Par. You are not a healer, Spock, and I do not think the healers would have allowed that risk under ordinary circumstances."

Spock looked over at Sarek. "She has to know."

"I agree," his father replied. "I had merely hoped that the story could come later, after she was rested."

"I won't stand for you two talking about me as if I'm not here, either!" said Amanda, her blue eyes flashing. "I'm rested enough, thank you! Now, let's have the truth. Spock, I assume you came home in case your father had need of you. How did you come to play healer for me?"

"It all started on the *Enterprise*." Kirk decided to begin, realizing that there was no use trying to keep it from Amanda any longer; the Vulcans could only agitate her further with their delays. "Spock was planning to come to Vulcan anyway, as you suggest, when one of our crew members was injured so severely that only the stasis treatment offered any hope for his recovery—"

McCoy took over to explain the medical aspects, and soon the four men were telling the whole story, with Amanda as wide-eyed audience.

"—and when I came to again, and found McCoy still sitting there," Kirk finished, "I was terrified that Eleyna had gotten to you."

"She had," said Sarek. "She drugged the guard, and somehow dragged him into an empty isolation chamber. Then she used my voice on the tricorder to enter your stasis chamber, Amanda. She started the release sequence, and smashed the mechanism."

"And all this while Storn and I were in his office, just across the hall," Spock put in.

"A masterpiece of timing," said Sarek. "She had already programmed the new computer to turn the central power off just after she left the stasis chamber, so that no one could get in."

"The airlock mechanism remained on the central power system," Spock explained.

"But Eleyna did not count on our bonding alerting me the moment you were in danger," Sarek continued. "I got there before the power went off."

"As did Daniel," added Spock, "for the emergency signal alerted him when the mechanism malfunctioned. By that time I, too, sensed something disturbing you, Mother. We all met in the hallway. The airlock has a maximum capacity of three persons. Father had to go in at once, and Daniel as your physician. Since Sorel was not yet there, it was logical that I accompany them. But then . . . the power failed."

"Then?" asked Amanda. "While you were in the airlock? How did you get into the stasis chamber?"

Sarek looked blankly at Spock. "I . . . do not remember."

"You tore the inner door out of its housing, Father," Spock replied matter-of-factly.

Amanda smiled, but there were tears in her eyes. "Oh, Sarek."

"Under the circumstances," he told her, "it was the only logical solution."

"No sooner did we get into the chamber," Spock continued, "than your stasis field collapsed. The power was still off; no healer could reach us. Thus I had to enter the meld with Father."

"I'm . . . glad it happened that way," said Amanda. "It was wonderful to find the two of you together."

"Well, *I'm* glad everything turned out all right!" said

McCoy. "When Jim finally told me what he *meant* me to tell Sarek about Eleyna—it was too late."

"Listen, Bones," said Kirk, "you were no dumber than I was. Neither one of us could for a minute think of Eleyna Miller as a murderer—until she proved it."

"Eleyna?" Amanda shook her head in disbelief. "She—she was always such a *nice* young woman. She casually killed two people—and tried to—?" She stared at Kirk.

"There is no hope of understanding the intentions of an unbalanced mind," said Sarek. "Of course it is incomprehensible to any of us why Eleyna would do such a thing."

Amanda studied him. "You are wrong, my husband. Eleyna's motive is the *only* thing I can comprehend out of all of this. What I do not understand is why, if she thought she could have you for herself if I were dead, she did not simply kill me directly."

"She could kill only at a distance, luckily for us," Kirk told her.

"What do you mean?"

"Eleyna could kill by programming the computer. She lured me out into the desert and pushed me over a cliff—but not one high enough to kill me in the fall. I think she *planned* that I would be injured, and if the flesh-eating plant didn't get me, I'd be killed by an animal or die of exposure the next day. She was not an efficient killer, you see—if she had been, she simply would have poisoned my food or stuck a knife in me. She had plenty of opportunity."

"She could not face the consequences directly," McCoy put in.

"Hence two people died who had nothing to do with Eleyna's plans," Spock added.

"Your young colleague," said Amanda, "and . . . T'Zan. Oh, poor Sorel!"

"His children were there for him," said Spock. "And Daniel Corrigan."

"Who is now bonded to T'Mir," said Amanda. "At least *he* was willing to share his good news with me."

"And so another offworlder becomes part of a Vulcan family," Spock commented.

"You disapprove, Spock?" Sarek asked, one eyebrow rising precipitously.

"No, Father. I think . . . I have come to understand that family takes precedence over tradition at times."

"My son, family *is* tradition," said Sarek. "If no families ever did anything new, where would traditions come from? And that reminds me—I promised you long ago that I would give you the lytherette that my grandfather made. Now seems the perfect opportunity."

He held the instrument out to Spock.

"I . . . am honored, Father. But—I cannot take it with me aboard the *Enterprise*—"

"Why not? Should not your traditions go where you go, Spock? Just as other traditions come to Vulcan? Consider Sendet and the others who were trying to turn back to the days before Surak—they have chosen to leave Vulcan, and been assigned a planet to colonize. They choose to take Vulcan's harshest, most ancient traditions with them. You represent IDIC, Spock—a new tradition, although no less to be honored. As a Star Fleet officer you are both scientist and soldier. Yet you are an artist as well."

Spock touched the ancient wood of the harp, and strummed the strings gently. Then, there in that Vulcan household, among his human friends, sitting between his human mother and his Vulcan father, Spock began to play. The music combined elements from Vulcan music, human music—Kirk recognized Andorian triplets creeping in, and even a Klingon drinking song they had heard on Station K-7. He smiled—perhaps the smile Spock would not allow himself—at peace with the galaxy, content to rest for now before returning to the *Enterprise* and the life they shared beyond the traditions of any single culture—a life among the stars.

ABOUT THE AUTHOR

Jean Lorrah is Professor of English at Murray State University in Kentucky. She is a first-generation *Star Trek* fan, having become a devoted viewer of the series when it first appeared on television in 1966. Her contributions can be found in *Spockanalia*, the very first *Star Trek* fanzine, and she has been active in fandom since its inception.

Although she learned the craft of fiction through Trek fanzines, her first professional science fiction sales were non-Trek. With Jacqueline Lichtenberg (whom she met through Trekfandom), she is co-author of *First Channel* and *Channel's Destiny*, and sole author of the forthcoming *Ambrov Keon*, all in the Sime/Gen universe created by Jacqueline Lichtenberg.

Jean Lorrah's own professional science fiction series consists of *Savage Empire, Dragon Lord of the Savage Empire, Captives of the Savage Empire*, and two forthcoming novels, one of which will be a collaboration with Winston Howlett, whom she *also* met through Trekfandom, and used as a model for one of the characters in her series!

"There is no untangling *Star Trek* from my life," she says, "what with all that fanzine writing, and all the friends I've made through fandom. Writing a *Star Trek* professional novel feels like coming home—I have known and loved Kirk, Spock, McCoy, and all the other characters for eighteen years! It's been delightful to spend some more time with them—like going on a trip with good friends."

Jean Lorrah teaches full time and writes full time, but still manages to get to several *Star Trek* and general science fiction conventions every year. She loves to meet other fans at such conventions, so be sure to say hello to her. Obviously, she doesn't have time for pen-palling or critiquing other writers' manuscripts when she is working, but she participates in writers' workshops at some conventions, where she *can* give you some of her time to help you with your writing. Watch the convention listings for such appearances. She is also co-editor, with Lois Wickstrom, of *Pandora* magazine, a small-press sf magazine which encourages new writers.